DOUBLE DECEPTION

C. A. MITCHELL

RAMPART BOOKS

Also by C. A. Mitchell

Beneath the Veils
Beneath the Lies
Beneath the Conflict
Girl in the Middle
Third Child
Sixth Victim
Double Deception
Angel
Tinker Tailor Conman
Children of the Mask
A Woman Called EVE

DOUBLE
DECEPTION

1

———

Shouldn't everyone have the chance to reinvent themselves and be happier to be the person they always wanted to be?

As a name, Cecelia had never worked for her, which was why she needed to change it. In Latin, it meant blindness. Previously, the name Clara had worked for her, and significantly, it meant light. She liked the idea of being a person of light. It gave her the sense she could always be hopeful, optimistic, and even enthusiastic. For a long time, she had been thinking about renaming herself, change her image, and leave the trap of herself behind to be different. If it didn't work, she could always revert to her old name. Yet, as soon as she changed her name legally, hey presto, she was offered a job.

But giving yourself a new name doesn't instantly provide a new personality. It needs working on. So, where had this depression come from? It was part of the person she used to be. On the first page of a brand-new notebook, Clara jotted down a few details of the person she wanted to be. Someone fantastic, smart, and who takes chances and isn't afraid of change anymore. Someone who recognizes the truth. Was this possible? Why not? It was who she would like to be.

Her first official job as an investigative journalist was to be held in a designer bar. And it was cool, so cool. You would need a mortgage to eat there. Walking into the restaurant with the attitude that I come here often was an approach that wasn't working yet. Nervous around confident people, for this was their territory. Were all eyes on her? Not really.

The restaurant shimmered with sophistication. When she whispered her names to the maître d, his eyes quickly flickered to attention before taking her to the table. So polite, so well trained.

Glad that she wore a suit instead of the jeans which laid waiting to be selected. Not so happy, though, was the fact that she was picking up the tab for this meal. Yet, this must be considered an investment, a cent for a dollar.

Settling herself into her chair, a glance at her watch confirmed that her guests were late. This meal would be costly, but they were worth it because they must have the money to live this lifestyle. Afterward, she would add the price of this meal to her fee.

Late, it was not a healthy sign. It said volumes about them not being responsible; to Clara, it said disrespect. But a job should not be about personalities; it should be about getting paid at the end of the day.

What Clara would get out of this, she hoped, was an interesting article. So desperate to get a job, she would say yes to anything. A missing daughter, who they were anxious about. And a nice expensive place to live in and be worried.

Two beautiful people walked towards her behind the maître d', smiling and nodding; they knew most people here. She was stunning and slender, about five feet seven, and could even have been a natural blonde. And as for how she dressed, wow, her clothes were beautiful and faultless; it made Clara feel awkward and dowdy, uncomfortable and even jealous.

'How nice to meet you,' the beauty settled herself into the chair.

Faultless teeth that were obviously unnatural. Everything was perfect about her. While standing behind her hovering around, was the maître d'. She smiled; she was used to this sort of attention.

'Shall we order and then talk?'

'Yes,' said Clara, feeling the silk cut into her purse.

Now that they were comfortable, and the fanfare had settled, the drinks were on the table; sips were taken from the wine, straight to business, and the reason she was here.

'It's Raphael's daughter from his first marriage,' spoke the wife in a relatively low and measured voice. She was at ease with herself and her delivery.

Anise, the beautiful long-haired blonde wife, took the lead by introducing the subject. She was a natural blonde and somewhere in her early forties, but she still looked exquisite and would always be beautiful. Expressive hazel eyes in an exceptionally balanced face. Not too full lips, sculptured eyebrows, which added elegance to her comments. Everyone would agree with her and like her just because she was beautiful.

'You have been married before?' this question was directed to Raphael but not answered by him because Anise intervened.

'It was a miserable marriage.'

This intrusion offended Clara. If Anise wanted to be the journalist and write their own story, then so be it.

'I am trying to understand what happened to your

daughter,' Clara directed her question again to Raphael. 'I take it your daughter did not live with you?'

'She lived with us until she decided she wanted to do just exactly as she pleased. She didn't want us telling her what to do.' Anise once again replied.

'Was she unhappy?'

This time, Clara didn't even bother to ask the father; she went straight to the beautiful tigress. 'Children only run away when they were unhappy.'

'Unhappy? I would call her ungrateful,' Anise spat indignantly. 'Everything she wanted—she only had to ask my husband; he would bend over backward for her. I tried my best to be an excellent mother, but she was impossible. It was a great difficulty for us because we had five other children. Charisse wanted such-and-such, and so she got it. Our other children wanted to know why she was so special.'

'And was she special?'

'If you call being very rich special,' Anise's eyebrows raised.

The Lamonts. Something from Clara's memory rang. She had heard the name before in the newspapers. She had to be right about this.

'Charisse Lamont? Is she the daughter of the late Natasha Hunter, an heiress of the Hunter tobacco fortune?'

'She was my wife.'

'I know something about her.' Clara was excited. 'Natasha was found dead from a drug overdose. She had a four-year-old daughter. I thought I had heard the name before. It was very tragic. A sad little girl completely alone in the world.'

'Not completely alone,' added Raphael. 'She had me. This is how the media wanted to present her to sell their fodder.'

'I took her in as one of my own.'

Anise again turned to Raphael with a look of concern.

'She was never alone. How can you be alone when you have a father?' she shrugged. 'It was my intention to adopt her, but because of her money, I found out that I couldn't.'

Pampering time, Anise stroked the ends of her blonde hair to settle herself down into her calm and beautiful composure.

'The fact is,' said Raphael, 'that we did the best we could. But we failed. We obviously weren't good enough for her.'

'She didn't want to be a part of our family. She wanted only her daddy, but not the rest of us.'

Clara stared at them both. No, she didn't like either of them; she particularly didn't like the wife. It was not difficult —not difficult at all. But maybe it was too soon to make a judgment?

'I take it you want me to find out where Charisse is and ask her to come back home?'

'We need to know what's going on with her,' replied Anise. 'We worry she may be dead.'

'Dead? Why?' Clara frowned.

Why did she have to be dead? Obviously, Anise didn't like her, which was probably why Charisse ran away. But there was no need for her to be dead because of that.

'Unfortunately,' Anise's beautiful eyes warned Raphael not to answer this awkward question. 'As much as we tried to be exemplary parents, Charisse was spoiled. Discipline was hopeless. She always seemed to find fault with me. She was always saying such dreadful things to me as if it was my fault her father left her mother for me. You remember?' Anise turned to Raphael. 'You heard her.'

'Anise—' Raphael's eyes pleaded.

'Her mother was a drug addict and an alcoholic.

Raphael tried his best with Natasha, but she was unbelievably controlling. He had to get away. Look at the evidence. She died from a morphine overdose. What more can I say? We're not the ones on trial here?'

'My daughter left our home of her own volition,' tried Raphael. 'If there was an impediment to Natasha and now Charisse, it was because of their fortune. I was in charge of Charisse's money until she came of age.'

'She was questioning everything,' jumped in Anise. 'We got a bigger house, a new car. Charisse wanted to know where the money came from and if it was from her money? I said to her, well, look, honey, we need to live if we are looking after you. She was paranoid about her money. She felt we were taking it away from her. Damn her, what we had used made no difference to her vast wealth. I put the problem down to the fact she was just jealous. She hated me—'

'When was the last time you saw her?'

'About three years ago,' said Raphael, now frowning.

'Three years?'

'Yes, three years—' snapped Anise. 'She was impossible. She chose to leave us, not us leave her.'

'Why do you need to know where she is now?'

'We know where she is. She's joined this commune, and now she's disappeared.' Anise couldn't help herself.

'You see,' began Raphael. 'The problem is, Charisse is a very wealthy young woman. People use her because of that.'

'And take advantage of her,' again Anise jumped in.

It was all now beginning to make sense to Clara. Thoughts were chasing one another with stimulating deductions, and she was about to crown her suspicions.

'When did your daughter come into her fortune?'

'Four months ago.'

Raphael shook his head while Anise's hazel eyes gleamed with sparkling hatred.

'Let me,' he put his hand over to stop his wife. 'We were receiving money from the trust—this is what the argument was about. Unlike my late wife, I was not in possession of a substantial fortune, but I still needed to live. We hoped we could talk to her about this. After all, I am her father.'

Seething with outrage, Raphael took a few seconds to breathe.

'The payments we received dried up when she came of age. I don't believe my daughter would have done that to me. Yes, we had problems when she was with us. Well, money creates problems. Unfortunately, she couldn't forgive me for moving on with my life and falling in love with another. And when she lost her mother, I had no choice but to take care of her.'

His eyes were gritted with anger.

'I love my daughter, but going without money is difficult when you've become dependent on it.' Now he was working to make this woman understand what their lives were like? 'I can't apologize for enjoying money.'

Anise enclosed her hand, now on top of Raphael's. It was a very special sharing moment for them both, which Clara noted.

A calm sensation followed in the wake of Clara's thoughts. The question compelling Clara to ask—was, when did you miss your daughter? When the money ran out? When the jingling of coins stopped filling from your piggy bank?

Taking her pen as if she were about to write, this little motion called these two people to her attention.

'You believe the commune had something to do with Charisse's disappearance?'

'Absolutely,' nodded Anise, and then to her husband. She waited for him to show the same loyalty.

He looked disturbed, as if losing his eldest born affected him. Sometimes, in life, people just want to get on with living. There was nothing wrong with that.

'Yes, I do. I know Charisse wouldn't have left us high and dry despite her feelings about us. She is a decent girl. The problem was her mother. It was Natasha's way of getting back at me by poisoning our daughter's mind.'

And then he stopped and stared at his glass.

'I just want to know if Charisse is all right. I want her to know I care about her. It's up to her what she does with her money.'

Stunned, Anise dabbed his arm as if he should not have said this.

It hadn't been an easy interview, mostly. But now Clara was trying to fight off the prejudices about this couple. A beautiful woman who had clearly intoxicated this man by making him her own and taking him away from his wife. Where were her scruples? But it couldn't matter and mustn't. Everyone follows the course of their lives, and we aren't there at that vital crossroads where decisions are made. The present has the power and knowledge, and this is what she had to work with.

There was one question she needed to ask, if only out of vanity. Why had they chosen her? But it wasn't her they had first selected. They wanted a proper detective, and they were going to pay him once the job was completed.

'Why was that?' Clara was forced to ask.

'Simple, because we don't have any money,' said Anise, insulted to answer this.

'I need money.'

Did this couple think she was going to work for them for nothing?

'But you would be prepared to work cheaper?' again Anise answered for them both. 'We can only give you what we can afford. And when we have the money, we will pay you the rest we owe you.'

How dare Anise look at her as if she were a grateful servant, pleased to be working for them? How dare she think their lives were more important than her own? The incense was almost enough to demand she walk out on these two spoiled people, but she had already drafted a story about Lamont's daughter. And this could be a big seller, and she certainly needed the money with a mortgage payment coming up and expecting to be paid. This arrangement required thinking about.

'How much can you pay me?'

She was looking at the clothes Anise was wearing, a beautiful dress in white with striped lemon. This was not the sort of clothing you bought off the peg. So perfect and untouchable, sitting there with one eyebrow slightly raised, as if Clara dared to touch her.

'We thought two hundred dollars.'

'For the day?'

Anise laughed. 'For the week. It is what we can afford.'

'Like you, I don't sell myself too cheaply. I have standards to keep, you know. Make it five hundred with expenses.'

'We can't, can we, Raphael?'

Anise turned to him and shook her head.

'Four hundred then, and you make a note of the expenses which I'll square up with you when the job is over.'

Two hundred and seventy-five would cover the cost of

her mortgage—something she couldn't afford to throw away.

'Very well, four hundred,' she nodded.

Clara was rewarded by a slow smile rising from both of their faces. She knew then that she had been duped.

'I hate that woman,' the cab she had promised herself vanished. Walking now was going to be the option of the day. Oh, how she hated Anise. She hated the fact that this woman had gotten her own way in everything. She was used to it.

But there was no use fuming over it. The bargain was made, and like everything, she would do an excellent job of it—a new way of thinking because of money. There was a story in it. And Clara could feel it. She was excited. Work towards the positive; make the best of any situation, and surely, by giving one's best, it will all work out.

The Lamonts gave her the details, addresses, and dates that she asked for, and, as usual, Anise took charge of this. After this, they stared at her; it was uncomfortable. When she told them she had to go, they didn't disagree. But what next? Should she offer her hand to them? No, she didn't want to touch this beautiful woman's hands.

Standing there gave an awkwardness about her presence. Clara looked at them as if she must ask permission for her to leave. Why didn't she tell them she wouldn't do this job and watch their expression? It might be worth it even to lose the paltry four hundred dollars.

'I'll let you know how I get on,' she said as she picked up her briefcase while trying to look efficient.

'We will pay you on a monthly term,' said Anise, picking up her glass of wine.

'No.'

They both thought this was novel.

'No?' questioned Anise, a smile, a frown, an insult.

'I need to have some money upfront; I too have my bills to pay.'

'We will give you the first four hundred, but it will have to be deducted from the monthly account.' Anise sipped her wine.

'Yes, I'll take the four hundred now.'

Clara was desperate; her house depended on it.

'Raphael,' said Anise to her husband, who, like an obedient child, went to his trousers and took out his wallet.

They had come prepared. From his wallet, he took out eight fifty-dollar bills and passed them across the table to Clara. Anise watched, clearly enjoying this exchange. Once she took the money, the deal was sealed, and there was no way for Clara to get out of this trap.

But now walking, the money was sitting in her briefcase while her feet paced the sidewalk. She had this month's mortgage; she wasn't going to lose her house yet. For the time she was going to work for this couple, she could pay her bills.

Plotting and planning. Some people have so much money that they don't know what to do with it. Well, she did. If they had too much money, they could pass some of it over to her. But life never pans out like that. These people like others to be beneath them. In this way, these poor people can always be grateful.

One day, she would be rich. She could feel it and see it. Only this interminable future always seemed so far from her grasp.

2

————

Walking always helped Clara to think and plot out her thoughts with every step she took. Charisse had gone to a clinic that specialized in rehabilitation, especially with drugs and alcohol. It was an expensive private clinic, which meant only the very rich could afford it.

Charisse had been in rehab for three months, and it appears she took well to the treatment. Even though she was still very vulnerable. Raphael and Anise hoped that she would return home for a while; they needed to see her. Clara could guess what this meant; money, and a comfortable life, but they didn't get this chance to talk to her before she disappeared.

Catching the 110-shuttle bus took most of the brunt of the walk. Sitting by the window and watching with a vacant eye as the city scenery passed by. Other passengers didn't interfere with her. The conversation she was having with the human dolls in her head was much livelier.

The first time she had been in hospital, she swore it was going to be her last. It was humiliating talking about things she didn't want to speak about while the nurses watched on with amusement. When she thought about suicide, everyone does; it's natural, but it didn't mean she would do it.

For this job, there might not be any alternative but to enter the clinic as a patient. She hated the idea, but trying out the other option to apply as a mental health assistant would not work. If she applied for a position, she could blow her cover for any further attempt. She would just have to submit herself to be a patient. At least she knew what they would expect of her, having already gone through the system.

An hour later, she was home. The telephone which she had been trying to avoid for the last week rang persistently. Only a week late, and already the bank was on her back.

'What is it?' Clara answered in a waspish temper, and then after a few minutes, she put the telephone down.

Impossible to know what to think at first. Wow, then really and then no.

Congratulations followed the expressions of sad news. The caller wanted her to sign some papers and bring some proof of identity to his offices; he was a lawyer. This was a nightmare gone crazy. How was it possible she had been left with all of Peter Thornton's possessions? He was terribly sorry for her loss.

'Peter is dead?' those awful words were spoken.

'Yes, I am very sorry to be the bearer of bad news,' said Mr. Anderson.

'Peter is dead—really dead? But he is not supposed to have died. I got a card from him just a month ago.'

'I am sorry to have shocked you, but I—'

'No, no, that's all right. He is never ill.'

She was grasping for contact, putting her hands out to grab hold of reality and that elusive question. Why?

'I am afraid to tell you he took his own life.'

'Suicide?'

'Yes.'

'No, Peter wasn't that type.'

And then she remembered the nature of his work. In those few seconds of discernment, it became clear. Peter didn't take his own life. Someone else did.

'Oh, poor Peter,' she held her hand to her mouth in shock. 'So young.'

'Miss Tinder, can I ask if you are all right?'

'Yes—well, no, but yes. When did it happen?'

'About six weeks ago. I've had trouble locating you. Originally, you were called Cecelia Clark.'

'Yes, I know—but I didn't expect to become rich. I didn't expect Peter to die.'

'Of course not.'

'Fortunately, I had your telephone number for this house—'

'How did he die?'

'Consider Miss Tinder if you want to hear this,' worried Mr. Anderson.

'I need to know because, if I don't, I shall still believe him to be alive.'

'Suicide is a very personal affair just as people take overdose—'

'He overdosed?'

'No, and he didn't step in front of a train either.'

'Was he pushed in front of a train?'

'No, absolutely no. When a man takes his own life, he will determine his own ending; he died the way he wanted to die or deserved to die. He jumped out of a sixth-floor window and landed on spiked railings.'

She gasped. The image of Peter falling through the air made her freeze. He must have seen where he was about to land. Poor Peter. A horrible death, even though he did this sort of thing to others, it became ironic and even in poor taste that this should happen to him.

'Are you still there?' Mr. Anderson tentatively asked. 'I am sorry I told you, but you insisted on knowing.'

'Yes, I'm okay, and thank you for telling me. It was a shock, you know. Poor, Peter.'

'Yes,' he muttered, aware that death greets most people either pleasantly or otherwise.

But the good news, when she replaced the receiver and still feeling a little strange and uncertain, what came out of it was she was going to be rich—rich. Rich, like in fabulously wealthy, if Peter was telling her the truth. He was a man who was incapable of telling lies. Clara was to meet Mr. Anderson tomorrow at eleven sharp.

How rich was she going to be? Should she say a prayer for dear Peter? A year had passed since she last saw him. Knowing him then, his face and slim yet very strong body did not warn her or him that he had only a year left. But he must have guessed this was a possibility. When you kill others, they will try to return the favor. If she had foresight, would she have told him he had so little time left? Would she have married him when he demanded? It was difficult to say, or was it? The truth—she would not have.

The call was over, and Clara was still in shock. Peter is dead. A thought she found almost impossible to take in. When Peter asked her to marry him, which she thought was what she wanted, her answer became no as soon as he asked. The idea had suddenly become abhorrent. Most peculiar, she had been attracted to him right from the beginning until he asked her to marry him. Bizarre, it didn't make sense; she felt panicky. A commitment she could not make. And the bewilderment came when she realized he was asking her to be his wife. And then, why? What did he see in her to desire her for the rest of his life?

The incomprehension of losing someone who had become a debt because she had always feared him. But now, the debt was gone. It was a strange relief. Did she miss him? Did she feel sad he had gone? Should she think it was sad he was dead? That strange word. Dead in that she would never see him again. For the first time, she didn't know. She didn't know how to think about him. It would be so ungrateful to feel relief when he had left her everything. But he had to leave it to someone, she supposed. How could she be so ungrateful?

But she was smiling, smiling big and bright. There was going to be a great deal of money in her bank, and no more worries about paying the mortgage or truncating her spending. She could spend as much as she liked without having to worry.

Arriving at Mr. Anderson's office, he invited Clara to dinner. He had a cancelation in his diary. Very convenient to offer dinner for this suddenly very wealthy woman. At first, she was about to say yes, that would be nice, but suddenly she realized her status had changed. Now, as a very wealthy woman, what were this lawyer's motives?

All these thoughts whizzed around in her head like feathers unable to settle in a breeze, until gravity finally pulled them down. Now Mr. Anderson was speaking again and asking if she was all right and if she wanted to come out with him for dinner. Popular now, she had come into fashion. A question, would you have asked me out before you knew I was wealthy?

So, she said no. Though it was generous of him, she was still suffering from disbelief.

Unimaginable fortune. Peter was right when he said he owned some works of art. She knew a few of the artists from Peter's collection, but of course, not intimately. The only two artists she truly knew were Picasso and a somewhat questionable Van Gogh, attributed to the confused artist.

Stocks and shares. She never had enough money for those sorts of things. She wouldn't know what to do with them, either. It was very daunting. Mr. Anderson told her not to worry because she would have a team of financial advisors, but only, of course, if she wanted these people to care for her finances.

Yes, she would. In her hands, she would probably lose everything.

A villa in Tuscany overlooked the sea and an apartment in a fashionable part of New York. Yet there was another which had been purchased just over a year ago in Los Angeles. Peter, Clara now realized, had meant to come back to her; he wasn't going to leave her. She might have said no to him the first time and even to the second, but he would not let her get away that easily.

'But it appears he was hardly ever in the country. Mr. Thornton was a traveler, a nomadic—' chatted Mr. Anderson busily somewhere in the distance.

Rich, I am rich.

There was no need for her to work anymore, and then she felt guilty. She wished she had been kinder to Peter and maybe even agreed to an engagement. But then he might be alive now, and he would have taken better care of himself. It was for the best this had happened to him. At least it was for her.

'Was there anyone else?' Clara asked, because, why her? Why leave everything to her, and only her?

'It was Mr. Thornton's money and property to do with as he wished.' A polite cough. 'Take it as an opportunity to enjoy this sudden wealth. He would want you to be happy. I feel very sure of it.'

'Did you ever meet him?'

Suddenly Clara was curious. What had Mr. Anderson thought of Peter? Would he have supposed this smartly dressed man, peculiar in his ways and habits and needing control over inanimate objects, was an assassin? Can you tell a professional killer from those who were managers, laborers, taxmen, or architects?

'No, I didn't. It was a unique situation. A colleague asked me if I could set out a last will and testament for a very busy man. What was he like? I would have loved to have met him.'

'He was just like everyone else, I suppose, except he was special to me. That's all I can say about him.'

She smiled. And that was all she was going to say about Peter. It was time to end the session before it became too familiar. But Mr. Anderson needed to see her documentation to say she was the person she said she was.

Producing her paperwork, he was happy with the proof. He was looking forward to seeing her again.

Clara then smiled politely and announced her departure.

Oh, what a wonderful life this suddenly was. And how quickly her life had changed. Money, or rather the lack of it, would never be a problem again. She didn't need to work if she didn't want to. And as for Mr. and Mrs. Lamont, she could tell this spoiled couple she didn't need their job. Find someone else for a beggar's salary. Her station in life had changed.

Now thinking about it seriously, for her mind had delighted in frivolity, repeatedly telling herself over again she didn't need to work anymore. Yet, something was intruding on her mind. Had she become what she never thought she would, a dedicated and polished investigative journalist? A writer of truth; someone who was questing to put things right in her own way and to be recognized for it? Yes, she had become that. She was picking up the gauntlet to slip it on. It fitted her well.

Yet, lying in the dark was a dormant instinct, twitching its nose, sensing evil was afoot. Charisse was a child who had grown without love. A pawn between her parents used in battle who needed someone like Clara to help her live her life.

Tomorrow, Clara was going to make an appointment at the clinic where Charisse went for her rehab.

There had been a cancelation at the clinic; Dr. Slanders could see Miss Tinder at three this afternoon. If Clara had any medication, she needed to bring them to the interview. Yes, she would do that, absolutely. Fearing yet grinning at the rules of the game. She had changed. She had become a winner. She had found that golden lottery ticket to make her a winner with the winner's touch. Whatever she did in life now was always going to be good. Simply because she had changed her name from Cecelia Clark to Clara Tinder. How simple was that?

This time, she would take the cab to the clinic. No more cutting back on herself; no more going without or living beyond her means.

It was not a huge clinic, yet it was sleek and tucked out of the way. The windows, unlike other places, were not open to the world. This clinic reminded Clara of the architecture she had seen in magazines of large houses in England. The structure of the clinic had a presence that gave permanence. A good sign?

Two receptionists guarded the front, beautiful women in smart clothes and well-checked voices. Taking a seat, Clara was requested to wait because she had arrived early. At three o'clock, almost on the dot, she was asked to follow one receptionist through the heavy wooden doors. The traffic noise was cut out once the swish of the door closed behind her—while heavy pale green carpet woven with woolen flowers conjoined and suffocated the rest of the world from within.

It was now Clara regretted her commitment. Why didn't she just cancel this job, blow some of her money, and enjoy her life?

The receptionist, who smelled of chemicals from hair spray and the many types of cosmetics she had applied to her face, opened the door for Clara. Inside the room and behind a desk, a man in a mid-brown suit stood upright, which was very gallant. He nodded to Clara to enter.

He must have been nearly six feet tall. Wearing a white shirt and a darker brown tie, and brown tortoiseshell rimmed glasses, he should have looked impressive, but he didn't. Mediocre colors gave a very dull look. His bored expression was, Clara supposed, very reassuring.

'Won't you take a seat? I am Dr. Slanders.'

No shaking of hands: this was not that kind of relationship. Waited for Clara to sit. He took his chair. Without taking his eyes off her, she guessed he was already making his first assessment of her. Her cautious but still intelligent gaze rested on him, waiting for the interview to begin.

'And what can I do for you?' a moderate voice asked. There was no drama in it. He was a professional man here to help.

'I am going through a bad time, and now I am unable to cope.'

He nodded gently, serious eyes waiting for her to go on.

'I've now concluded I need help.'

'And what happened to you to come to this conclusion?'

She looked down and thought of Peter. 'The man I was to marry has just died; it was sudden. A tragic accident: I don't understand why it happened to him; it shouldn't have. And now I fear I'm going out of my mind.'

'I am sorry for your loss. Grief is difficult to come to terms with, but it doesn't always mean you should go into hospital as a full-time patient to overcome your tragedy. Counseling can help with the aid of medication.'

What was going on? Was he refusing her?

'You don't understand.' She looked frantic. 'It took a great deal of strength to get myself here. I have suicidal thoughts, and I am afraid. I can't see anything in my life to live for.'

'I understand.'

Dr. Slanders looked thoughtful for a moment and still with his eyes on Clara.

'I have been like this once before. I know the signs, which is why I came to you.'

'You were hospitalized before?'

'Yes.'

As she clutched her hands together, his eyes went straight to her hands. She realized then that he was watching everything she was doing and making detailed mental notes. What must it be like to be him, devoid of living his life for himself while hanging on to the tail strings of others?

'Tell me about the other time.'

She must tell him about Thomas. That harrowing and embarrassing episode she needed to forget.

'I fell in love with a man who was already married, although I didn't know it at the time. I followed him home —he never took me anywhere. We always met on the beach; I assumed he was in love with me as much as I was in love with him. I didn't know he was married with children.'

'Yes,' he said when she stopped.

'His wife knew what he was doing.'

She was cringing under his curiosity, his clinical mind poking around her lather of emotions and seeing her shame with medical disinterest.

'His wife didn't mind what he was up to. She probably had suspicions, but as long as he didn't tell her, she could keep on pretending. They had two children together; that was what mattered to her. That he kept a floozy on the side was nothing, because she had the wedding band on her finger. She was unattractive and overweight, and she knew it, but he had asked her to marry him, and she said yes and closed her mind to the rest of his world. I can't believe she ever loved him. She was probably very grateful he was handsome.'

'Did you love him?'

'Yes, I did. I would have looked after him—' she trailed off into silence.

'Do you believe he loved you?'

'Yes.'

She suddenly felt lost and tragic. His cold detached

hands were handling her experiences like an exercise of actions and results.

'I had to believe he loved me after the things we did together; he had to love me. And there was Peter—'

'And did you love Peter?'

He was watching her. She was trapped. Swiftly, he was moving from one man to another as if there wasn't any comparison between these two men. Thomas had become Peter. Did she love him? No, she couldn't. He had been sent to kill her. Peter never wanted her. He only wanted her because she refused him. While she was attracted to him because she was running away from—oh, did it matter? Sometimes everyone messes up.

'I could never love another like I loved Thomas.'

His eyes became brighter; this was the first honest word she had spoken.

'But I came to care for Peter. I'm sorry, this is confusing. Perhaps it was a mistake to come here.'

He blinked, glanced down at his notepad on his desk in front of him, and picked up a gold nibbed pen and wrote a few notes.

'When you say you felt suicidal, what did you intend doing?'

'If I didn't get any help from you, I intended hanging myself.'

A response which raised an eyebrow, and again he applied the pen to the notepad.

'To hang yourself is usually the reserve of men. Women usually overdose or cut their wrists.'

Had she interested him enough to take her on?

Lifting his face, a frown nipped his brow. He regarded her again clinically and thoughtfully.

'What do you think we can do for you?'

'I don't know. It was just a hope,' she sighed. 'I don't know if there is anyone who can help me.'

What was he doing, thinking through things as he shifted his face in consideration?

'How long have you known of his death?'

'Nearly three days.'

'And what have you been doing during those three days?'

'I haven't been able to cry. If I could cry, I might get some relief.'

Why was he so reluctant to take her on? Had he sensed something about her which disturbed him? Was she not a good enough actress to convince him she was ill, or had she forgotten how to be a mental cripple, a leper to society? Peculiar to find she didn't feel like she did when she first had that breakdown over ten years ago. What a mess. She despised herself then. But time had passed, and the person she once was had gained strengths, learned about the world and herself and what other people had mastered to play this game of life.

'I am uncertain how we can help you,' he still held on to the pen, a necessary prop to show he was in control. 'You are going through a hard time, and you will need support, but it doesn't mean you have to be in the hospital for that.'

Was he going to fail her? If there was something she was good at, she always thought it was her mental instability. Gosh, had she become balanced without knowing it?

'Have you checked this hospital out?'

'I don't understand.'

'Well, this clinic is geared up mainly for people who have drug-related problems. There are some exceptions, of course.'

She listened while she felt the embarrassment creep up

her back, blushing swept deep into her cheeks. A mental hospital was a mental hospital; she didn't know she had to do homework before applying.

'The reason our system works is that we are a community. Everyone is expected to support each other. Life is being a part of a community. Our community is a rehearsal for the next stage. Most people fail in life because they do not have a proper network. We educate the people who come here to succeed where possible. And as a result, I don't know how you would fit in. You are older than our usual subjects.'

'Just give me a chance. I will do everything to help myself.'

He listened to her remark as if it was a frantic call of no consequence.

'The clinic's day is based on group therapy, where discussions are held on how their experiences of life affect the residents, and why they resorted to drugs instead of sorting out their actual issues.'

'I can do that.'

'Perhaps,' he said, holding her attention.

Did she really want this? To enter a madhouse and abide by these rules.

'We can give you a go.'

Again, Dr. Slanders became thoughtful.

'This is an expensive paying hospital. People who come to us are rich—'

'I can pay.'

And so it seemed all was settled. She was to sign in with them tomorrow morning at ten. Never had she worked so hard to be accepted as a mental health patient.

3

G oing into a psychiatric hospital as an inpatient was something Clara was not looking forward to. Packing her case carefully, Clara thought of her previous experience, something she had cared to forget, but now it appeared imperative that she remembered. The balance from being ill to being stable was precarious. That time from the past became so thoughtfully close. The question again, how does anyone allow themselves to get into that state? But she had. These days, it was not something to be embarrassed about, that's what they say, but somehow Clara didn't believe it. Try for any job, and you will find out the hard way.

Having sorted out her new wealth with Mr. Anderson and how she could start using it was followed by several signings of forms and copied proof of her identity. Then on to the most interesting part, most of the money was tied up and working for her. But a sizeable steady trickle would enter her bank every day to keep her going and providing the idea she was wealthy.

Everything was being taken care of; the only task she

had to do was sit back and enjoy it. Secure and safe; no one could touch her anymore. Such a wonderful yet strange feeling to have, though she knew she would never take her sudden wealth for granted. If she wanted, she could pay off her mortgage straight away and sell this house and buy herself another one, a bigger one. Chuckling to herself as the cab made its way to the clinic the following day, again and again, she thought how wonderful it was to be rich.

Already the staff was expecting her. Clara checked in with the reception and was taken through to the building's central part. Although she had signed herself in by choice, she still held a feeling of revulsion as the memories flooded back. But this time, it was different. She was here of her own volition. There was nothing to fear but fear itself. Do not fool yourself, Clara; mental illness is always to be feared by pretense or for real.

A smart woman calling herself Nurse Jones took Clara for her medical; she had forgotten about this embarrassing episode. Stripped to her undies and in one of those gowns, she waited behind a screen for the doctor.

The door clipped snap as the soft brown leather shoes tread almost quietly across the padded flooring. Dr. Slanders was going to do the medical examination while Nurse Jones stood by watching. He wanted to check her heart, so she had to remove the top part of her gown and take off her bra. Nurse Jones did this.

Was this really necessary to demoralize a person with the pretense they were interested in your health? Resentfully, Clara stared angrily over Dr. Slander's shoulder. He had seen her bare-breasted and invaded her personal privacy; she would have to live with this. But this medical determined her resolve to do the job better, if only now out of bitterness.

'You can sit up now.'

Dr. Slanders took a step backward, still holding the stethoscope.

'Are you taking any medication?'

'No.'

She sat with her breasts still uncovered.

'When was the last time you took medication for depression?'

'Can I get dressed now?'

'Help Miss Tinder to dress,' he said, looking at the nurse.

She could dress herself, thank you very much. Hopping off the table, Clara quickly put on her bra. He had hardly touched her, and yet she still felt dirty.

'I can't remember,' Clara said, doing up her bra. 'Years ago. I didn't expect to have another breakdown again.'

'And what did you take?'

'I can't remember that either.'

Taking her blouse, Clara hurriedly put that on as well. Nurse Jones was not even bothering to help but continued watching her with cold and dispassionate eyes. If Clara were to sketch this woman of about thirty-something, she would credit her with beauty and sophistication, but that's where it would end. Her heart, Clara felt, was set in ice. With no conversation, Clara had already judged her hard. Instinctively, she knew she didn't like her.

As if Dr. Slanders knew what she was thinking, he turned to Nurse Jones.

'Nurse Jones is one of our senior nurses here. If you have any problems, such as the food, your room, or any other complaints, you can first turn to Nurse Jones. We want your stay with us to be without trouble; that way you will get the best benefits from it.'

A quick glance over to Nurse Jones's icy face, she

thought if there were anyone in this place she should turn to, it would not be her. Already Clara could sense there was a mutual dislike between them both. Couldn't Dr. Slanders, who dealt in psychology, not see this?

Clara was shown to her room by Nurse Jones. Walking behind this slim lady, her hair dressed in a French twist, Clara fancied if she caused any problems, this woman would be the first to stab her in the back.

After she was given the schedule for the week ahead, Nurse Jones reiterated Dr. Slander's expectations of her. That she should go to each therapy group unless excused by a team leader. They stared at each other, and in those three tense seconds before Clara dropped her eyes, the evidence of Clara's instincts showed this woman had no compassion, only hatred for her.

It was a relief when the icy woman left the room. Looking around her room, she realized this was her home for the duration. Her bags had been installed in this beautifully decorated room with a magnificent view out onto the garden. If she were really mentally ill, this would have been an ideal place for recovery. In the middle of her room, a table waited with a complimentary bowl of fruit. Very nice. In every way, this was a beautiful place. It should be, considering the cost. Something now she shouldn't worry about.

Lunch was at one in the afternoon, and for the first time, she would meet the other residents.

It would be her first chance to socialize with the others. Again, Clara reminded herself this was work and not social entertainment.

At ten minutes to one, Clara took the elevator down to the ground floor, where instructions from the timetable on how to get to the dining room were conveniently left on the table. She couldn't help but be excited. Upon entering, there were already people sitting at the four-seater round tables. Everyone was happily chatting with each other.

No one here looked particularly psychologically ill. From experience, Clara knew what mentally ill people looked like, especially after they had been drugged. But there again, mental illness had become fashionable as a growing trend from fast living.

In hospitals, as in any institution, seating places would be taken. Not wanting to risk upsetting these people, she waited until everyone else took their seats for that vacant place.

Standing there on the edge of society was something she was familiar with. While she waited, in the background came the chimes of a piano playing, which was good living. Actual waitresses were also serving, a far cry from the other psychiatric hospital.

'Hello, I take it you are the new resident?'

A nurse who looked to be in her early forties had touched her on her shoulder with a smile.

'I am Nurse Ryan, and you must be Clara Tinder. Why don't you take a seat?'

As instantly as Clara disliked Nurse Jones, she immediately took to Nurse Ryan. Brown hair and eyes, pleasant features, and a kindly smile were attractive but not like ice, more like russet.

'I thought it would be better to let everyone take their usual seats first before taking mine. I don't want to step on anyone's toes.'

Nurse Ryan smiled enchanted and raised her eyebrows in approval. She looked about the room before stopping at someone in particular.

'Come with me. There's a seat over there with Argenta; she always sits on her own.'

Taking Clara by the hand, Nurse Ryan led her to the table.

'Argenta, this is Clara Tinder. Clara, this is Argenta. Argenta, Clara, is new to the clinic; remember how it felt. Perhaps you can help ease her first day here.'

Eyes too large for her face, possibly because this slight figure was so slim, looked up with interest at Clara. Her deep blue eyes sparkled with mischievous interest.

'It's good to see a fresh face. I will do my best to look friendly. Take a seat, but don't take it away with you.'

The corner of Clara's mouth lifted, hearing this young woman's childlike humor. A promising start. She was convinced she was going to like this woman-child. There was something very innocent about her, with her baggy trousers and her hair in a ponytail.

'So,' Argenta's eyes detailed Clara while she made herself comfortable in her chair. 'Which bins have you been in?'

Clara forgot about the hospital language.

'Just the one, and that was ten years ago.'

'Which means you are not a professional nutcase. I'll have you know I am gaining the most wanted title in psychiatric history, which is to be completely mad. Very few make it to this stage. I am hoping Dr. Slanders will give up on me and tell me I have no chance.'

Surely, she couldn't mean that. Nurse Ryan had moved to the edge of the room to keep her lookout.

'They watch us,' said Argenta, noticing Clara looking. 'They watch us all the time. They don't want to miss anything.'

'Don't they trust the people here?'

'Who knows? Probably not. They're trying to learn the art of how to go mad. What are you in here for?'

'Classified as a broken heart. The man I was to marry suddenly died.'

And even though she said this, Clara still couldn't believe that Peter was gone.

A look of passing puzzlement ran across Argenta's face before breaking into a smile.

'Perhaps it's for the best. At least you will remember him with passion. He will always be romantic to you.'

A shocking remark, but Argenta was right after thinking about it. Peter would always be a romantic figure to her now. The shining knight in armor, a slayer of rascals. Peter, who walked on the wrong side of life, had now found his place amongst them. It was a beautiful paradox. As much as Clara tried to stir up that feeling of loss, nothing came except one feeling, gratitude. An involuntary smile triggered Clara's lips —he would approve of this emotion by considering this as a step towards love.

'Why are you in here?' now it was Clara's turn to ask.

'Money.' Argenta said, lightly lifting her neck into the air. 'I came into my inheritance last year and the responsibilities that go with it. My guardians want me to marry someone my parents wanted. But I want to marry the guy of my choice, which just happens to be the same guy. The point is, I didn't want to be told who to love. I want to choose for myself.'

'I still don't understand why you're here.'

'Because I tried to slash my wrists. They kept going on at me and telling me it was what my mother and father wanted.'

'Are your parents dead?'

'They went off a cliff when I was a baby, twenty years ago.'

'I'm so sorry.'

'There's no need to be. I don't remember them at all.'

'Do you have any brothers and sisters?'

'Not one, and I like it that way. My guardians say I'm spoiled, but they're always saying things like that when they can't get me to do what they want me to do. Apparently, I drive them to distraction, but as I told them, they are getting paid for it.'

With her elfin chin tilted upwards, Argenta came across as confident and arrogant. But she was far from that; a glance over at Clara implied she was trying to be brave. Shocking people was her way of gaining attention. She looked younger than she was, which could hinder others from taking her seriously. When so young, losing one's parents must have a devastating effect on a girl growing up.

'And what about you? Do you have any siblings?'

'No, but I would have liked to have had a big brother, someone I could look up to,' said Clara.

'When you've got money, you don't need to worry about having someone to look after you.'

This slight child was trying so hard to be brave, to be fierce and careless of what others should think, but it only made Argenta appear more vulnerable. So thin, her hands a little more than bones bothered Clara. What had done this to make her resent her own body?

'Now,' began Argenta again. 'You've got to plan what you are going to do with your life, and especially how you are going to live it.'

'What do you mean?' such a grownup statement to make.

'I mean, you must know what you want to do with yourself. Do you plan to have a career, get married? Do you want to be happy? There is no good going through life hoping these things will happen. My guardians want me to marry.

Unfortunately, they are more worried about my money rather than whether I will be happy.'

It was hypnotic; this was a conversation that others had had with Argenta, perhaps her guardians. She was not looking at Clara as she busily rearranged the cutlery's setting. The knives slid across the tablecloth in a practice of turns, just like a young boy playing with his toy cars. At the same time, the spoons became traffic lights. The dessert spoon and a soup spoon placed head to head became barriers. When the fish knife and the dinner knife met this barrier, Argenta bounced on her chair from side to side as if she were counting. And then she drove the knives through the barrier.

She looked up. 'You didn't answer me.'

'I have a job. I work for my living.' Being wealthy, she didn't need to work anymore. 'I chose to have a career.'

Now puzzled, she leaned towards Clara. Argenta stared at her with sudden distrust.

'What is the matter?'

'Why are you here?'

'Because I'm not well.'

Argenta's insight was disconcerting. They both were now spooked by each other.

'Have my guardians sent you?'

'I don't know your guardians. I never knew you were here,' and then she saw the fear in Argenta's eyes. 'No, they didn't.'

'I wouldn't be surprised if they did. I wouldn't be surprised at what they get up to. It's the money; that's the only thing they care about. I had to be sure of you.'

'I understand.'

'There's nothing they wouldn't do to get at my money.'

'I'm sure they wouldn't do that.'

'Oh, you don't understand. I live in a far different world from you.'

This time, those big dark blue eyes were hungry with suspicion. Her world had been made unsafe. She looked behind Clara and then nodded to her.

'The food is good here, but you want to watch it—they drug it.'

'No, surely not.'

'You are very innocent. I wish I were still innocent. I lost my innocence years ago. Eat up; it's delicious. The chef is first class.'

'Excuse me,' one of the two waitresses wanted Clara's attention. 'I am Dilly, your server. I've come to ask what you would like for lunch. We have a choice of three dishes on the menu. There is a lamb hotpot, fish salad, or a vegetarian.'

All attention was on Clara; Argenta watched curiously to know what she was going to choose.

'What are you having, Argenta?'

'I'm going for the vegetarian. I'm not a meat eater.'

'Then I will have the same. Thank you,' she smiled back at the waitress. 'Is the vegetarian good?' she asked when the waitress had left their table.

'I suppose so.'

There was a jug of water on the table. Seeing it, Clara poured them both out a glass and then settled back, glancing around at their neighbors who were still chatting brought on a feeling of calm.

'So, what happened to you?' Argenta's forks were making their way to the barrier of spoons.

'About what?'

'Your breakdown. What did you do?'

'Nothing really, except I gave up.'

'Were you in love with him?'

The second person to ask this question. Did it really seem impossible for her to love someone?

'Yes, although he was usually off somewhere and very busy. He worked very hard?'

'Did you cry?'

'No, not really. I was in too much shock.'

Her questions were unsettling and invasive. It was almost as if she didn't know she was being rude.

'Look, do you think we could drop this line of questioning? I feel I am under attack.'

'Oh dear,' Argenta looked up from her roadblock of forks. 'You are going to have to get used to people asking questions like mine. It's part of the therapy. You have to talk about things which upset you. But I guess while we are eating lunch, I can ease up a bit.'

'How long have you been here?'

Most of the residents had been served their meals and were enjoying their food.

'Nearly four months. I plan to be out of here in a month or so. They are fitting me up to join their commune.'

'A commune? Why do you want to go there?'

'It's better than the alternative, which is to go back to my guardians. I figured when I get back on my feet, I might get myself a job.'

She had replaced her cutlery to their right places because the waitress was now heading towards their table.

'What are you thinking of doing?' Clara was interested.

'Something like what you are doing. I want to be like you.'

Confused by this answer, Clara had to ask. 'How do you know what I am doing? I never told you.'

'I can guess. Thank you,' she said to the plate which had arrived in front of her.

'Okay. What do you believe I do?'

Was there something about her that said she was a journalist? The idea others could tell she was an investigative journalist was worrying. It almost made her feel paranoid that she had broken her cover.

'You are a businesswoman.'

Such relief, Clara smiled.

'How clever you are. Not many people guess this about me.'

'I can tell what people do; it's one of my skills. I sense different things about people. I knew it when you came here that it was because you had a broken heart. It was obvious. I could feel it in your soul. It's almost like words are floating above your head telling me this.'

Was this strange woman-child serious, or was she just having a joke? But the look on her face showed she was very confident in what she said. It might be better if she changed the conversation.

'Are you looking forward to going to the commune?'

Two plates were now set in front of them. The food looked interesting—a Mediterranean stew with chickpeas, which not only smelled good but promised to be tasty. Argenta eyed the stew before looking at Clara. Her face was fearful.

'This is nice,' Clara said encouragingly, after taking the first spoonful.

'You don't find anything strange about the taste.'

'No,' again, Clara smiled and nodded to Argenta, inviting her to try her own. She could do very well to eat.

Still watching as if she were just about to plunge straight

down into a deep ravine, Argenta picked up her spoon and put it into the medley.

'Do you want to see my friend?'

'Your friend?'

This was a distraction.

'Yes.'

From under the table, Argenta produced a strange looking soft toy.

'This is my friend. He gets real hungry, don't you, Leon? He's super friendly, and doesn't enjoy being on his own, so I have to take him with me everywhere, especially at mealtimes.'

Embarrassing, Clara inwardly cringed when Argenta produced this child's toy. Surely, Argenta didn't expect her to take this seriously.

'I know you are hungry, but you will have to wait.'

Taking up her spoon, Argenta stirred it around her plate with that interested attention of appetite. Complete fascination in the dish while surreptitiously glancing at Nurse Ryan. She was on lunchtime duty. Fascinated, Clara ladled her spoon with a few chickpeas. What was Argenta going to do with her spoon? Clara saw Argenta take the spoon to her opening mouth and from the side of her eyes, she saw her wipe her mouth. The food had disappeared off the spoon.

The sleight of hand was truly professional. But why? Why was Argenta choosing to starve herself? A demonstration of her protest showed she had no power or control over her life, which was her way of revealing her anger. Not her affair, though. Time to mind her own business. Clara couldn't allow herself to be involved in this young woman's life.

'That was nice,' said Argenta, putting her spoon down, pleased she had cleared most of the food off her plate into her lap. 'I think we've done very well today, haven't we, Leon? I'd better take you up to our room and get you cleaned up.'

And then her eyes grew large because Nurse Ryan was making her way to their table.

What was this? It was disgusting. Something wet and soft was deposited on to Clara's lap.

'Argenta, what have you been doing?' Nurse Ryan stood over her.

'Nothing Nurse Ryan, I promise. Look—' she raised her hands into the air. 'I've eaten nearly everything. Aren't you going to congratulate me?' she grinned hard.

'Stand up first,' said Nurse Ryan, 'before we do any congratulations.'

Argenta stood, her eyes beaming, knowing she had won. An empty victory to believe she had fooled a person who cared about her. Yet, in the fooling, she continued to endanger her life, and there was nothing funny about that.

Clara found it very difficult to continue a conversation after Argenta had implicated her in this childish plot.

4

After lunch, there was a compulsory meeting in the conference room. Taking the toy containing Argenta's wasted food, Clara had time to dispose of it down the toilet. Repulsive, but Argenta made no apologies. This was the last time she was going to share a table with this socially inadequate woman for two reasons. Not only because it would jeopardize her mission, but also because of the childish nature of this exploit.

Two o'clock and the meeting begun. In command, Dr. Slanders was sitting at the front, viewing the semicircle facing him. In good humor, he sat awkwardly cross-legged. It appeared as if his legs were too long, and he didn't know what to do with them. Head slumped to one side, held up by his raised shoulder. For a psychiatrist, he wasn't in command or at ease in his own body.

'Before I start the lesson today.' Dr. Slanders' smile was hanging limply around his face. 'I want to introduce you to a new resident. You've probably seen her at lunch. Can you please stand, Clara, and introduce yourself briefly to the rest of the group?'

They knew where she was, eyes on her like sticky fingers of curiosity, demanding she stand. Embarrassing, the last thing she wanted to do was call attention to herself.

'My name is Clara Tinder, and I am pleased to be here. I want to get well, and I am prepared to be supportive of the rest of the community.'

How loud her voice sounded in the meeting of so many.

'Thank you, Clara,' Dr. Slanders replied, pleased with Clara's introduction.

Almost as if he had orchestrated the meeting's smoothness into the more serious business of the gathering. She settled herself uncomfortably, feeling she had become a puppet.

'In the previous meeting, and I know some of you have heard this before, but it is important. We need to understand what our responsibility is to each other. This applies to when you leave this community for the bigger one outside.'

He looked at each one to make sure they understood what he was telling them.

'You may have problems at this moment in time, and you may feel bad about yourself, as you may wonder what you can bring to this community. You may even think you are not worthy. But you are. Each of us can contribute in different ways.'

His eyes fell on Clara. She thought he had brown eyes because everything about him was brown. Brown office, brown clothes, brown personality, but his eyes were sharp like ice. They were blue. But they were too light for her taste.

'With some, they are excellent orators; they can mesmerize people by using their words. With others, it's their hands; they can create and make the world beautiful for others. It is a gift and one which I wish I had. With others, there is a finer gift.'

He looked around the room again.

'Has anyone any idea what this gift is?'

They looked to their hands and their laps, and then to each other.

'Anyone?'

The silence grew heavier.

'Then I will tell you what it is. It is obedience. Now I can see the look of surprise registering on everyone's face. You thought it was something far out of your range of abilities. But it isn't. Everyone can be obedient.' Nodding with encouragement, he smiled, his eyes once more circled the room.

'Everyone has a place in the community—and being obedient is not an inferior quality. It is the model we approve of. It makes for a happier life not only for the individual but also for the community as a whole. Society is more productive because of it.'

Everyone focused on him. It was not only what he was saying, which had such power. It was also how he spoke. The tenor of his voice, and the way he used his hands, and his eyes, this gave a convincing demonstration. Astonishingly, Clara was much affected by what he said. And his smile. He used every orator's instrument of power. And for those looking for a direction which most of these vulnerable people were, this was the ideal prototype and a shape they could mold themselves into.

Emphatically, carefully breaking down any opposing argument with what became common sense, Dr. Slanders' logical deductions produce an optimistic view of living in a commune. They were mentally at default in the world. Well, look at them; they were here. Going out into the world again for some would be dangerous. However, there was an alternative. Somewhere they would be safe. But would they still be able to contribute to the world by living in the commune?

Right from the beginning, Clara had denigrated this man. As a psychiatrist, it was enough for her to think badly of him. What did he know about mental illness, anyway? People like him had never suffered; they learned their science from a book on what it was to be mentally ill. But sitting in this group amongst these others and sensitively picking up on the group's feelings gave an oppressive conclusion inferred that anything other than this was bad.

He waited to see that digestive look of agreement before continuing.

'Most of you have stayed outside of society to observe your fellowman with revulsion. You think to yourself you cannot fit in.'

Dr. Slanders smiled. It was the smile of power which made him ready for any opposition. Total control in a subject close to his heart. Nobody moved. Clara felt afraid to move; she was even terrified to blink. While breathing now became controlled.

'But you can fit in. You are showing this capacity just by being here. And this is because you trust us. You trust this therapeutic community. And you trust me. We have shown you it is good to be you. You are safe in this community. You know no one here will harm you. I can see it and read it in your faces.'

What was it he saw written on her face?

'In here, you are all special people and chosen because you are wanted.'

Lowering his voice and his head, he revealed his bright blue eyes. Had he practiced this before? Suddenly, eyes were trapped in his brilliant radiation, caught in the limelight of his celebrity.

'But you will not be staying here forever. You will move on. But will you fail when you walk out of this door for the last time? Perhaps. But I would like to think that everyone will succeed, but they won't. I am not pessimistic that doesn't come into it. One has only to look at the facts because seventy percent of you will fail. I want to look at that seventy percent and ask myself, what can I do for these people? How do I care for these important individuals? This has been my mission to be there for the ones who don't make it. Look about you. Who do you think will fail, and who will be successful? Will it be you, or you?' he pointed a random finger.

As if permission was given, sitting tight in their isolated chairs, faces turned to look at their neighbors. Eyes now not so confident as when they first walked in to take their places.

'Ask yourself, why have I failed? Is it because my peers do not accept me? Do I feel so different from them? The answer is you differ from them. You cannot help it. And it is not because you are weak or even stupid. You will always stand outside of society. Society out there does not have a place for you. Unfortunate, but true.'

The room had become uncomfortably quiet.

'So, you are thinking, where shall I go? Who will have me? Will no one notice my qualities? Will I always be despised?'

Raising an eyebrow, he shrugged; this was likely their future.

'No one can save you from yourself. Look at yourself and recognize your flaws. So, you are here. You are special to us, but where do you go from here? I apologize for painting a bleak picture, but you will be right back in the place that made you ill unless you face up to it. But this time, you will go further, and your despair will be greater.'

Someone had moved. It was Argenta. Not only had she moved, but she also sighed. All eyes went to the traitor. Straight as a poisoned arrow, they collectively ousted her out. Dr. Slanders was the sharpest of eyes. While all eyes, like warriors, chased their leader in anger, they trampled over Argenta.

'I am sorry we are boring you, Argenta.'

'No, that's perfectly okay.'

Dr. Slanders' teeth bit hard on his smile; his lips drawn apart with the grin of a dagger.

'We were talking about people's future and how we can help them.'

'That's fine by me. You don't need to apologize. Carry on.' She waved irresponsibly, as if to dismiss him.

'You would do well to take an interest in what is being said.'

'I'm sorry, I was just, well—tired. We talk about the same thing every time, and it's never pleasant. Can't we talk about something else?'

'Would you like to leave us? Have a rest if you are feeling tired.'

'Yes, that would be nice.'

'Then I suggest you go now. Nurse Jones, please, would you take Argenta to her room?'

Nurse Jones stood immediately, proud to serve this important man. With stern eyes, she fixed them on the culprit, and anger in her hands, she helped Argenta to stand. The room remained quiet, waiting for these two to leave.

'I am afraid you have just witnessed an example of someone who will not make it in this world. You understand, we can only go so far towards helping you—but you have to do the rest.'

Was it Clara's imagination that she fancied Dr. Slanders' eyes fell pointedly on her? A lesson he felt was relevant for her, but did she already feel guilty being here on false pretenses?

'I want you to think about your future seriously, and what will happen when you leave here? Have any you got any questions?'

For Clara, it had been a creepy meeting, for it searched for undertones of failures when in truth, there were none. Dr. Slanders' technique had worked. Doubts were stealthily creeping in, uncertainties and fears. The confidences Clara had collected little by little over the years were put on trial and found wanting. Was she really sure of herself? Did she believe in what she was doing?

It was ten years ago when Clara had her breakdown. Such a long time ago, or so it seemed. A devastating experience she felt happened overnight. Such was the destruction that she was reduced to levels of despair and self-loathing— where had it come from? But she never wanted to go back to that place again. Until now, she never had. She had survived, but her spirit had suffered. Even so, though her life after had never been what she would have liked it to be, it was, in essence, reasonable, and she appreciated it. An almost impossible struggle upwards, but she gained each step back to health. Yet, never had she suffered the prediction which Dr. Slanders forecasted for these people.

When everyone left the room, Dr. Slanders put his meaningful eye on them. He had looked at her in the same manner, which was alarming.

But as an investigative journalist, her only problem was it felt like she was too close to home.

Instead of going for tea with the rest of them, Clara sat in the armchair, leaning forward with her head in her hand, deep in thought. She needed to ask questions, and there was no use in being friendly and being the perfect patient. It wasn't easy being here; the ghosts of her past were still hanging around; it wasn't as easy to be objective as she had hoped.

The commune was a place spoken of with reverence. Promising to give hope to those people who thought they wouldn't make it. During the meeting, questions were asked about what it was like and what was expected of them should they think about applying.

'Well,' began Dr. Slanders. 'Are you happy here?'

No one answered. Heads moved as they looked once more at their neighbors. Being here was easy because everything was done for them. The staff thoughtfully and carefully prepared their meals. Here they would be kept busy; there was no chance for boredom, the sin of a creative mind. No one was lonely, and people were kind and happy—a wonderful place to be if you were never ambitious. Life went on easy enough, and most importantly, society didn't poke its nose in with trials people couldn't handle.

'That is what it will be like in the commune. There is no difference. You will not be expected to do anything you don't like. You are people who need to be protected from the rest of the world because you are special. It is an ideal life.'

And when Dr. Slanders said it like that, the appeal was powerful. As easy as ice-cream on apple pie, Clara saw herself projected into this life with all its ease and convenience, always to be surrounded by friendly faces. Why did she need to push herself into this awkward life? She had all the money now to enjoy herself and be waited on. But it was a fool's paradise to think it's possible to hide away from life, a niggling voice reminded.

Charisse, a troubled heiress, had taken this route. As much as Raphael claims he loves his daughter, it was actually the money that provoked him to look for her. That's the trouble with money. Would Clara now only be measured by how much she was worth? A thought which shouldn't be dismissed, always the silent partner in a relationship. She never flinched when Dr. Slanders told her the magnitude of their fees. It appears her money bought her admittance.

There was one thing that trouble Clara, and that was the clinic's policy. There were to be no cell phones. The excuse was that while they were in here, they needed to work on themselves. The outside world for the duration was banned. This was a problem. Clara hoped to contact the Laments, as there were always questions that had been forgotten.

A busy day with a new routine in a new environment was tiring. Yet, there was another therapy session she had to attend. It was a choice of either art or drama. Art was more restful, although she was hopeless at painting. But what did it matter? While she was here, she might as well have fun.

Looking at the large Victorian tub in her bathroom, it became an invitation to have a long soak after dinner and curl up with a long glass of wine—not that she had any. Alcohol was banned, which was understandable. Some were here for alcoholism.

Changing into jeans might help her mood. Outside, the sun shined lazily. It would have been nice to sit out there with a glass of excellent wine while making her notes. She could do with a long drink.

Ten minutes later, with a change of clothes, quick freshen up, and brushed hair, Clara felt more herself. It was the thought she had voluntarily entered a nuthouse that disturbed her. It shows you that you shouldn't close the doors on anything in life.

Walking along the corridor to take the elevator down, Clara was as surprised to see Nurse Ryan coming out of Argenta's room as she was surprised to see her. Closing Argenta's door, she then locked it; something wasn't right. Perhaps it was also because Nurse Ryan had fallen in step with Clara.

'Are you going down in the elevator?' she asked to Clara's ruptured silence.

Clara nodded, wondering why Nurse Ryan would lock Argenta in her room.

'I'll take the elevator with you.'

'Why did you lock Argenta's room? She's all right, isn't she?'

Nurse Ryan stopped in front of Clara.

'Let me ask you one thing. Did you see Argenta eat?'

The face in front of Clara was frowning. Nurse Ryan didn't want any lies, just the truth.

'She didn't eat her lunch,' Clara said, hating herself for sneaking on Argenta.

'Thank you for your honesty. What did she do with the food?'

'The food never touched her mouth. She put it into a bag, and when you came along, she passed the bag over to me.' Clara squirmed at the memory.

'And what did you do with it?'

'I took it to my room and disposed of it. I'm not here to spy on her. I have my own problems.'

'You're right,' Nurse Ryan's anger turned to sadness. 'It isn't your problem. It's Argenta, but she doesn't know how to help herself. We are losing her fast. I am doing my best to help her, otherwise—'

'Otherwise, what?'

Horrors were gathering in Clara's mind. The wickedness of all illnesses is always mental.

'Force-fed.'

'But I thought that was illegal.'

'What alternative is there? To watch someone die when they can't help themselves?'

Nurse Ryan held her hand to her mouth because they both had raised their voices.

'Do we have any other choices? Argenta is killing herself, and she can't help it.'

'It's against her human rights.'

'But to watch someone die is aiding and abetting suicide. We have to intervene, and I will, even though it repels me. In fact, it would disgust me even more to witness her death.'

This must be one of the cruelest tricks to become a care-giver, as the love you impart is rejected. But why was Argenta starving herself? Did she really have no choice?

'Was she like this before she entered the clinic?'

'She was slim, but not underweight. A bright and happy young woman, and very outgoing. I couldn't think of any reason she was here. Having mental illness is not a holiday.'

'Was she,' murmured Clara.

'For the first week, she was fine. Very engaging. Everyone liked her. Like a bright star, all the residents and staff were attracted to her. And then one morning, she awoke, and everything about her changed. As if she went to bed that night and thought enough of this, she would reveal her true self. Argenta repulsed everyone, and she believed they were in a grand plot against her. Quickly, the residents turned away from her, as did the staff. I could see she was heartbro-ken, although she never told me so.'

Nurse Ryan could have been talking about her as she was once upon a time.

'I don't know what to do for her, I despair. I'm a member of staff, but first I'm a person. Dr. Slanders has been very patient with her while I've been, I suppose, overly protective. But I shouldn't be telling you this. It's very unprofessional. Argenta is dying right in front of our eyes.'

It was on Clara's lips to say perhaps she should let Argenta die, yet how callous this sounded? This nurse was more involved in her patients' lives than Clara supposed. To care about someone was crippling, like dying an extra death when yours wasn't enough.

Then Nurse Ryan became conscious of herself and what she was doing.

'Aren't you meant to be somewhere?'

'Yes,' this abrupt question startled Clara while her eyes looked at the locked door with thoughts of the person lying asleep inside. 'Will she be all right? Do you think she will pull through?'

'I really don't know, but I shouldn't be talking to you about her.'

'She said that she plans to go to the commune, the one which Dr. Slanders was talking about. Do you think that will help her if she gets there?'

What was that look on her face, a wry smile coming from prejudice? Nurse Ryan was thinking about something, but she wasn't prepared to share it. That cognizant look of understanding as Clara walked away. Nurse Ryan had views on the commune. Come the right time, when she was plump with anger, perhaps she would share it.

5

————

Painting was relaxing and harmless. Mixing up paints and applying them to an empty canvas was a solitary excursion, like taking a walk. Strokes of greenery plowed on to the paper with the life of an imaginary countryside. Broad sweeps of calming colors had a soothing effect on the soul. And this was what she was painting, moving away from the bright artificial lights of compact living. Now glad she had come to this class. The therapist was friendly and encouraging, and afterward, they had one of those discussions.

Clara would never be an artist, no matter how hard she tried. Thank goodness she didn't desire to be one, as neither did she have an artist temperament or Bohemian mind.

'I was interested in your painting,' said Sarita, the art therapist. 'You've caught the essence of calmness. Do you know what I was reminded of? Kashmir, my homeland. It's such a beautiful place to live, pungent, spicy, and warm. My family and I were most upset about leaving.'

Attention from others was alerted and directed to Clara, who would rather move about these people unseen.

'Thank you.'

'What were you thinking about when you painted your scenery? Was it anywhere in particular?'

'No, nowhere but a place in my head. A place I would like to imagine exists without the flaws.' Her attempt at humor wasn't taken. That her painting could make Sarita think of her homeland was absurd.

'That's a fascinating thought, Clara. Can anyone else comment on Clara's painting? Show us your artwork, Clara. Bring it into the circle.'

No, she didn't want to. This was embarrassing, but this was also a community where everything is shared.

'I am really not that good. I can't paint, and I don't try to.'

'It is not how well we paint, Clara; it is the feelings we inspire into our work which moves others. Don't be shy, Clara. We are here to learn from each other.'

Distressing to have so much attention called to her. While the others looked at her painting, Clara's heart bled with despair and humiliation. The critical appreciation seemed to go on forever. Then, at last, after each of the other paintings were looked at, the session was over.

'Clara,' asked Sarita, coming across as Clara put her painting away. 'I didn't upset you, did I by asking you to bring your painting to be viewed?'

'I can't paint.'

'You have good use of color. The way you paint and the colors you use say things about yourself which you are hiding.'

What did she mean by that?

'Each of us has sides which we keep from the public eye. You ought to reveal that side of yourself. What have you done in life? I'm sure your life has been more exciting than most.'

'I am the daughter of a mother who hates her. The only person I really loved killed himself, and that was my father.'

Spoken in anger and temper, and it showed. It was violent enough to make Sarita take a step backward in startlement.

'I'm sorry to hear that, Clara, when inside of you, you reveal a caring soul. I wish your mother could see you as others like myself see you.'

Such a gracious lady, gentle and positive, and someone who really cared about the people she worked with.

Strangely, she didn't feel bad anymore since she had inherited Peter's money. Funny how money can make you feel so much better about yourself. Oh, it was good to be rich—no wonder those people who have always been rich feel smug about themselves. Rachel always believed she was more superior, but where was she now?

If Clara had hoped she would see Argenta at dinner, it was received with disappointment. Clara was going to have to eat alone.

While others chatted at their tables, Clara didn't feel awkward or left out. She had always been a solitary person. Nurse Jones, who was on dinner duty, often glanced at Clara with disapproval. For her own reasons, or it might have had something to do with Dr. Slanders, she didn't like Clara. Which meant she didn't want people who wouldn't fit in.

Why should she care about what others thought? Imposing their ideas on how she should behave wouldn't happen anymore. She was her own person now. But this wasn't the right attitude while she was here. If anything, she needed to show that she had problems.

Argenta's room was silent when Clara walked past her door. Looking at the door handle, she felt tempted to try it. But this was her first night here, and it had been a very tiring day. With thoughts of the bath and a good long soak, such things as worrying about Argenta could be left for another day.

Yet, looking to Argenta's door, Clara was smitten with sudden concern because there was a person quietly dying? It pulled a shudder from Clara. But this was what life was about, people trying to live while others are also wanting to die. It would never be easy being here.

No locks on residents' doors made for another vulnerability. Swimming backward and forward from the past, again, Clara thought of her parents. Her mother fought to live, using her father's shoulders to pull herself out from the mire. But putting her parents into the past was something she really ought to do. Don't allow them to define your future, and yet it was difficult. Emotionally, if her mother were to die right now, she would say good riddance; she wouldn't be going to her funeral.

It was a humid night. After dinner, Clara had taken a tour around the dayrooms. No one invited her to join them. But this didn't matter; she was used to being and living on her own, yet it was strange no one other than Argenta had befriended her.

Was there something about her which they objected to? Was she giving off some sort of bad chemistry?

Throughout her life, she never had friends, only acquaintances. People rarely fell in love with her personality. It had to be something to do with her early life.

As a young child, hearing the door crash told a young Clara that it was her time to creep downstairs and be with her father. He would always be pleased to see her. They would have something to drink, a cup of hot chocolate usually, and sit together to watch the television.

'I love you, daddy.'

That had been enough for him then, and enough for her also to have her father completely to herself until she got older. The hardest problem for Clara was finding fault with him. Why didn't he stick up for himself? Memories: they follow you.

Poor dad.

This evening, she was going to take advantage of the large Victorian bath. The wide, white, and deep basin was very generous. Standing on elegant feet in the middle of the room, it was the perfect host. Getting her large towel and her bathrobe, Clara sang about the forthcoming indulgence. A lot was going on in her head, and a good soak would help to reason out her thoughts.

The plumbing thumped as Clara turned on the hot water faucet, threatening to throw out large splashes of hot water with promises of a decadent hot bath. The tub began its journey to fill slowly, rippling and rising further up the white enamel with the plug firmly in place. It was going to take ten minutes at least to fill this vast bath. She touched the fast rapids of waters; it ran over her fingers like a heavy waterfall and fell onto the white enamel of the tub. This was going to be a great pleasure, a great luxury.

The steam was already drifting into the cooler air like the impenetrable fog of pollution. Going over to the window, noisily she pushed up the old-fashioned sash frame. Drawing it up, the cooler air rushed in. Those two climates rapidly found each other to become a war of weather.

Out went the fog, and in came the cooling air and then the smell of cigarettes. Someone below was smoking. Oh, how foul? If she didn't have the steam to deal with, she would have shut the window. When one has been a smoker and given up, there is nothing more repelling than returning to the haunts of that obnoxious wafer.

Though smoking was forbidden in the hospital, an outside convenience was in place for people still addicted to the weed. Why didn't they use that instead of sharing their unsocial habit out of their window with others? She could imagine him or her by the window blowing out their poisoned breath.

'Same old thing again,' a man's voice said from below. 'How wonderful commune life is.'

'It appeals to me,' answered a woman.

'It would do. He likes his women. They are easier to manipulate.'

'That's not a very nice thing to say.'

'But it's the truth.'

'Maybe he prefers women because they're nicer.'

The man laughed. The silence which followed suggested he was taking another draw of his cigarette.

'Women like him because they find his age and position attractive. Women like power.'

'That's true, but it's also because he is kind.'

'Then, women like father figures.'

'I know you don't want me to go into the commune. I don't know why.'

'Because I don't trust him.'

'You've been listening to the rumors.'

'Where there are rumors, there is also some truth.'

'You won't put me off, so there's no use in trying.' she said defiantly. 'I have made up my mind. I like the idea of people working together for the common good.'

'There is nothing wrong with the outside world. Like most people here, your problem is you don't want to take responsibility for your actions. Once you take responsibility for yourself, then you'll take back control of your life. Accept what you have done and don't become a victim. It's become a fashionable problem these days. People are always whining and whining that it's never their fault when they have manipulated the entire scenario.'

Clara listened, stunned there was someone else who didn't trust Dr. Slanders. To hear better, she leaned her head over the window ledge.

'Perhaps some people can't help themselves. We are not all as strong as you.'

'I don't claim to be strong; I went off the lines and found when I experimented, I liked it. In a way, I suppose I am lucky my parents are forgiving and are prepared to take me back. I have a future to look forward to instead of the alternative Dr. Slanders is holding out.'

Again came another thoughtful silence, as if whoever the female was—was sulking.

'You're lucky.'

'I know I am.'

'My parents are divorced, and neither of them give a damn. They have no time for me now they've got new families.'

'I know, Lulu, but you've got to forget them and make your own future. Come and work for my family.'

'I don't have to work.'

'Yes, I know. You are independently wealthy like the rest of us in here. But that's the problem when you are rich and young. You need to work to have a purpose in life. To get up every morning with something structural to do. I see that now. I don't want to mess my life up anymore. Look what it's doing to Argenta. She doesn't want to get married and have children, which is impossible now because she is so freaking thin.'

'Do you really think she wants to die?'

'No, I don't. But she doesn't want to go to the commune either. But don't allow her to pull you down. We all have to be responsible for ourselves in the end.'

'You're lucky to be leaving here. I'm going to miss you. You are about the only sane one here.'

'You'll be all right, but if not, there is always a place in my family's business.'

'Thanks.'

'Cheer up. It's not as bad as it seems. But I tell you what strikes me as odd, and that's the people who go to the commune are usually female, and who are usually fabulously wealthy. Thirdly, they don't have either any family or, like Charisse, their family has moved on.'

'Are you adding me to that list?'

'Well, there are some similarities. Dr. Slanders has never pressed ganged me into joining the commune. He usually wants females in distress like Argenta and Charisse. Charisse said herself, her father and his wife only wanted her as the cash cow.'

'Yes, I know.'

Whoever the male was, laughed.

'Except that poor little rich girl when she came of age has cut them off, good and proper. I bet that hurt them.'

Some seconds passed, another cigarette had been lit.

'She said she would keep in touch with us,' said Lulu. 'She promised she would.'

'She obviously lied, or perhaps she is enjoying her life in the commune. Time passes when you are happy.'

'I was hoping she would let me know how it is.'

'They have rules about correspondence, which is another thing I find suspicious. My advice to you is to avoid the commune. Come and work with me.'

'No, I can't. I need stability and a home.'

'That's what Dr. Slanders has drummed into you. What he is clever at is making you doubt yourself. You know, Lulu, you have many skills which you haven't tried out. Try to be more positive about yourself.'

'It's easy for you to say that, Dirk. You didn't hit rock bottom like I did.'

'I had a good try at it.'

'Can you hear something?' Lulu asked again.

'What does it sound like?'

'Running water.'

'Now you mention it, I can just about hear something in the background. You've got better hearing than me.'

'Do you think someone is listening to us?'

'I don't know.'

Running water, the words hit home; they were talking about her. Craning over the window ledge to hear what they were saying, she had forgotten about her bath. The bath-water was still running. Now to the top and already spilling over. Grabbed by panic, Clara spun off the faucets. The water, spiteful to the touch, promised to scold her. The scalding water was too hot to plunge her hand down to pull out the plug, but it had to be done. With such a weight above it, the plug was reluctant to escape. Brow burning hot with panic and exertion, a large burp as the water gurgled out.

It was awful, but since Phoebe, Clara had lost some of her confidence. Watching the water disappear, she wanted to cry, and she did. Tears of self-pity came from a well that hadn't been touched for many years. There was no harm in feeling sorry for herself, just don't make a career out of it. All over now. But as for a bath. Not now. Not after her stupidity. Oh, life, what was she doing here? Be glad for your life; it was Phoebe. No bath then, instead have a shower. Compromise.

On a positive point, she had gained some important information through eavesdropping on their conversation. Lulu knew about Charisse. It would be a good idea to make friends with this young woman. An excellent idea, Clara. Well done. Clara smiled to herself; it was good when she was on her own side.

Wouldn't it be a good idea to spend some time in the communal lounge? It would be a good idea, but no, not tonight. An early night and writing some notes was more of her style, for now.

But it wasn't to be a good night. As being in a strange place brought noises Clara was unfamiliar with. At half-past nine came a knock on her door; the staff were doing their checks to find out where everyone was. Two night-nurses had started their shift. This time one of them was a man called David, here most of the nursing staff were young women. David looked to be somewhere in his fifties. Lined with graying hair, he came across as friendly. If she had any problems, she should ring the bell or alternately come to the staff room. Nurse Jane was the other nurse on duty.

It had taken Clara a long time to get off to sleep. Thoughts rushed around her mind about Charisse, and now Argenta. It was then she realized how vulnerable she was. No one knew where she was except the Lamonts. If she disappeared, would they be interested? Somehow, she didn't think so. She had gone into this blindly without letting anyone know where she was. Yet, people, Clara argued, don't suddenly go missing during the night, do they? Oh, Clara, stop predicting disaster. For goodness' sake, give it a break. Counting backward, she blocked out her thoughts and fell asleep.

A door slamming woke Clara with surprise. In a daze, she lost all sense of where she was. The moon, gliding in strong and bold strokes through the limbs of a tree, told her it was not in her room. Sounds erupted again; someone passed her room as they ran along the hallway.

'Is everything all right?' She had rushed from her bed to peep out the door.

'Yes, go back to bed,' said Nurse Jane, her nurse's hat cockeyed as if she had been in a brawl.

'What happened?' still half in sleep.

'I said go back into your room. There is nothing for you to worry about.'

But there was. Along the other end of the corridor, with the lights full on, Clara saw Nurse Jones coming out of Argenta's room. Nurse Jane looked to where she was looking and then turned back, but not in time to catch Clara because she had closed her door.

Was Argenta dead?

6

It had been a frightening night for Clara, which had been made worse by no one else mentioning the disturbance. The breakfast room, another sunny day, the other residents happily chatting. Clara wandered to the table where she and Argenta ate. Could she have imagined last night? No, no, she didn't? Natural to take a seat as before where yesterday she had sat with Argenta. No, this was a time for progress and not regress to move on and mix with the others.

'Hello, I am Clara. Is there room for me to sit with you?'

She took the table with a man sitting at it, hoping he would be Dirk. There were only three men in the clinic, which narrowed the odds. All four faces looked up. They had been in private conversation, and if they could, Clara felt sure they would have excluded her. She felt this by how they looked at her with reserve, the reticence to include her in their circle. Uncomfortable, Clara forced herself to smile. With Anise in her mind plus the idea she should become this other personality that needed to push herself forward, you know, claim that positive identity, no one else would do this for her. She smiled hard, and she meant business.

One of the four seated around the table, big enough to take six, stood to fetch her a seat. Nothing was said as he went to an empty table and picked up another set of cutlery. She was made way for, but she wasn't included. It was very awkward.

The three women remained in intense silence even while the man took his seat. She had gatecrashed, and Clara felt the wrath of their mute temper. Hadn't she observed their rules? The tweaked hostile glances, the slight raise of their chins. The cold frontiers which set the perimeter of their courtesy. She was frozen out. There was no meeting of minds. It just wasn't happening.

In all societies, there must be some negotiating, but only Argenta had warmed to her. More puzzling was why were they so unfriendly? Of course, mental hospitals were peculiar places to find friends. These people were the debris of society, and they were all pitched into the same pot.

Sensitive enough to feel the hard-icy daggers aimed at her. Even if she left their table, she knew there would be a group mutual sigh of relief. But she was going nowhere. She would not give up and walk away with her tail between her legs. Did they believe themselves to be more superior to her? A problem Clara needed to resolve as she looked at the stark tempered faces around the table. Almost as if they had just sniffed something distasteful. But the trick is not to mind.

'I was sitting with Argenta yesterday,' Clara addressed the male. 'But she hasn't come to the table. I do hate sitting on my own,' she smiled.

'I'm Dirk,' said the man, who looked to be in his late

twenties. Mid-brown hair and already age lines from anxiety probed his forehead.

'Hello, Dirk.'

She held out her hand across the table to shake. He took her hand reluctantly; she had broken into their clan. While the icy eyes of the other three still made her awkward. She had been correct in her assessment of who Dirk could be. Lucky.

'I'm Clara. Have you been here long?'

'Long enough.'

Just two words squeezed from his lips.

'And has it been helpful to you?'

'Yes.'

Oh, dear. This was going to make life very difficult. The rule was not to give up on the first hurdle. Faint heart never won fair lady, a very apt proverb at this moment. What was wrong with them? Was there something more personal about her that declared she was null and void? She looked at her clothes, then made a quick comparison to theirs.

Then it hit like a bullet. Of course, they had to have known each other before they came to this clinic. They had a history together. The common denominator between them was they were born of the same clan, wealth. It was not her gender or her skin. It was the color of her money. They had judged she was a nobody who came from that distasteful order, poverty.

'I believed,' said Clara, 'if I stayed in England, then none of this would have happened. But my late husband, Lord Dover, wanted to move back home. They begged him to stay, as they feared the government would collapse if he was not there to advise. But that was a year ago. I hoped we would go to Tahiti. You see, we were always traveling around the world; my Peter was always in great demand.'

The click, click of necks turned to look at her. They had taken the bait.

'We arrived back here, and then he died.' Clara stopped to collect the effect. 'I call him my husband as tragically for me; we were always going to get married. But I had this awful feeling that marriage would put an end to our relationship and firmly put it in the garbage can. Of course, I got the inheritance—the money, properties, and also the paintings. But if I could, I would give them all back to have my Peter,' said Clara.

'I'm Emma,' said the dark-haired girl in her mid-twenties, stretching out her hand to Clara.

'I'm Lulu,' said the blonde-haired female sitting next to her and in between Dirk. At a glance, she was of a similar age. Quite pretty in an expensive way, right clothes and correct makeup and manners always do wonders for presentation.

'I'm Joanne.'

The same could be said about this one. Dressed differently, but with lank brown hair, she was a remarkably uninteresting person whose only quality was her money.

'I'm in here because of heartbreak,' said Clara, intrigued as to what brought them here.

'We are here because of drug abuse,' added Dirk.

Clara was about to say how interesting, but then forbid those words from gaining reality. It must be unbelievably fashionable to have drug abuse as your break in life, as it now seems rather sloppy to have an emotional problem.

'I'm sure it was his fortune which killed him, working so hard for others. I would trade everything to have him back, but I know he would never be happy without his money. It's a crazy world we live in. It makes me almost hate the money. When you're rich, you can't help being wealthy, but it's this which makes you hated.' Clara carried on with her story.

She could feel the anger of curiosity hopscotching crossing to her like the dancing spangles on the casino spin. These people were so rich they didn't talk about money.

'Money doesn't do anything evil,' said Dirk. 'It's the people that have it and how they use it. That's where the unhappiness arises.'

'You are absolutely right,' said Clara quickly. 'But would you say it is the people who don't have it but want it who are the most dangerous?'

The table went quiet. What was she saying? They were all looking at her, unsure of what she meant.

'I am trying not to believe Peter was murdered for his money. I have been told I am in deep grief, and I am not accepting what has happened. I am afraid for my future. I feel I will be targeted next.'

From around the table, there was only silence. It was as thick and dense as the wooden chairs they were sitting on.

'I'm getting so paranoid; it's driving me mad. I don't know what to think anymore.'

'Have you spoken to Dr. Slander about your belief?' asked Dirk, unable to make any sense of what Clara said to them.

'No. I don't know who to trust, but I have to trust someone before going headlong into madness. I'm terrified of everything at the moment. I feel like I'm being watched, and I don't know if it's just me or my imagination?'

'You should tell Dr. Slanders about these fears,' said Dirk. 'I can't say for sure if they are real or absurd. To you, they're real. I hasten you to talk to the doctor about them.'

'The problem for me is I don't know whether to trust him.'

All four stared at her; Clara had quite bewildered them.

'Do you trust him?' asked Clara.

'Dirk doesn't like him,' said Lulu, eyeing him with something like, well, you don't, do you?

'I don't take him as seriously as the ladies do,' Dirk stared sideways at Lulu. 'They trust him and like him.'

'But that's because you have your future all mapped out. You don't need him as others do?' Clara frowned.

'' Dirk took an inward sigh of resignation.

His eyes were still affected by illegal drugs. Blue eyes, but his pupils were bigger than they should be. Could he see as well as he used to before taking the drugs?

'I've found Dr. Slanders has more impact on the ladies. A man like him, strong in mind, is very attractive. Personally, I feel he thinks far too much of himself, but he means well, I suppose.'

'He has dedicated his life to people like us,' jumped in Emma.

'And he gets handsomely paid for his time,' replied Dirk.

'Are you saying I should trust Dr. Slanders?' asked Clara, her eyes wide open to persuasion.

'The girls' trust him, and you're a girl. He appears to treat the ladies well.'

'He's good to you,' added Lulu. 'He has helped you.'

'It's more of a question of me helping myself. I was the one to gain from working on myself. But yes,' he said after a couple of seconds of thought. 'He has helped me in some ways.'

With great interest pushing her eyes out as far as they would go, Clara listened.

'He talked about a commune at the meeting yesterday. I found him very convincing. Are there any of you thinking about joining this community?'

'Lulu intends to join the commune. I'm right, aren't I, Lulu?' smiled Dirk.

'Yes,' she muttered between her teeth.

'I think this could be the answer to all my problems,' Clara enthused. 'A place where I will feel safe and secure and be happy.'

'It isn't the place for everyone,' said Lulu. 'You need to work on yourself before you are accepted.'

'Yes, naturally, I understand that. I'm curious about it. Have you ever been to see it? What is it like?'

Between the four, appreciative looks were exchanged. Knowledge is as powerful as wealth. But did they want to share it? Fascinating to know what they were holding back, which meant that Clara had to probe deeper.

'Depending on who you are—not everyone will benefit from this way of living,' said Lulu.

'Okay,' Clara listened.

'The commune is based on everyone being good to each other.'

'I like that idea.'

'What Lulu is trying to say in her own special little way is a lot of religion is preached. Prayers are said several times in the day. It's expected you should be grateful for everything,' said Dirk smugly.

'Well, we all know this sort of lifestyle isn't for you,' said Lulu, who felt herself to be under attack. 'Just because I feel I need something different doesn't mean that it's wrong. You've gone for commercial life, business. There's nothing wrong with that either.'

'I could do that if it made me feel safe,' began Clara. 'To be secure and not have to worry about anything is worth a lot.'

A channel was opening on how these friends thought about themselves and their friendship.

'It sounds very safe to me,' continued Clara. She giggled, embarrassed now. 'I have always wanted to be a nun. I think every woman does when they are a child. Either to be a nun or a ballerina.'

Emma, who had been listening, had engaged in her own daydreams.

'I wanted to be a nurse, if not a model. What does that say about me?'

'It doesn't say anything bad except the future is big for everyone. Each has hopes, but life shows you differently.'

'This is a table full of women. No wonder I want to escape from you all. I love you and leave you,' said Dirk, standing to attention, saluting. 'But I am going to get on with my life.'

And then he left the table to a hush of silence. The four females sat there wondering either what they had done or what was going to happen next.

'Why do we need men?' said Joanne, feeling the vexation of rejection. 'We don't. I don't know what we did to offend him.'

'What are you going to do when you leave here?' asked Clara.

'I don't know.' Joanne shook her head.

'She is going to be persuaded to join the commune. It's what she secretly wants,' smiled Emma.

Clara glanced from Emma to Joanne.

'Do you want to be persuaded?' asked Clara.

'I don't know. I'm trying to get my head together. I don't know why we are talking about this or how we got on to the subject. Please drop it before I also leave the table.'

A silence grew around the table, as did the feelings of

hate towards Clara. An ugly cloud of thoughts became more solid as the seconds ticked past. Resentment was building, and she was the target. But if Clara gave in now and removed herself from their table, then they would have won, and her investigation would become more difficult.

Yet, it meant more for Clara; she always felt she was on the outskirts of society and friendship. It was the sisterhood of rules and acceptance. From what she saw looking from the outside of the circle was a pecking order—she was stumbling to understand where she could fit in and what she could bring to this group. But they had more than enough tough friendship. She was not welcomed.

Such people like these, Clara would see seated outside or inside a restaurant. Long-haired beauties, highly made-up, often with brightly colored clothes, but they all looked the same. Their clothing was a uniform of commitment to each other. If she had wanted to be like them, she knew that wearing the right clothes, having the same ideas, and changing herself to become someone she was not, was not what she wanted. Join in, speak the same jingly language, like the same things, admire and admit to ideas and ways of life which she didn't believe in. She was rich, but she would never be one of them.

Why did she always have to be different and difficult? And always the outsider. Yes, that's right—always.

It came as a bright light, a called for thought that dashed in her head, demanding to be heard. She had come to this table with preconceptions. She didn't like these women; she had never intended to like them. Her prejudices led to the idea they were life's wasters, pointless and straightforward, and it was just because they were rich. But now, so was she. What she wanted from them was answers to her questions, and that—was as far as this feigned friendship was going to stretch. These women were below the evaluation of herself. Did it show what she felt? Could these people pick up on her contempt for them?

What we carry with us is another language. A smile is only genuine when it comes from the eyes. A look, a pose, the hand under the chin. Why don't people warm to me is only matched by what Clara had said? These were as false as the smile she carried when walking to their table.

'I am sorry,' began Clara. 'I had no right to intrude. I was just so desperate not to be on my own it made me selfish, and I sometimes forget I am not the only one to have suffered.'

The three listened first with a frown and then with surprise to Clara because she was honest. They found themselves ready and even willing to adapt their ideas. Do people want to be led to the side of their better nature? It's likely being sorry and contrite is the best white flag to wave. She wanted to be liked, and that came as a surprise.

'Is everything okay here, ladies?' asked Nurse Ryan again on duty.

From the side, she had been watching Clara with puzzlement and then concern. She was a new person here and a potential intrusion for these friends. How was she going to be accepted in this community? To her prying eyes, Clara differed from the usual people who came to the clinic. For one, she was a little older than the rest, although not by much. And by the way she held herself, her composure, and even her confidence suggested she had a goal in life and more direction hinted at strength. Her diction was also different from the rest, showing she had a much different life. Clara was an interesting anomaly, a puzzle.

You get an idea about people especially working here, and listening to them, but not always to what they say, but in the way they said it. Who was Clara Tinder? She had a sophistication about her which belied the reason for her illness.

'I have been—' but Clara was stopped.

'Yes, we are fine, thank you, Nurse Ryan,' smiled Joanne. 'We were just seeing who could resist saying something. Clara felt the tension, and so she lost.'

Laughing, Joanne's eyes were bright with intelligence. How interesting this situation was becoming. Joanne looked sharply at Clara, daring her to refute her lie. What had been hostility was now an invitation to join their side? You can play with us if you want to. We have opened a space for you to connect.

Nurse Ryan looked at Clara; the newcomer was wheedling her way in. She should be pleased for her because it wasn't an easy group to enter. They were possessive of each other, which sometimes was detrimental to their own welfare. Taking a step backward, Nurse Ryan walked away.

Back down to the four of them, they took a moment to reflect on their new relationship. What were the rules of their sisterhood?

'We are sorry you felt you were left out,' started Joanne. 'We often forget what it's like to be new.'

'We have known each other since we were children,' smiled Emma as if by ways of an apology.

'Went to the same social gatherings, schools, universities —you name it,' said Lulu.

'And by the looks of it, did the same things.' Joanne rolled her eyes. 'Drugs.'

'It must be something to do with the lifestyle we led. Don't blame the parents for everything, but you will find they had a bit to do with it,' said Emma.

'It looks like you got away from bad parenting and too much privilege,' launched Joanna.

Their breakfast sat in front of them for the last ten minutes, but nothing was touched because this was the time when Clara had joined them.

'I certainly was told how lucky I was and how I didn't appreciate what I had. But as I said to my nanny and my parents, how would I know what I had when I have never been without? It's not my fault.'

Emma and Lulu both laughed at Joanne's dry humor. This should have been Clara's cue to laugh also, but she couldn't. Her childhood had not been wholly deprived, but it had been very different. The uncertainty of her life had made her nervous and always anxious.

'Which group are you going to go to this afternoon?' asked Joanne.

It was then Clara knew she had been accepted.

7

———

It surprised Clara how easily she could forget Argenta now she had other friends. She liked to think she was virtuous with all the other qualities, like kindness, generosity, compassion, and forgiveness. But the surprise was, she only held on to the understanding of them in the passing. Was it possible to be so good? It depended on how much you wanted to survive.

Perhaps this was who she was, and it had taken an actual incident to show her this side of her personality. And while she chatted and laughed with the other three females. Subjectively, she could see herself as that other person watching and noting their behavior. Was she really so false? Her observations about others had always been sharp, and dare Clara say it, well on target.

'Careful what you say about Dr. Slanders, he is a God, and you must bow down to him, and I am the one he loves.' Clara was good at mimicry.

'Clara, you give me goosebumps. You sound just like Nurse Jones. How did you manage to get her voice?' so startled, Emma couldn't help laughing.

Emma was not a pretty young woman. Although youth was on her side, she was not going to be protected by this fleshy face for much longer until, of course, she had cosmetic surgery. Money, though, insured the looks, while those large bulbous eyes were hideous. God had protected her from being ginger.

'I don't know,' Clara smiled. 'It just came naturally to me, I suppose.'

'Can you do anyone else?' Emma stared at the others. She was incredulous at Clara's surprising talent.

'No, not really. Although I haven't tried, to be honest, I find I can mimic her because I don't like her, which might be why I am good at it.'

As if they were in on the conspiracy, the other three laughed like school kids.

Had she become popular by trying to be liked? By smiling, baring her teeth, and opening her eyes, and making that pose which had suddenly become fashionable. Like me—I am really nice. Perhaps she had a few changes here and there, nothing dramatic. By remembering Rachel and the impossible person she could be, Clara chose to think and be like her. It was easy to be liked when trying out all the tricks. Neither did she have to change herself too much, either. All good fun that perhaps she might have forgotten herself because when she looked up, Nurse Ryan from the edge of the room had been watching her.

The day was spent with the three friends in the day groups. Being friendly, though, used up a great deal of energy; it was tiresome. The ever-smiling face and too interested enthusiasm of what one of them was saying was unnatural work. But it had to be done, and she had to keep up with this as if they were in on the conspiracy friendship act just in case there was knowledge to be had.

Three days later and nothing of importance was said. Dr. Slanders had another one of those meetings about their future and what they would do, but it didn't have as much impact on Clara as the first one did. But Clara was all eyes, watching and waiting.

Dirk was going to leave at the end of the week. His time was up, and he felt it was time to go. He told everyone at the meeting about his plans, which had taken Dr. Slanders unexpectedly. Dr. Slanders' quiet, immobile face showed cold symptoms of anger. He was furious that Dirk had taken away something of his morning's message.

'Oh, we will miss you,' said Lulu turning to Dirk when he finished his emotional departure. 'You never let on that you were going to leave tomorrow morning.'

'That was because I hadn't yet decided.'

'And when did you decide you were leaving us?' asked Dr. Slanders? By his manner, Dirk had clearly spiked his guns.

'Just now. You were talking about everyone leaving again and what were their plans.'

'You are lucky you have parents who want to take you back. Most of the people here do not have such a fortune. Some are orphaned, others have divorced parents that have perhaps remarried. These are the vulnerable people.' Dr. Slanders' eyes didn't quiver.

Mischief must have been in Dirk, for without warning, he suddenly grinned.

'I just had an idea. Why don't you all come and work for my parents? It will give you structure and keep you out of vice. There are no rules except you turn up for the day's work, and you get paid for it.'

Everyone looked at Dirk with this sudden change of events. Another alternative. The inevitable didn't have to happen, leaving without a future or the other of joining the commune. And new thoughts grew into other possibilities. No one needed to work, but they needed to fill their time.

'Dirk, if you don't mind,' interrupted Dr. Slanders. 'But the ground you are treading on is not in your territory. There is no point in giving these people ideas and hopes of something they cannot do or achieve.'

'Oh, I don't know. Like you said before, everyone has potential. We just need to try at life and believe in ourselves. There are great untapped abilities to be found within us all. You said that—I remember?'

'What I said was that the commune was a supportive arena where people could lead their lives. It is a safety net. It doesn't mean they have to commit themselves forever. You are giving false hope to these people who are weak and vulnerable at the best of times.' Dr. Slanders kept to the tune of his voice, slowly and methodically paving the way for the logical deduction, not a quiver of worthless emotion. 'Supposing one of these people you are inviting has a relapse, and it's possible. Once a person has been subjected to addiction, they are never fully cured. The best they can do is take one day at a time. Do you understand what I am talking about, Dirk?'

Flushing to his hairline, Dirk received the embarrassment as if he were a young cadet in the army.

'I know you mean well, Dirk, and I congratulate you for trying to do something for your fellow man.'

Dr. Slanders smiled; the tension which had built up in his neck gradually relaxed.

'But I have to stop you here with caution. Do not give false hopes. I have been a doctor for over twenty years. I have learned and understand people with severe problems, and they are serious, Dirk. And you, too, have been broken.

But I also want you to know that when the time comes, and life becomes too difficult again, we will be here for you.'

Crimson now, yet it wasn't all from humiliation. Dirk turned on his heel and walked out, hating this place he had once needed.

When Dirk was out of the room, Dr. Slanders turned to everyone with a demonstrative shrug. 'What can you do when someone refuses your help? Nothing, at least not until they need you again.'

Over ten years ago, Clara would have been affected in the same way as Dirk. And it was so subtle the underground indignity placed on being mentally ill that it could be put down to you being paranoid. Don't ever become mentally ill, for it is a hell of a hole to get out of. And those who oppose you use your illness against you.

Clara felt sorry for Dirk, but there was no way she was going to follow him and show him loyalty. This was a battle he would have to fight himself, and she wished him good luck. Even being here in a mental hospital subjected her to doubt if she was as well as she thought. Everyone has a dark shadow slipping through their thoughts, which could become the virus of madness if held on to and worked upon.

'Can I have a word with you, Clara?' asked Dr. Slanders when the session was over.

She stopped, unsure of what this meant. Her sudden hesitation suggested she should flee. There was time to. But she stopped and turned and smiled. After all, he was in charge of the clinic. He studied her as she walked towards him, analyzing her every move as if she were a lab rat whose examination was devoid of feeling. But she carried on smiling because this was not a time to reveal fear.

'Yes, Dr. Slanders,' she halted in front of him.

He made no attempt to stand. He sat on his throne, resplendent as a king.

'You've been with us for nearly a week. I wanted to know how you are settling in. I meant to have a chat with you before the session, but never mind.'

It was impossible to see his eyes now, as his glasses had been caught by the sunlight and reflected it as a visor that made him appear blind. Perhaps he was in some ways.

'I'm getting used to the place, and going to groups has been very helpful.'

'Yes, so I have been informed. You have been making an impact on certain people.'

His voice was soft and insidious, almost as if it were veiled by threats. She had never liked him and doubted his sincerity, but now she realized she also feared him. He had so much power in this place, and it oozed control out of every one of his pores.

'I don't know about making an impact,' she said shyly. 'I am trying. I want to get better.'

'Yes,' he murmured under his breath.

That thoughtful expression suggested he had something on his mind, but was toying with the idea of whether he should mention it.

'Which therapy sessions have you found to be the most interesting or, should I say, helpful?'

That audible suggestion of thought made her hesitate for a moment while catching up before she uttered from her lips.

'I would say the art session was helpful. It made me think. I liked the therapist particularly, Sarita.'

'Yes, I heard about you.'

Was it because she looked trapped like a bird, which netted his smile?

'I make it my business to know everything about everyone here. If I didn't, I would be failing in my profession. So, tell me, what have you gained from your stay?'

She knew what he was asking, and that was what was she doing here? She had shown no signs of mental illness.

'For me, the main thing is I have been able to distance myself from my grief.'

Still, he smiled.

'Being here has given me a break from my sadness.'

'You could have gone somewhere else for that. On holiday, for instance. I am certain it would have been a great deal cheaper.'

He waited most patiently to see how she would answer.

'But I would not have felt safe. I feel safe here, and if I were to break down, at least I would have the support I needed.'

'Yet, you haven't shown any sign of distress. You have actually acted as if you were part of the staff, and I am not the only one to have noticed this.'

Who could have rat on her, who wanted her out of this place? There was only one person who came ready to mind, and that was Nurse Jones.

'I don't like Nurse Jones.'

This raised an eyebrow.

'Nurse Jones?'

'Yes, Nurse Jones. I don't know why, but she has taken a dislike to me.'

Rubbing his hand slowly over his mouth, Dr. Slanders became thoughtful.

'Let me put it to you—Nurse Jones said the same about you.'

Clara mimicked Dr. Slanders' hand expressions. She was treading dangerously; she knew he had a special relationship with this nurse. An understanding which was mutual for both of them. That spy in the camp who gave him private access to what was going on.

'She told me she found you very aggressive when she spoke to you.' Dr. Slanders wearied her with an eye of caution.

'She probably did because that was how I felt about her. I felt she couldn't be trusted. I have no other real reason except I don't like her as I don't trust her.'

He frowned because he got on famously with Nurse Jones, and why not? They were the same kind of person.

'It could be something to do with my mother. She reminds me of her. The way she speaks and looks at me, it's exactly the same as my mother.'

This could turn into a therapy session. He could ask her about these provoked memories of her mother and what it meant to her, but this wasn't what he was interested in. He didn't have time for analysis.

'Yes. Well, I suppose like all chemical reactions, each of us has an aversion to certain personalities. But I ask you to be at least polite to Nurse Jones.'

'I can do if she too respects me.'

'I shall see you again in two days.'

A glance towards the door told her this was her cue to leave. Again, Clara hesitated. It was noticed by Dr. Slanders as his eyelid keenly raised itself in expectation of this faltering moment as to what she wanted. Nothing, there was nothing in the end. Perhaps they were playing the same game. A quick smile and she was off. At this moment, she judged this wasn't the time to give voice to her thoughts.

She hoped these new friends would speak about the clinic and if they had noticed anything unusual. Mentioning a friendship with the Lamonts as casually as she could, it went on to the subject of if they knew about Charisse Lamont. It was asked in a direct and very crude way. Charisse was leaving the hospital as they arrived, so they hadn't got to know her that well. The odd thing was, she never appeared to be happy.

'That's a nutty thing to say,' said Emma to Lulu's observation. 'People are rarely happy when they are ill, especially people like us. But she seemed all right. I thought she was more angry than unhappy.'

'What did she look like?'

'Thin, like she had been on a starvation diet,' answered Joanne. 'She wasn't very popular with anyone except Dr. Slanders. She absolutely doted on him like he was a God. He could do no wrong. You could see he cared about her. He was kind and gentle to her, which was what she needed. You could say like a father figure missing from her life.'

'But she had a father,' remarked Clara.

'Yes, but not a good one, according to her. I remember overhearing her say that once she turned twenty-one, she would come into her fortune. Well, she said she overheard her father, who was her guardian, and one of the people supervising her money, saying he wouldn't be able to touch a penny of her money anymore. She also said that Dr. Slanders would help her do a business course or something like that to take care of her money, which I found strange. In some ways, it looked like she was getting her act together.'

'Did she ever come back to the clinic?'-

'Why would she want to do that?' asked Joanne.

Clara shrugged. 'Therapy sessions, maybe?'

'She doesn't need to come back to the clinic for that. Dr. Slanders also spends time in the commune. After all, he has part ownership of it.'

As if Clara should know this. 'Shares?'

'Yes, he part-owns the commune. This is his thing. He sets everything up. The clinic—everything. He and another doctor called Dr. Barnet. Dr. Slanders runs the clinic while Dr. Barnet runs the commune. They are about getting people healthy and back into society. There's nothing illegal about that. Didn't you know this before you came to the clinic?'

'No, I didn't. I never thought to read up on this when I was having a breakdown. A friend recommended this place as one of the best clinics to go to if you are ill.'

'It shouldn't make any difference to anyone where they go for treatment as long as they recover. Just because Dr. Slanders is getting rich from his investments shouldn't be anyone else's business but his own.'

'You're right. It was strange.' Clara smiled. 'I guess I didn't think he had any part in the monetary side.'

'We've all got to live,' smiled Emma. 'I suppose you thought he ran this business out of love?'

'I guess I did.'

'There is nothing wrong with doctors having a vested interest in something he strongly believes in.'

'Now you put it like that; I suppose there isn't.'

At times like this, when someone disagreed with Clara, she would automatically decide she didn't like them. How did they think so differently? Was it her fault, or was it theirs? Whatever it was, she suddenly realized she didn't like them. And coming across this picture spoiled her idea because she did not want to be the one that was wrong. This meant they weren't honest; they had deviated from the truth. And the truth was always important.

In this frame of mind, Clara returned to her room. Looking across the hallway sparked her curiosity and made her pause. The door to Argenta's room was open and enticing her to enter. An invitation which would be rude to refuse. The truth was, Argenta had not been on her mind at all. She had forgotten her. She had forgotten how sick, weak, and small she would have looked lying in her bed, tired and weary of life. Her unusually pale face was so close to haunting. And yet, Clara had forgotten her own life was more pressing.

The bed was now empty of her presence. New bedding had been laid out, and the room which had, she remembered, been cluttered with enchantment told that Argenta had never grown out of her much-needed childhood. The room had become a startling reality, and adulthood had now replaced the past to reveal a divine revelation. 'You shall grow up. You shall become an adult. You shall take your place in society and become a woman.'

It was such a shock to walk into a room devoid of Argenta's presence that Clara found herself stepping backward in wariness. Was it must be the wrong room; it had to be because she could not shift the idea Argenta was still living and sleeping here.

There had to be an answer to this puzzle. There just had to be. Quickly, Clara ran down the stairs instead of using the elevator. Nurse Jones came out of the staff room just as Clara passed. Clara, though, kept walking. It wasn't her she wanted; it was Nurse Ryan. And there she was, coming through the door from the garden, having enjoyed her daily dose of nicotine. This was what Clara had smelled on her breath a few days before.

'What's happened to Argenta?' Clara demanded, pulling up with anger in front of her.

'And good afternoon to you as well, Clara. Argenta has moved on. She left yesterday.'

She was surprised Clara had asked. And besides, what was it to her?

'But I thought she was ill. In fact, I know she was ill. Was she taken to another hospital?' why hadn't anyone told her? Why wasn't this announced in the morning meeting?

'Argenta has recovered, and now she's moved over to the commune.'

So incredible to be told this—Clara couldn't answer. Argenta was ill. She remained fast, blocking Nurse Ryan's way.

'Are you all right, Clara?'

'Firstly. The last time I saw Argenta was nearly four days ago, and she was unconscious.' Clara held out her hand to count her arguments on her fingers. 'Second, how did she manage to become well enough to eat and gain the strength to stand? And third, from what I saw of her, she was closer to death than life?'

'Well, Clara, she has left us, and we should be happy she is able to do so. Dr. Slanders obviously thought she was well enough to be moved; otherwise, he wouldn't have given his permission for her to go.'

'Dr. Slanders, Dr. Slanders,' Clara muttered angrily to herself as she walked away.

He was just a man. A few letters after his name and a distinction in front of it. What did it mean if no one took any notice of it? And yet, this accolade gave him such power and control over others. She hated all psychiatrists; they were pompous and disinterested, and always believing they knew better—she just hated them.

Like a breakaway tornado, Clara battered across everything which came in her way. When in a temper like this, reason was no good to her. She would have to wait until it blew itself out.

8

———

'I understand you have been upset hearing that Argenta has left us,' accused Dr. Slanders. Hiding behind his glasses, his thoughts were focused on Clara.

An hour had passed since Clara had been summoned from her singing group to talk to Dr. Slanders. She had chosen singing instead of martial arts. It would have been sensible to pick up on the little she had already learned with the physical program, but the memory of her past still had a constant presence.

'Argenta was the first one to befriend me. I was naturally shocked as well as grieved I had let her down.' Clara lowered her head, feeling the weight of her shame.

'But, as I understand, you never kept up this friendship by asking how she was?' Dr. Slanders scrutinized every movement and expression that Clara revealed.

'I supposed I had shown some disinterest, but that doesn't mean to say I was.'

Knowing that every marker she revealed was serving Dr. Slanders' analytical observation of her state of mind, she was thinking and thinking.

'I felt I had upset Argenta, and it made me nervous.'

He didn't answer, only listened, and always with that impenetrable expression. Clara could read from his face whatever he wanted her to read. This was his power.

'I just wanted to know if she was all right.'

'Did you believe something had happened to her?' Dr. Slanders asked, but not giving her the much-needed appeasement she wanted. Was Argenta all right?

'She was so ill,' Clara pleaded.

'All the residents here are ill. There is no exception to that.'

And then he smiled because he was proud of himself. His vanity—this was his biggest weakness. The belief he was always right. It was what made him smug and how he viewed life from behind his glasses.

Could it be he had no compassion or empathy towards the people he helped? A shocking conclusion, for it meant so many things but always ended up being cold-blooded.

'It would be nice to know how Argenta is, so I can stop worrying about her.'

'Let me ask you, Miss Tinder, why do you worry about others when it is yourself you should worry about?'

'I don't usually worry about others, but isn't it normal to care?' indeed, he should understand that.

'I have noticed you have been caring about a lot of people just lately. I am wondering where all this care is coming from.'

Prickles of fear traveled up Clara's spine. This had become a mind game, and he was so much better at it than her.

'I don't know.' Feeling lost, as well as fearful that he had been smart enough to have worked her out. 'I am trying to fit in with the community. Perhaps I have been trying too hard. Christ, I don't know how to behave towards these other people?'

This was becoming a therapy session, and his eyes bored into her lowered head while she desperately strived to think of what else to say.

'It's all been so difficult just lately, and I know I should be grateful for receiving the fortune, but it feels like blood money. Do you understand what I am saying?' Clara asked, swiftly lifting her head.

'Tell me what it feels like to you?'

'That somehow fate has tested me. I have never been an emotional person—correction, except for once when I lost my mind and believed myself to be in love. But never again. The humiliation of emotions is such a big uncertainty I had believed I could never love again. And the worst thought of all was that Peter must have really loved me.'

Was it going well? Did she sound convincing? She hoped so because she was trying desperately to look for things Dr. Slanders would find interesting.

'The worst thing, though, is I doubt if I truly loved him —or even cared about Peter.'

Slightly bored and unimpressed, Dr. Slanders continued to listen.

'It's as if I should do some sort of penance for his money.'

His eyes, which had wandered to his notebook so neatly placed on his desk, square to the edges, three inches exact, and still blank of words, looked up.

'What penance did you have in mind?'

'Well, I thought about giving my money away, but then I decided that would be stupid. But I would still like to do something with a part of it.'

'I think I understand you.' He linked his fingers together

and leaned back in his chair. 'You feel you haven't earned the money.'

'Yes, yes.' Clara replied anxiously to please.

'I tend to agree with you. Money has no value unless it is used. But if you want to give so much away, you must be sure of what you are doing. Do not act rashly; this is my advice. Be sure of yourself and consult a lawyer.'

Had she got him wrong? Clara was surprised Dr. Slanders showed consideration of her supposed problem with money.

After a half-hour session, she left his office with renewed views that didn't fit in with her previous ideas. In his brown suit and white shirt, he had emerged as a boring and uninteresting man. So much so, she felt contempt for him. Again, Clara was shocked she could dismiss people in such a way, even to the point of feeling herself to be superior. These thoughts had kept her perfectly safe from others, in that she always found a reason to dislike them. Was this where she went wrong? To have no real friends, not even the three people that sat with her at the table.

But Dr. Slander never said where Argenta was, which was the only annoying part about their session. He left her to guess at what happened to Argenta. The chances of Argenta going back to her guardians were slim. That's the problem with life. Trying every variant one can think of, and it always ends with the one you never thought about.

Argenta wasn't the only one to leave the clinic in a hurry. In the middle of the night, Dirk left. He packed up his cases and walked out of the hospital, and no one was any the wiser until the following morning.

Clara's actual mission was to find out about Charisse, and Lulu hadn't been exactly honest when she confessed she knew nothing about Charisse. She knew a great deal more than she was saying. Out of the three friends, Lulu was the most reluctant to like Clara. She held back her approval, but in the company of the other three, she was bubbly and friendly. Clara had seen this when she approached the table, and upon looking up and seeing Clara approach, the shutters were pulled down hard over her lips.

It would be a good idea if she caught Lulu on her own to get her to talk about Charisse. The opportunity came that evening. Just when Emma and Joanne decided they would go into the communal lounge, Clara moved to walk with Lulu back to their rooms.

'Have you thought any more about your future?' asked Clara in a gentle and kindly tone to get Lulu to speak.

'Have you?'

This question was quickly returned as a line of defense.

'The more I hear about the commune, the more I am interested in the idea.'

'That surprises me.'

'Why?'

'Because you don't strike me as a person who needs that sort of support.'

'Really?' Clara shrugged. How could Lulu come to this quick assessment?

'Yes. You said once you had worked for a newspaper.'

When had she told anybody anything about her history?

'Oh yes, I almost forgot about that. I worked to earn my keep while going to university.'

Lulu's eyes sharply scanned Clara's face. Clara again had underestimated Lulu. What a fool she was making of herself.

'So, by having a job, you think it makes me able to survive better in the world?'

'I got the impression you had worked longer than a few months.'

Clara smiled. When did she have this conversation about her work? She couldn't remember. Was Lulu able to read minds? Who knows? People with disturbed minds have a connection to strange gifts.

'I suppose I present a positive person, and that pleases me, but it also puts people off when they believe I can take care of myself.'

Lulu stared at Clara as if she were unconvinced by whatever she said.

'My problem is, I don't trust anyone. I am trying to change that side of me. It's not good being a loner.'

Yet Lulu remained unmoved.

'I would like to be friends with you.'

'You are friends,' said Lulu.

'But I feel you don't trust me. I want to improve myself, and I want to be accepted. You know, I really liked Argenta, but I was told to back off because she was unwell. Still, I want to know how she is, but no one will tell me. It's like a big dark secret.'

'Who told you? Did it happen to be Nurse Jones?'

'Yes,' Clara looked startled, as if Lulu had hit it right on the button. 'How did you know?'

'Only a few residents like her. You just have to keep on the right side of her.'

'Oh dear, I am not very good at that. I tend to let my feelings known.'

'You're just like Charisse.'

'You know Charisse?'

'A little. I came here a few weeks before she left.'

'Do you know she is the daughter of friends of mine, but I've never met her.'

As if she had offered Lulu a cyanide tablet, she retracted right back into herself, poisoned by her mention. What did she say wrong? And again, why this secret society?

'Have I said something wrong?' Clara was now annoyed with the hints and dances of secrecy. 'I can have friends. I am allowed to know the people you know, even if it is a big world.'

'I've heard everything I need to know about Charisse's father and the woman he's married to. They don't care a damn about her; they are just trying to screw her out of her money.'

'I don't believe you,' suddenly, Clara's eyes opened wide because she too had formed unsavory thoughts about them, especially Anise. But this antipathy had been blamed on her jealousy of this beautiful and sophisticated woman.

It was amazing how Clara was prepared to hear bad news, mainly when it would confirm her thoughts about this malevolent, untouchable couple. Lulu had just been about to confide to her when the door to the fire escape opened, and out came Nurse Jones. Seeing these two together provoked her suspicions; she needed to know what was going on. Her eyes narrowed, ready to pounce on them.

'Quick,' muttered Lulu under her breath. 'Come to my room.'

Like mice scurrying from a starving cat, they moved frantically. Clara and Lulu bumped into each other in their rush to escape.

'Where are you two going?' Nurse Jones called out, annoyed, knowing they were running away from her.

'Don't answer her,' again muttered Lulu, catching hold of her door handle to get inside.

She pulled Clara into her room, laughing at their childish prank. Then she pressed up against her door and took in a deep breath. Her eyes were a darker blue now, and her small nose, which was not her best feature, was perfectly sculptured, yet too well composed to be an original. Nice teeth: these also had been veneered with money.

Noticing all of her features gave Clara an interesting profile for her writing, but it was not something she could use.

A rap on the door took them both by surprise; they stared at each other, wondering what Nurse Jones was going to do next.

'Don't say anything,' whispered Lulu, warning Clara.

Clara had already decided to keep her silence. Lulu could trust her for that. Putting a finger to her mouth, Lulu shook her head and blew a silent shush.

On the other side, with invisible feet, the muffled footsteps after thirty seconds or so of frustration strutted away.

'I was so nervous,' said Lulu, landing on her bed. 'I thought she would open my door in a temper and march in. She could do that; she has the authority, and Dr. Slanders always listens to her. He believes everything she says. She struck Charisse once around the face. The blow was enough to knock her over, but when Charisse told Dr. Slanders, he didn't believe her. He said he needed proof and told her she could have done it to herself just to get attention.'

'Did she do it to herself?'

An innocent question and harmlessly meant, but it drew an adverse reaction from Lulu. This was the height of disloyalty.

'I trust Charisse more than I trust Nurse Jones.'

'Yes, you're right. It was a silly question. But why would Nurse Jones strike Charisse? I would have thought this would have been instant firing. Were you there when it happened?'

'No, it happened a week before I arrived. Nurse Jones was jealous of Charisse because she was popular with Dr. Slanders, and if you haven't already noticed, Nurse Jones is very possessive of him.'

'I sort of guessed she was keen on him. Does he feel the same way about her?'

A deep smile radiated across Lulu's face with pleasure.

'He uses her. He allows her to think she is special, and something is going on between them, but all the time he is playing with her.'

'He isn't married, is he?'

'No. He has never been married or engaged. He is a cold-blooded reptile who probably thinks there must be something sick with the female if she makes any confessions of love. You've got to keep your wits about you, especially when you're here. Mental hospitals are the worse place to think you're safe.'

Here was Clara's invitation to be real friends with one of her own sex. Of course, there had been Phoebe, but their friendship was so fleeting and tragic, something she had put at the back of her mind as a place never to go. This journey was always painful. In the months that followed, Clara had never forgiven herself, believing Phoebe's death had been her fault. She must forget her and quickly if she wanted to keep her sanity.

'It's not the first hospital I've been in,' said Clara.

'You told us about it on the first day when you joined us.'

'Will you ever forgive me for doing that? Crashing into your party, that is.'

'Probably not. I tend to have a long memory. But an excellent memory is not necessarily bad. People I care about tend to stay with me longer.'

Lulu had a sweet smile when she wasn't defensive, and it was charming—choosing a lighter note.

'Don't you think the psychiatric staff is sometimes nuttier than the patients?'

'Sometimes? I think it's fair to say they are most of the time,' grinned Lulu. 'In fact, I would say there is something seriously wrong with Dr. Slanders.'

'In what way?'

'Haven't you noticed the classic symptoms?'

Puzzled, Clara shrugged. Instinctively, she hadn't liked Dr. Slanders, but this didn't make him a nutcase.

'He is cold and distant and very manipulative. He makes me shudder when he comes near me. But when he asks to speak to me, I behave myself. My addiction was drugs, and I won't be doing them again. I've learned my lesson; I'm going to keep myself straight; the best one to trust is yourself. Don't allow anyone to take control of your mind.'

'I have no intentions this time,' Clara smiled, now wondering what next to say.

Clara needed to probe more about the setup, especially that of the commune.

'I understand you are going to the commune after this. Can I ask why?'

'Because Charisse is there, I want to support her.'

'That's very loyal of you.' And very puzzling for Clara. Why?

'I don't know about loyalty; I feel it's the right thing to do. Did you know—' and then Lulu stopped as if she didn't trust Clara?

'Know what?'

'How well do you know the Lamonts?'

'Not too well, but there again, I haven't got many friends.

Although, to be honest, I am not keen on Anise. She's the boss in the family.'

'You are right not to trust Anise. I feel so angry at what they were trying to do to Charisse, and I am sure it was all Anise's idea. Charisse told me her father and his wife wanted her to make out her will and leave everything to them. What made them think she was going to die before them? How can her father and that woman be so wicked?'

'Yes,' murmured Clara, more to herself. 'How can one's parents be so wicked?' Lulu had forgotten she didn't know Charisse that well, despite her wonderful memory.

'Charisse was distraught by their suggestion, and she asked them why they should want her to do this. They said they were only being sensible. Charisse's mother had died suddenly, so it was a precaution just in case anything happened to her. If she made out her will to them, it would solve the problem.'

'She didn't do it, did she?'

'No, at least, I don't think so. That was when she left. She ran off without any help or support. Her father and his family had been everything to her; she loved her father, but he broke her heart like he did Natasha. They only cared about her because she was wealthy. Her guardians and her father had protected her from the rest of the world. I figured they didn't want her forming any other relationships, just in case she signed her money over to them.'

'I find it very scary,' said Clara, 'and hard to believe.'

Surely even the worse of parents wouldn't do this to their children, but then her mind returned to her own mother. There were good people in the world, like Detective Patts and Travis. It was the world she had moved into, which showed her these types of people, good people.

'I find it also hard to believe, but it's true. I believe

Charisse. Her father is weak, while his wife makes him do the things she wants.'

'I can believe that.'

In that instance, the world felt cold around her. She looked up; Lulu was watching her.

'Have you heard from Charisse since she's been at the commune?'

'Just the once to say she had arrived, and she was getting to know people. She said she thought she had made the right choice but then added she didn't have any alternative. She was more afraid her father would try to get her back; she didn't trust him or, rather, Anise. But at least being there, she was protected.'

Lulu's voice dropped to a whisper, as if afraid to speak too loudly.

'It's a private commune. The new people are treated like novices and kept away from the rest of the world. You have to earn your freedoms. For the first four months, you are not allowed any contact with the outside world.'

'Why?'

'Because you are vulnerable. Most of the people who join the commune are still susceptible to the influences of their problem.'

'How strange. The way Dr. Slanders sells it makes it more like an extravagant holiday where people are pampered.'

'This is what I mean about Dr. Slanders; he is not to be trusted. He just seems to lie to get what he wants.'

Clara could not help staring at Lulu. Her rude thoughts were now coming alive with what she supposed was happening here. This was an entirely different reality from the one Clara was prepared to believe. Too bizarre and inconceivable. Should she believe this young woman who had come into the hospital with her own unique problems? This could be a part of Lulu's madness. And drugs could have altered her reality, making this possible.

'Poor thing,' Clara muttered loud enough for Lulu. 'When do you intend to enter the commune?'

'This weekend. Dr. Slanders assured me this is when they will take me in. Then I will see Charisse.'

9

Madness, Clara had pondered often why some people find themselves on the rails and heading fast down to that station. The people she met suffering from this illness have always shown themselves to be kind, brave, but suffering. The blame for this was solely placed on their shoulders, and they accept it because they don't want others to be hurt. Clara should know that. The flame in Clara's mind had been ignited by passion, and the sense of being wronged had, by intelligent reasoning, been dampened. But not completely. If she were to concentrate on it, she would relive that passion and the anger with the strength of a rebel. Thomas had used her when she had given him her heart. This was when she felt herself slipping and falling apart. But she had never accused him. She bore it like it was his right.

In the beginning, the desire came fitfully in bouts of frustration that if she couldn't have him, then no one else could. She had planned to kill him, shoot him dead when he walked out his door. She could see his face and the look of surprise when she shot him, and the blood pouring down from his chest where his heart should have been.

And then if the aberrant wife came to the door, she knew she wouldn't have any choice but to shoot her too. One body falling on top of the other. The sound of the gun would surely attract the children. Bang, they were dead, the two of them. Once that was done, she would have to shoot herself. Clara saw her mouth open with the barrel of the gun filling it.

Again and again, she saw herself killing Thomas and then going over to him, falling on her knees, and asking for his forgiveness. She could not believe he had tricked her; she had loved him with a heart of beauty. What she should have done was to hire a private contractor and pay him to complete the job.

But then it occurred to her this was not enough. How would Thomas know the depth of her pain if he was to be quickly and efficiently finished off? The best way was to shoot him herself. But first, she must explain why she needed to kill him, which was, of course, that he had broken her. It then, with that same distorted argument could be used by him.

'If you truly love me, you would be happy for me and let me live.'

Inevitably, he would never know what he had done to her. She could not hurt him because she had loved him. Now she would carry the memory of him in her heart, making her a martyr to love. And when she was alone with those strange nostalgic memories playing her thoughts repeatedly. The idea romantically of what she had lost and the sacrifices she had made for him, a beautiful peace came over her. The whole concept of loving someone and carrying on loving them faithfully made her feel like a hero-ine. This was how she redeemed her dignity.

As for Lulu, she had her own battle, which made her feel like a heroine. It was something the damned could do by restoring their lives.

Strange lives. Each of us lives in our own world, choosing to believe that whichever makes us beautiful.

Something about Argenta's room fascinated Clara. There could be hints, little bits of evidence here and there that could put some answers to the puzzle. When Clara left Lulu's, she trod quietly across the hallway to the other side of the hall, where the other five bedrooms waited. The door to Argenta's room was closed; Clara hesitated, but not for long.

Opening the door, she went inside. Everything had been shut away, which made it seem sad. This was the room where she took her vigil over Argenta. If she thought hard enough, she could see the covers and sheets materializing as an image on the bed; next came the pillows, and about the room, dolls and teddy bears appeared, and last of all, the small head on the pillow. When she had been here before, she was convinced that Argenta was dying. No one so slight could survive what she had done to her body.

'What are you doing in here?'

It seemed like the voice came from another dimension. With this, Clara felt as if her body had been pulled back so rapidly that her heart and lungs would explode from the shock. The images of her fertile imagination on one strange note instantly disappeared while the magic which had come willingly dispersed into evil.

Shaken up at finding herself here in this different reality, Clara found it difficult to speak. Nurse Ryan's smart and pressed lemon and white nurse's uniform was waiting for her answer, yet she could have been an alien who had dropped from out of space.

The alien walked in, frowning.

'Why are you in here?'

'Have I done something wrong by being here? I was curious about Argenta. She was so ill when I saw her the last time.'

That anger relented quickly as Nurse Ryan walked to the window.

'No one else is worried about Argenta except you. She didn't make herself popular.'

'Probably not, but I still liked her. Anyhow, no matter how horrible you are, everyone should have a friend.'

An odd thing to say, but it was enough to make Nurse Ryan laugh.

'If you must know, Argenta went to the commune.'

Her answer was enough for Clara to look astonished and reveal a degree of disbelief, which presented some compassion this time.

'Dr. Slanders felt anxious about her.'

Difficult to believe this with Dr. Slanders' brown suit and cold-eyed, glassy stare.

'He asked Argenta what he could do for her, and if she wanted to leave and go somewhere else because he could see she was clearly unhappy here? He also warned her that if she persisted by not eating, then she was going to die. It was a sobering talk, but he had to let her decide.'

Should she interrupt the nurse now and tell her she couldn't believe this story?

'I believe that inside Argenta's starved head was the idea she would never die. With this frame of mind, she had gotten herself to where not eating would keep her in a state of perfection. It was one of those wake-up talks when she acknowledged and accepted what she was doing to herself. She didn't want to die. She was scared, and she didn't know what to do to help herself. Probably it was the only time she asked for help.'

Again, it was difficult to believe Argenta would ask for anyone's advice, especially Dr. Slanders. But these opinions she reserved for herself so she could listen to Nurse Ryan first before asking those questions.

'Argenta was desperate to get herself out of this crippling circle of starvation. In Dr. Slanders' opinion, she needed to go to the commune, better to go now than later. I believe he took her there himself, late at night. So, Clara, there is no good worrying about Argenta. She is still ill, but I believe she will get better and start putting on weight.'

These toxic lies tasted vile. And now she felt the reckless impulse to tell Nurse Ryan she was lying lay firmly cemented to await its chance. And it would come. Everything does in the end.

'Thank you, Nurse Ryan, for telling me this; I've been worrying about her. I am glad Argenta is getting on well. How did she look when she left? I wished I had been there to give her my farewells.'

'I didn't see her go either, but Nurse Jones did and collaborated Dr. Slanders' story. She went with Dr. Slanders to escort Argenta to her new home.'

Was Nurse Ryan really at peace with herself while she was relating these set of events? If she was, why then did she also come to this room as if on a pilgrimage? Clara had witnessed her expressions of concern and worry when they had been in the room together. Did Nurse Ryan choose to believe the story Dr. Slanders and Nurse Jones had told her? But this bordered on paranoia, the inability to believe the truth and to accept it. By the same token, the truth was also found in the borderland of paranoia.

Now looking about the room, as it was apparent Nurse Ryan wanted her out. She glanced down and beneath the bed was a sad and lonely soft toy, the same one that had sat at the table with them on her first night. For some inexplicable reason, Clara knew if Argenta had been leaving for another new place, this soft little toy would have gone with her.

'I shall miss Argenta,' she whispered, going to the door. 'But it's for the best, and I am glad for her. Like you, I wish I had been able to say my farewells.'

Tonight, when it's dark, and everyone should be sleeping, Clara was determined to come back and retrieve Argenta's little soft toy. Perhaps one day, and soon, she could return it to her.

The hush of the still dark night came in hundreds of breaths. Behind closed doors, people were sleeping, catching their dreams, and knitting them into woven stories, which made Clara more conscious of herself and what she was doing creeping along the hallway with all the machinations of drama.

Like we all do, finding ourselves behaving eccentrically, Clara saw how she must look if someone should come out of their room. How bizarre she would appear to a saner mind, because since she had been here, she had to fight a war of weird and toxic thoughts. Now, with this mad sneaking, Clara felt a great need to laugh at herself. The more she pulled that face of retention, the more she wanted to hail for the mockery of it all.

But no one should know what she was doing. What would Phoebe think of her or even her father if they had been here?

'Oh, daddy, please don't,' her cheeks were full and rosy with the most tumultuous grin. Almost as painful as if she had been badly hurt to make her feel sick.

But here she was, outside Argenta's old door, and it was a relief to let herself in. But inside the room brought another set of feelings. The main one was she should not be in here. How mysterious was this world with all its rules?

And next came the questions. Would the toy still be there? Had Nurse Ryan also seen it and taken it, then gave it to the lost property? Or maybe she just forgot about the young child and threw it away. No, Nurse Ryan wouldn't do that. She respected those silly feelings drawn from innocence. When she saw Argenta next, she would hand it across to her personally, knowing how much she would have missed it.

Yet, it was still there underneath the bed. Waiting and looking at her with that eye, a pretty bead sewn to the fur.

'Got you,' she grasped the soft toy, kneeling on the floor and stretching under the bed for it.

Grabbing the toy and pulling it across to herself, Clara was pleased to have it. But then she stopped horrified, for the soft toy had a life and revealed its history. Its head and that dedicated face which had faithfully kept its silence were nearly torn off. Such was the toy's ugly suffering, she dropped it just as if it had screamed at her. While the stuffing poured out of its neck, it flowed red, blood carmine.

Scampering back, Clara couldn't touch it again, but already on her hands was the peeled blood of its sufferings. The poor little thing, the innocence of the inanimate, the vessel for all our thoughts so designed that we can form our life. We buy it—we sell it—and then we disown it.

She was staring at this soft toy. What had it been once? A modified idea of a dog. Pricked ears formed for interest, while enormous eyes made copiously bright with shared thoughts and a mouth that measured a smile. It had promised to love Argenta, while she had torn out her heart to love it. The pain of days and hours had been invested in it. Impossible to leave it lonely under the bed. Someone will come along and clean it up, ignorant of all this love.

Tenderly and gently, Clara stretched out to pick up the scraps of stuffing and held its neck together. She would mend this dear little creature, and between them, they would put this experience behind them.

How horrible people can be to each other.

Like someone on a mission, Clara stood with this treasure. The world was an evil place, but she would show others how by evoking dignity with respect and honesty with sympathy. Turning at the door, Clara took one more look around. Argenta had lived some of her life in here, and all of it had been in suffering. What do we do with our secret selves when we are on our own? For many, they are their worst tormentors. The evil owners who have to face the truth about themselves. But not for Clara, not anymore.

For me, I write the truth because I care.

Though how honest and pure were Clara's thoughts about herself? She now felt like she was being pierced and analyzed as she made her way back to her room. Money, it was all about money. The world had sucked up to money, and everything one does has a cost to it. But frankly, what was she all about? She wasn't counting her steps anymore as she walked back to her room. Well, yes, she was doing this for money, but she also had principles; she needed money to make the truth work.

That clutch of fear was real. A tight grip on her shoulder blunted a scream, which should have been released.

'What are you doing, Miss Tinder?' the question came from Nurse Jones.

Like burning coals, Nurse Jones' hands penetrated through Clara's blouse into the ribs of her flesh. If she could, she would have carried on walking, pretending Nurse Jones had become a phantom. But she was real, too real to be dismissed.

'Hello Nurse Jones,' Clara was too afraid to smile. She had been caught when she believed she was safe.

'I asked what you are doing?' Nurse Jones's eyes ran over Clara to fall upon the stuffed dog.

'Where did you get that? It's not yours. I've seen it somewhere before.'

'I rescued it from Argenta's room. I feared it might have been thrown out.'

'Argenta,' Nurse Jones turned from the toy to Clara. 'What were you doing in there?'

'I missed her. I wanted to see the last place where she had been.'

'What do you mean by the last place?'

Her face became ugly with frowns. The defensive look of hate indented itself in her features. Eyes like liquid daggers cutting away as it pushed through the forest of imaginings. Her question, though, became a statement of facts.

'What happened to Argenta?'

'It's time that you mind your own business, Miss Tinder, and concentrate on your own health. Mischief and malice bound up in curiosity will get some people in trouble, and if they seek it, they will find it.'

'Is that a threat?'

Clara was startled. It was supposed to be a hospital to help you get better; it shouldn't be another battle arena. But hospitals were also about money. Honestly, it is naïve to think any differently.

'However you choose to see it,' and then Nurse Jones smiled, her eyes closing in satisfaction.

'What have you done with Argenta?'

'Argenta is at the commune. It was her decision. I went with Dr. Slanders to escort her there. Now give me that toy, and I will make certain she gets it. Come along now, Miss Tinder. You are very distressed, and your mind is everywhere; you imagine things and see situations that have never happened. It's called paranoia. I will mention this to Dr. Slanders. He will probably give you something to calm you down.'

Holding out her hand for the toy, Clara didn't have any choice but to hand it over. The dog she fancied had looked from Nurse Jones to her with appealing eyes. Please don't hand me over. He knew its death would not be long after this.

Oh, what am I to do? I have to save myself first.

Snatched, Nurse Jones had captured the stuffed toy and was returning along the hallway. Her back held straight with determination. She was furious. Left, right, left, right, back to her leader.

Unreal this night had been chimeric in so many ways. Walking back to her room, Clara reflected on the coincidence that Nurse Jones, of all people, should pace the corridor, waiting and ready to pounce. Had she been prepared for someone like herself to be curious?

This was a night Clara didn't want to remember, but it stalked her like everything else about this place. There were so many anomalies about this hospital whose only redeeming feature was most people could not afford to go there.

But to forget and sleep was the only way to get through this, and if she were clever to hold on to her health, she would have nothing to fear.

Wearied of body and mind, too tired to take even a shower, she climbed into bed, patted her pillow, and turned on to her side to sleep. Closing her eyes to await that blessed oblivion, the images of the day and thoughts ran across her retina. Peter was staring at her with eyes of expectation. People paid him to finish off their problems while he had no conscience about taking someone else's life. I wish he were here to do this for me. Situations of this kind could be taken care of just like that. Wouldn't it be nice?

10

———

The sunlight was just gliding in, peeping through the chinks of the curtain, when Clara heard a heavy noise going on outside. Still steeped in sleep, to be intrigued. She was lounging in bed when the door was abruptly opened. Looking up, she saw Nurse Jones had entered. Behind her was Dr. Slanders.

'We are going to help you,' said Dr. Slanders, walking forward in front of Nurse Jones.

'What are you going to do?' Clara, now receiving a big dose of reality, panicking, Clara tried to raise herself up on her arms.

'Nurse Jones, you had better help Miss Tinder to relax. She is getting very anxious.'

'What are you going to do to me?' and now, Clara was scared.

Her eyes ran all over their persons, looking for something. And there was something in Dr. Slanders' hand—a hypodermic syringe.

'No, no. I don't want that—'

Alarm was setting in, and the need to flee became paramount. Her legs were caught in the covers while Nurse Jones traveled quickly to the other side of her.

'No, no. Why are you doing this to me? I haven't done anything wrong.'

Clara's eyes were full on the needle, and now the silver dagger was about to enter her flesh. The muscular arms of Nurse Jones tightened her fingers on Clara to hold her down.

'No, you can't. I haven't given you my permission.'

Nurse Jones was so strong, she pinned Clara to the bed, and by the determined look in her eyes, she was enjoying herself. But Clara had legs, and these were still free. She kicked and thrashed her legs for freedom.

'Oh, to hell with it,' snapped Dr. Slanders while his eyes caught on Clara's bare arms. 'Is there anything you can do about this? I can't catch hold of her arm while she is intent on breaking my back?'

'No, this is illegal. You can't do this to me,' cried Clara.

'You think so,' smiled Dr. Slanders, his face moved across to hers with those watery ice-blue eyes staring down into hers. 'You forget, you voluntarily signed yourself into my responsibility. Miss Tinder, you are sick, and you need help. This, as you know, is a mental hospital. Whatever I do to you is for your benefit.'

Nurse Jones had climbed on to Clara's bed while holding Clara's arms down. Now sitting on top of Clara's legs, she panted.

'No,' screamed Clara. 'For pity's sake, don't do this to me.'

'For pity's sake, Miss Tinder,' grinned Dr. Slanders as he lowered the hypodermic into her arm. 'We are saving you from your poor self.'

The red-hot needle traveled into her arm's virgin flesh to

pump in its intoxicating draft. Were they trying to kill her? For death at its worst would come as a memory. She felt the light spinning around and then retreating while she was going under.

'She is going now,' Dr. Slanders' voice came as from underwater. 'Well done, Nurse Jones.'

'Can she hear us?'

The remaining bit of consciousness was slowly ebbing away. A large face looked into her eyes and grinned before this, too, disappeared.

ONCE AGAIN, the beginnings of another day, a second chance, as the last one had been a mistake. Opening her eyes, Clara felt she could appreciate it better.

To her surprise, she found she was already sitting up, or perhaps it would be correct to say her head was raised. Automatically, she went to stroke back her hair, but another pair of arms this time were on her, tugging at her to stay where she was. No, this was silly. She should be able to do what she wanted, and that was to push her hair back from the side of her face.

Restraints secured her, and there was no option for her to move her arms. Her legs, too, were also bound to the bed at her ankles. What had happened to her? What had they done to her?

'You're awake,' smiled Nurse Ryan, standing from the chair she had been sitting on. Slowly, she walked across to Clara. 'How are you feeling now, Miss Tinder?'

'What's happened to me?' her mad eyes stared at the nurse.

'Well, let's say you haven't been at all well. Dr. Slanders

thought if you were to drop into madness, there wasn't any hope of ever getting you back.'

'I don't understand. There was nothing wrong with me—'

'Now, now, don't get yourself upset again,' this time she stroked Clara's hair away from her face. 'Everything is going to be all right, I promise you.'

'Tell me what happened to me. I need to know.' This was a scene out of someone else's madness.

'You had a fit, Miss Tinder, a terrible one. You started screaming and crying out loud that there were monsters in your room. Nurse Jones, who was on duty up here, dashed into your room. You would not be comforted. She paged through to Dr. Slanders, who had just entered the hospital.'

'No, no, I don't believe you.'

'Don't get yourself upset; you will undo all the good we have done for you. Lay still, Miss Tinder; we are all rooting for you to get well. You must cooperate. It was touch and go with you. You were fortunate Dr. Slanders acted so quickly.'

'I don't believe you.'

'Oh dear, if you don't keep yourself calm, I will have no choice but to call Dr. Slanders again. My strict instructions were to keep you calm.'

At the mention of another visit from Dr. Slanders, Clara sobered up dramatically. Play the game, she reminded herself, if you want to get yourself out of here. Be sensible, get smart, and don't, for goodness' sake, allow anyone to see your fear. Her palpitating heart had sprung into action, and it was prepared for a war which, if she were smart enough, could avoid. Think calmly and take back control, and don't act as you feel. After all, this was not the first time.

'I supposed I didn't believe I was that ill,' she looked at the straps which were holding her arms down.

'Oh, I know dear,' Nurse Ryan was genuinely worried. She leaned further towards Clara in empathy.

'And now I feel embarrassed about the way I behaved. Do you know what triggered it?'

'I overheard you accused Dr. Slanders of being the anti-Christ. Nurse Jones was going past your room when she heard shouting coming from it. She looked in to see who it was and witness you shouting at something. She feared you were delusional, and that's when she called for Dr. Slanders.'

'It sounds like you are talking about someone else. I don't remember anything about it.'

But she did. The scene was coming back vividly to her. The stealth with which they had taken her by surprise, they had struck without thinking about their actions. It was as if they had something big to hide.

Nurse Ryan was thinking, and her frowning face appeared uneasy. Clara laid her eyes carefully on the nurse —something was puzzling her because she didn't look comfortable with her thoughts. Doubts were also running through her mind. She was making equations that were not adding up.

'It's embarrassing to know I behaved that way,' Clara began, still with her eyes on Nurse Ryan. 'What was I shouting about?'

'Something about evil when you saw Dr. Slanders—now try to relax. Something bad must have happened to you?'

Her frown became more profound.

'You know,' Clara smiled. 'Nothing like this has happened before, and I've never heard of anything like this happening to anyone else?'

Clara looked at Nurse Ryan's lowered head and enjoyed the discomfort she was witnessing.

'Have you?'

'I've known it to happen here.' She looked up, now smiling. 'So, you see, you are not the only one.'

Such a strange thing to say, and to expect her to be heartened by her supposed outbreak. Was this not unusual? Should she be relieved about that? And then that thought came to her. Who else had suffered an outburst like this?

'Did Charisse have an attack like mine?'

This question startled Nurse Ryan.

'Yes, she did.'

Clara could see Nurse Ryan was in a tumult about answering this question, but Clara had caught her out unawares.

'Why do you ask?'

'I heard rumors about her.' Another calculated risk with this question. 'Did you witness it?'

'I shouldn't be talking to you about it.' Nurse Ryan looked very uncomfortable.

'And I shouldn't have asked, but I need to know how she managed to deal with it.'

The pressure was taken off the nurse, who suddenly saw where this question was leading.

'Well, Charisse was different from you. As you know, she came to the hospital for substance abuse.' Nurse Ryan cautiously went on, thoughtfully making her way through the angles of accusation. 'She had what was called a drug-induced fit. She, too, was seeing demons and calling poor Dr. Slanders all types of names. But he managed to help her. She was put out for several days as well. That was when she decided to go to the commune.'

'So, she recovered. Did she have another fit?'

'No, she didn't.'

'Is that what happened to Argenta?'

'Argenta was different. She was starving herself to death.'

If only Clara could plead with Nurse Ryan and ask her to speak the truth. If only she could tell her what her suspicions were about Dr. Slanders, in that she didn't believe he was the man he purported himself to be. Was it possible to trust Nurse Ryan enough to say to her, let's pool our thoughts together to find out what is going on here? But she looked on and nodded while trying every way she could to get the answer she needed.

'Then Argenta didn't have a fit? She looked so weak when I last saw her, I was certain she would die.'

'Yes, I know,' Nurse Ryan smiled gently. 'I thought that as well. Thank goodness she pulled through. If it weren't for Nurse Jones sitting beside her night and day, the chances of Argenta surviving would have been very slim.'

This was a surprise. To hear such good things about Nurse Jones when Clara was only prepared to listen to the worse about this woman was awkward.

'Have you heard from either of these two?' again Clara smiled encouragingly.

'Yes, they are both doing well, and both are settling in well. It's so satisfying to hear such good news like that.'

Clara smiled while picking up the threads of thoughts to weave into an interesting pattern.

'I expect they would both know each other. I wonder if they're friends.'

'I never thought about that, but I don't see why they shouldn't be friends.'

'When did you last hear from them?'

'Last week.'

'And what did they say to you?'

'It was, in fact, Dr. Slanders who told me. He visited the

commune, and he thought I would like to know how the two young women were.'

'That was kind of him. So, you didn't actually speak to them?'

Nurse Ryan suddenly looked puzzled, as if Clara had caught her in some sort of trap.

'Miss Tinder, why are you asking me these questions?'

Dumbly, Clara smiled.

'I was just curious, that's all. It has come as a bit of a shock to me to find out I have been so ill. I just wanted to know how people who have been in my situation have progress.'

'I see,' but in her tone, there was a ring of doubt.

'I'm really sorry to have been a nuisance, and though I can't remember, I apologize for what I have done and for my behavior.'

'It wasn't your fault. You couldn't help it,' Nurse Ryan's willing eyes tried to comfort Clara.

'Perhaps not. I don't know what came over me. And these restraints, are they really necessary now? I can't do anything; I can't even scratch my face.'

'Where do you have an itch?'

This service, which Nurse Ryan was prepared to do, fell short of her releasing Clara from her bondage.

'Can't you please loosen my straps for me? It's causing me a great deal of distress.'

'They are there for your own protection.'

'But I am not benefiting from them anymore.'

In a temper, Clara had raised her voice, an act she regretted instantly, for this could get her into trouble. Stay calm and controlled. Otherwise, she would be playing their game. A game that didn't allow her to have what she wanted at all. Like chess, each move of a piece was carefully calculated because there could only be certain correct moves to win.

'Dr. Slanders said that you are not to have your restraints off until he has examined you.'

A rage blew up in her head like a ticking time-bomb. She never had a fit or gone mad. It was Dr. Slanders who played this sneaky game on her. Oh, how unfair? Yes, very unfair. But she prevented herself from this outcry with an act of courage. She would win in the end, so lie low and play the game. You will get your opportunity. Humiliating to realize she had already shown her hand by giving Dr. Slanders all he wanted on her. She was in a mental hospital. What more did she need to say?

'Can't you at least undo one of my restraints on my arm? I have sobered up to what I did before. Please. I feel like I am being punished for something. Just undo my left hand if you have to instead of my right.'

Nurse Ryan's eyes returned from the restraints to Clara's. Dare she?

'I feel like I am being reprimanded as a criminal. Only criminals get more rights than me.'

Again, the battle went on in Nurse Ryan's mind. If you were to ask her if she was happy about Clara's incarceration, she would tell you this sort of thing disturbed her, and she was also shocked when she found Clara subjected to this kind of treatment.

'Just one arm,' she stood. 'And no more.'

'Thank you, Nurse Ryan. I am very grateful to you.'

The door to Clara's room had to open just then; the timing could not have been more orchestrated. It was as if Dr. Slanders had been listening and waiting outside the door and expecting to find his nurse being deceitful. With her hands on one of Clara's buckles, she had begun unloosening it. In a few seconds, Clara's hand would be free.

'What are you doing?' Dr. Slanders' raging eyes were on the buckle.

'I'm loosening these restraints for Miss Tinder. It's making her uncomfortable, and she has complained she is in pain.'

'Leave that well alone,' although his voice was low, the sound of anger resonated. 'Please be so good as to follow my orders. You are a nurse; remember your place.'

Dr. Slander watched with a temper as Nurse Ryan's nervous fingers hurriedly carried on undoing the bindings.

'This is inhuman. You are punishing Miss Tinder. Look at her. She does not deserve to be bound up like this any longer.'

'I will decide Miss Tinder's treatment, not you. I am the doctor here.'

'But I am also a nurse swore to be the caregiver of professional treatment.'

'Nurse Ryan, please stop undoing the restraints.'

'Miss Tinder has apologized for her recent behavior. Anyone can tell she is in a much saner mind than she was before.'

The buckle was undone, Clara's hand was out and free. Another person entered the room. Nurse Jones, hearing loud voices, walked in. She instantly saw the tension between these two people.

'Nurse Ryan, will you step out with me for a minute? Nurse Jones, please be so good as to fix Miss Tinder's restraints.'

Nurse Ryan's eyes spoke quickly to Clara. She was sorry, and then she reviewed her opponent. With renewed spirit, she followed Dr. Slanders out of the room. The door closed quietly behind them both.

'No,' cried Clara, pulling at her hand from Nurse Jones' grasp. 'You can't do this to me. I have rights. You mustn't treat me this way.'

Her petition was heard without mercy as Nurse Jones dug on to her hand and pushed it into the strap. Outside the room, the raised voices continued.

'I shall report you to the psychiatric board,' said Nurse Ryan. 'You have exceeded your rights to treat a patient like Miss Tinder in this manner.'

'Who on earth do you think you are talking to me like this?'

'I have watched the methods you have practiced, and honestly, I find them despicable. I have been in nursing for twenty years, and I have never come across anyone as dishonest and ruthless as you. I am determined to report you. And how you run this hospital needs to be investigated.'

'I think you have said enough, Nurse Ryan.'

'No, Dr. Slanders, I have only just begun. I know how you bullied Argenta; this was the reason she stopped eating. You were determined to have her enter the commune. Let me ask you why? There are many questions that need answering, and many things are not adding up either.'

'Nurse Ryan, I am terminating your employment. I shall not have a member of my staff threatening me or questioning how I treat my patients. That is enough. Please go instantly and do not return.'

'You think I would continue working for you? I never want to see you again. And as for this hospital, where people without warning vanish. I am going to report all of this to the authorities.'

Leaving Clara's side after having secured the wrist restraint, Nurse Jones hurried to the door.

'Everything you are saying is being overheard,' whispered Nurse Jones.

'Good,' said Nurse Ryan. 'This is not the last you are going to hear of it.'

From her bedside, and restrained by the leather straps, Clara had a tantalizing view of the hallway from her bed. The lemon and white dress of Nurse Ryan stood up to the tall washed-out brown suit of Dr. Slanders, who remained like an impediment. A signpost which had been influential in its fashioned world, but now the place names had changed, and the world he had been formed in had moved on and disappeared. Yet, he was still issuing directions and orders, which weren't valid anymore.

'Please leave Nurse Ryan. You are a discredit to your profession—'

'I'll go, don't worry.'

The tense argument had blistered the air, and the vulnerability of Nurse Ryan's position showed clearly to Clara how imprudent she had been to accept the mantel of mental illness.

'Miss Tinder,' the head around the door was Nurse Ryan's. 'I will be back for you, I promise. You are unsafe while you are here.'

'Nurse Ryan.' An unemotional man, Dr. Slanders' calm face was becoming progressively angry; he was trying to keep hold of his self-control while the stress mounted in his pulsating temples. 'Please leave now, or else I will have no choice but to have you physically ejected from the premises.'

'You haven't heard the last of this.' Nurse Ryan's voice

disappeared along the hallway; she had lost all fear of this man.

The silence which came afterward was like the aftermath of shock. Two sets of eyes were taking stock of each other; Dr. Slanders and Nurse Jones were left to clear up the debris of this open disagreement.

Lying tightened by tension, Clara wondered what was going to happen next. Without Nurse Ryan, she was afraid for herself, but what could these two do to her? Nurse Ryan was going to the authorities.

A fair few thoughtful seconds passed before the door to her room was opened again. Two faces had cast off their threats and now were smiling at Clara.

'Good morning, Miss Tinder. I hear you have had a better night. How are you?'

Clara stared at Dr. Slanders. Was he serious? No one has a personality change in five minutes. And then she understood.

'I'm not pleased to be tied up.'

'Yes, I think we can do something about that now. What do you say? We will take them off if you promise to behave yourself,' he smiled.

She wanted to tell him he had exceeded his authority, but that would be foolish, wouldn't it? Play the game, Clara. Be wise and don't be indignant. That is a luxury you can't afford—yet.

'I promise to be good.' Clara looked at her wrists.

'Good. I think we understand each other now.'

He looked so smug with his absurd confidence, as if he had always won at whatever he tried his hand at. And seeing Nurse Jones smiling with pride, adoring him as if he were a god, the false sham of his troubled world could never be toppled.

11

———

D r. Slanders was pleased he could be lenient with Clara. So pleased he could release her from the restraints. He even had Nurse Jones do this for him. And how do you feel? Dr. Slanders asked when the bounds were finally removed from Clara as she rubbed her wrists symbolically.

'I feel strange,' and now she rubbed her ankles. 'And disorientated.'

'You know why we had to do this to you?' began Dr. Slanders. 'It was not a pleasure for anyone to curtail someone else's behavior. You understand why we did this, don't you?'

'Because you said I was violent.'

'You were violent—have no doubts about that, Miss Tinder. Have no doubts.'

'To be honest, I don't remember anything about it.'

'And why should you? The mind is kind, and it protects you from those ugly things which you cannot handle. Perhaps the day will come when the memory will return, but if it doesn't, don't worry yourself about it. It's just as well.'

Then he turned his attention to Nurse Jones, favoring her with one of his special looks.

'Nurse Jones, do you remember what we were talking about earlier? Do you think you could carry out our mission? It has to be done. If you cannot do it, then I will have to find someone who will.'

Unnatural charm on not a handsome man was almost hideous. The chill of ice was in his eyes when he tried a smile at Nurse Jones.

'Yes, Dr. Slanders, you can trust me,' said Nurse Jones, avariciously eager to please.

Her face, which had never been darkened with blusher or bruised with crimson lipstick, was even now whiter. She looked as if a vampire had stripped her of the living blood, yet she lived, and her eyes became larger and darker.

She left the room quickly and yet dejected as if horror had claimed her with its dark and vile thoughts.

'Now,' Dr. Slanders said, returning to Clara. 'We have to get you well and healthy. You need to get back to your hectic and new life.'

Was it relief she heard in his voice which heralded in the false smiles and cheered fake happiness before bringing in the line of attack?

'I suggest you rest here today,' he said, tapping her shoulder in an avuncular manner and was proud of her. 'I will look in later before I go to the commune. Oh, I forgot to mention the good news. Argenta has put on two pounds, and she wished me to tell you she is happy. Now that is good news, isn't it?'

'Yes, it's excellent news.'

'Good.'

His world, which had been rattled and distorted, had now settled down without even a crash.

'Yes, yes,' he smiled, touching his face as if to reassure himself. 'Everything works out in the end. Everything.'

Would Nurse Ryan go to the authorities and report Dr. Slanders and what he was doing at the hospital? Clara hoped so. She really hoped so. Then Argenta could go into another hospital if that's what she needed. She could restart her life and get on the right path, this time to happiness.

Good to be free of those torturous restraints, but Clara was left unexpectedly weak. Her legs shook when she tried to stand while lifting herself from the armchair was impossible.

No one had told her how long she had been unconscious with whatever Dr. Slanders had injected into her. That story had to be forgotten, and quickly. Now she must concentrate on getting better, but it was nigh impossible to think of doing anything strenuous. Trying to stay away from her bed was almost intolerable. The worst thing was she felt sorry for herself, as if she had genuinely suffered. She laid there waiting. Waiting for something. What that was, she did not know.

Why had she expected someone to come and visit her to see how she was? But Clara was hoping. No one came, not even Lulu. The last time she and Lulu had spoken, Clara felt there had been a connection, and that she had broken through that impenetrable barrier. But serves her right, she had been obnoxious initially, and besides, they had their own lives to lead. It just would have been nice to see a friendly face.

'You should eat,' said Nurse Jones, the only nurse who came to check on her.

She had brought her meal in on a tray and laid it on the table beside her bed.

'I don't feel like eating.'

Clara looked at the fish, which once would have been tempting to her. But now, the mere smell of it turned her stomach.

'What is going on with you?'

Taking out a thermometer from her uniform's top pocket, Nurse Jones motioned for Clara to open her mouth. While this was going on, she then looked at Clara critically. Her icy hands pulled down Clara's eyelids and then checked for her pulse. A minute later, when she took the thermometer from Clara's mouth, she regarded Clara in the eye.

'You've got a slight temperature, but stress can do that. I will mention how you are to Dr. Slanders and ask him to have a look at you. How long have you been feeling like this?'

'Since I awoke from the—'

'Yes, undoubtedly you have undergone a very distressing time. You look very white as well, and the coloring of your eyes doesn't look healthy. Have you ever suffered from anemia?'

'No, never.'

'It could be something as simple as that. A course of iron tablets should do the trick, but of course, that's for the doctor to say, not me. Now, though,' she alluded to the tray. 'I recommend you try to eat something. Being healthy has a lot to do with eating. I'll come back in half an hour. When I return, I expect you to have eaten at least some of your meal.'

Nurse Jones could never be said to be a friendly person. It was apparent charm had bypassed her. But she was proving to be efficient and competent. Clara was thinking this when the nurse left the room. She didn't like the woman, would never like her, but whatever she felt about her, it could not take away from her skills.

Some people like that, and then again, and for no reason, she thought about Peter, and a wave overwhelmed her. Was he the only one who cared about her?

How silly, she was crying. Crying for Peter, but really for herself. The world was such a dreadful place these days. Perhaps if she had a long cry, she would get this out of her system. She felt so low, which was understandable.

With a disapproving eye, Nurse Jones returned at the hour, looked at the plate before picking up the tray. No more needed to be said; Clara got the picture. Although she had looked more than once at the inviting food, Clara couldn't find the energy to take up the knife and fork, nor could she bring herself to eat.

Dr. Slanders had knocked at her door before entering her room. The good manners he had dropped previously had now been reclaimed.

'Nurse Jones told me about your temperature and loss of appetite. I want to know, Miss Tinder, if this is part of a rebellion or are you really feeling weak?'

'I'm just very sad,' she thought about not telling him, but suddenly it seemed pointless. 'I feel very low and very sorry for myself.'

'Do you mind if I check your heart?' he raised his eyebrow. 'I have to admit; you don't look too well.'

Clara nodded; even this was exhausting.

'Can I part your nightdress to examine you?'

She nodded again. The stethoscope was cold and unemotional; although professional, she still couldn't help feeling embarrassed.

'Hmm,' he said, now looking thoughtfully at her. 'Your

heart is racing a bit too fast for my liking. We need to give you some help. I suggest a course of iron tablets, and because your temperature is raised, it might be a good idea to give you some antibiotics as well.'

She had wanted to ask him. Was she really ill? And if she was, how did this happen? Both Nurse Jones and Dr. Slanders implied it could be stress which was robbing her of energy. She couldn't remember when she had felt so tired. She would take anything—anything to stop his awful inertia.

'I suggest complete bedrest,' he said, towering over her.

There was no kindness in his eyes, except perhaps the look of concern which rather disconcerted Clara. She would sooner dislike him than like him, but because she was weak, so very weak, she felt she needed him. When we are ill or afraid, it's natural to look for a parent in others, Clara reflected. Now she wasn't well, and she didn't have the strength to despise.

But what on earth was wrong with her? She was scared —no, terrified. Never in her life had she felt this helpless by being physically ill.

He had prescribed complete bed rest, which made her feel grateful. Just to lie on her bed and watch the world go by and not worry about anything seemed an odd way to spend one's life.

The chatting of people walking past her room filled the air. The sounds of their voices came so healthily; it was exhausting just having to listen to them.

Had she been asleep, she couldn't tell anymore, drifting in and out of consciousness, or so it seemed. Dr. Slanders had given her an injection of vitamin B12; he showed her the vial from which it came. The pink liquid in the tiniest of bottles with a silver-colored lid and labeled with B12. He knew she didn't trust him, which made her grateful. Never an emotionally demonstrative man, but he knew how to be gentle.

Laying there reviewing her life, thinking was now the only task Clara could do, but even that was exhausting. Another stage to help her recovery was when Dr. Slanders and Nurse Jones connected her to a drip. They felt her skin; it showed signs of dehydration. Something had to be done, as she could not help herself.

Time passed; hours melted away. Despite that, Clara lay in her bed. Dr. Slanders made constant and regular visits to her room, looking into her eyes with a show of ready concern. He pulled the light skin under her eyes now and speculated on the color.

All thoughts about Nurse Ryan and what she was going to do disappeared. No one from the board of health had visited. And as for the police shutting down the clinic, that also never materialized. So full of righteousness in the beginning, but now she was ill, and it didn't matter anymore.

That awful thought came along. Was she dying? Perhaps she was. If death were like this, then it wouldn't be so bad. At least she wasn't in pain—no pain at all except the vigor of energy ebbing away.

Sunshine and darkness were like two pillows of matter switching from one side to the other as if to make themselves comfortable. Sometimes she felt herself floating towards them, beautiful and more beautiful; this was a beautiful world.

Had she really been ill, the next measured thought came trifling through the windows. She had been seriously mentally ill in the past. Sometimes, something like shock or too much stress had stirred up her tangled psyche to blow her into space.

It could be this which had happened to her. She could have suffered a breakdown. These things come creeping along, catching one always unaware. She must have had a breakdown; she must have been paranoid; it suddenly seemed very clear to Clara this was what must have happened.

Perhaps the health authorities had come and made their examination. She wouldn't have known anything about it, and she would have been out of it in her own little world, an untouchable asteroid spinning free.

Having been drip-fed intravenously helped. For nearly a day, she was being brought back to life, and she welcomed it. Good health is a wonderful friend, and it comes running with gifts. A deposit of optimism and encouragement; learning to live again and appreciating it. But after that day, these friends became elusive, as if they were just visitors passing on to a more deserving host than her.

In this dreamy state of mind, she lay there while Nurse Jones came in and out, washing and changing her. Something that she would have hated once upon a time. But how things change when there is very little one can do for oneself. Hang on there, she told herself, too weary to speak and an effort to think. She couldn't do anything, so why should she worry? Why should she worry about anything?

Days glided by nicely while interesting thoughts poked snugly in her mind, some stranger than others. It then occurred to her as she lay there looking at the floral curtains trembling in the breeze that perhaps it was poor Nurse Ryan who had gone mad. So, Dr. Slanders was right all the while about her madness. Difficult to make any logical analysis except to have complete bed rest. This was such a comforting thought.

'I need to take a few samples of blood, Miss Tinder?' said Dr. Slanders. 'Unfortunately, you will feel some pain because you have lost a great deal of weight. So, I must apologize to you if it hurts.'

Clara could only look at him because it cost too much to speak.

It hurt. He was right, but the odd thing about it was she was pleased, pleased to have actual physical pain. It came as a relief to feel something; it was the evidence she needed. She was still alive. Her body was still fighting to hold on to its dignity. Fancy that, her body still cared that she should live. She should be more like this more often, Clara thought. Strange thoughts. If she were healthier, she would have laughed them off.

Why did Dr. Slanders want samples of her blood? It was only a thought and not a criticism. He was a doctor; he must know what he was doing.

And now Clara was waking up at strange times. In the dusk, her mother walked past. She didn't even stop to say hello, but that was Tina for you. Only here for herself. She must remember to be kinder to her mother, not that she deserved it, but it would be better for herself if she did.

A time to make amends, so whatever happens next would be kinder to her. Was she really going to die?

On the following day, after Nurse Jones had sloshed out Clara's tubes before being fed intravenously. It was funny to see these drips hooked up to her. It was as if she were becoming more like a robot than a human. The door opened quickly after a quick tap, revealing Dr. Slanders. Of course, it was him. Who else could it have been?

'Do you mind if I sit down?' he asked.

She hoped the expression in her eyes was enough to say she welcomed him. It must have done, as he pulled a chair towards her bed.

'I have been concerned about you, Miss Tinder. You don't appear to be responding to anything we are doing for you, which is why I did some tests. I sent them off to the laboratory for examination.'

A shrill of absolute fear, cold as ice, sharp as razors on the tip of the skin, ran jumping and leaping across her body.

'I had hoped it was just a suspicion, but it came back confirming my suspicion.'

Her eyes suddenly, with a will of their own, ran straight to his face, daring him to refute what he was about to say.

'You, Miss Tinder, are seriously ill. I am sorry to have to tell you this.'

'What?' Clara tried to croak.

Nurse Jones, who had been standing behind Dr. Slanders, came quickly across to Clara. From the table, she picked up a swab, undid the wrapper before dipping it into some water, and gently, yet firming, opened Clara's mouth to run the moisten swab around her dry and parched lips.

'What is wrong with me?'

Her voice sounded strange and almost surreal. She hadn't heard herself talk for several days.

'I suspected that you might have leukemia. And unfortunately, today, this was confirmed.'

'What does this mean?'

She was staring at him with hard, hollowed eyes.

'There is a cure for me, isn't there?'

'No, Miss Tinder. You have a rare form of leukemia. It is very virulent. There is nothing we can do for you.'

'Are you saying I'm going to die?'

'Let's put it this way; everyone is going to die. Most

people don't know when they will die, but in your case, you will. And now I must add that I am very sorry.'

'But I don't want to die. I am not ready for it.'

'That's understandable, Miss Tinder. I would have been happier if I could have given you better news, but the tests are conclusive. It could have been the reason you had a fit.'

'Isn't there anything you can do for me? I don't feel ill, just tired. What about bone marrow treatment? I could have that.'

'I am afraid it is too late for that, Miss Tinder. It has unfortunately spread to your brain.'

Such an awful sound came out of her mouth, a moan which sounded inhuman.

'Please don't let me die. I promise that I'll be good. I promise you I will be a better person. I just don't want to die.'

'Miss Tinder, please, it is as difficult for us as it is for you.'

'But you are not the one who is dying. There must be something that can be done? I promise you I will start eating properly. I didn't realize I was so ill. I thought I was only tired. Why didn't you tell me before about your suspicions? It would have given me a better chance. I could have been saved if you had told me earlier.'

'Miss Tinder, I understand you are very upset about being given bad news like this. I had hoped my suspicions would have been proved wrong, but they weren't. I was trying to spare your fears.'

'The doctor was only trying to do the best for you,' intervened Nurse Jones.

'That's okay, Nurse Jones, it is only right Miss Tinder is upset; she needs to come to terms with what is happening to her.'

'No. I will never accept what you have told me. If I accept this, it will mean I have given up when I haven't,' cried Clara. 'I want you to help me. There must be a cure. You could have got the diagnosis wrong.'

'I wish I had. That is why I took several samples of your blood, and the results always proved to be the same.'

'Please, please,' tears squeezed from Clara's eyes. 'Please don't let me die. I promise to be good. Please tell me there is a chance for me?'

He looked at Clara to assess how well she was taking this awful proclamation.

'There is something. I was going to pass it by you. It's an experimental form of treatment which has shown some results—'

'What is it?' Clara grasped at any hope.

'Stem cell transplantation, but it isn't a guarantee—'

'Yes, I'll take it.'

It had been a black hole that Clara had stared into. Dark and endless, with no reprieve, but now there was hope, like a small yet twinkling star in the very ebony of the blackness in another galaxy pushing its way into relief. It brought her the light of hope.

'But it might not work.'

'I don't care. If I believe it will work, it will. Faith,' Clara said, her eyes now radiant. 'Is what gets us through—'

'Yes,' Dr. Slanders said with a sigh. 'The only problem here is that we do not have the facilities or equipment to care for people with your diagnoses.'

'Well, I can't pack my bags and go back home.' Clara was astonished.

'Yes, I understand that. But for your recovery, we cannot help you here. It sounds like we are callous, but we have to think of everyone's wellbeing.'

'I don't understand what you are talking about. I have nowhere to go except back to my house.' impossible to believe this hospital could do this to her, abandon her when she was so vulnerable.

'Well, actually, we have been thinking about that very thing. Haven't we?' he looked at Nurse Jones, who too looked concerned. 'But before we proposed the suggestion to you, we contacted the people that carry out such procedures.'

Clara was listening and waiting. Her entire world had been turned upside down to find herself waiting at the mercy of others.

'We spoke to the commune about it, and they suggested that looking after you would be workable and possible.'

'The commune?'

This idea came as a complete surprise. Clara's vision of being cared for would be done in a hospital and not in a community of Bohemians.

'Yes. I could monitor you, and the community could take care of you. Of course, it will cost, and I can't promise that it will work—'

'I don't care. I will take my chances. What is the use of money if it can't do anything for you? It's no use to you when you are dead?'

There, she had said that word. The startling fact she might be dead in a few months was horrific.

'This is a decision which cannot be taken lightly. I want you to think about it, Miss Tinder.'

'I have thought about it. When can I go to the commune?'

He sighed; he shook his head as if he regretted making this suggestion to her.

'Please,' Clara cried, squeezing all the energy out of her.

'This, I know, is my only chance. Please make this happen for me.'

'Well, before we start, you will need to sign all the paperwork to confirm you understand it is just a clinical trial that may or may not work, and you have to accept the responsibility for any failure. No one can predict how your body will tolerate this procedure. You need to know what is going to happen.'

'Yes, whatever. But the more you are talking, the more time is passing by, and I feel with every second passing, my rights to life are denied.'

Why didn't he understand? Why was he putting so many problems in the way? This was a nightmare, and the irony was she had wanted to die for many years. But not now. Not now she had something in her life worth pursuing. A goal to reach to say she had existed, and that she had lived and stood amongst others to say she had made her mark.

12

____

Never had she been so conscious of the seconds passing. She tried to listen with patience as he told her about the procedure. Necessary to listen because this was part of her responsibility.

I will live. This chant played in her head as Dr. Slanders explained what would happen. Life, I want life; I have something important to offer. I am more important than most. If you're going to bargain with your life, you have to fight for it and use all the dirty tricks at your disposal.

There was a donor. Certain people have been checked out as potential donors, and because it was leukemia cancer, the success rate was higher.

Yes, she nodded impatiently. Carry on, get the documents, and she would sign whatever they wanted. The entire trial was going to cost. Yes, she nodded, don't worry about the money. And then she saw in her mind's eye Peter smiling at her as if he knew that one day this would happen to her. Here he came as her knight in shining armor. When she recovered from this, she would visit his grave and thank him personally.

Poor Peter—but thank you so much for the money.

The legal documents would take a day. Why so long? But never mind, carry on. In between this time, she would be taken to the commune. He just had to telephone through and ask them to get her room ready.

'You will need a full-time nurse.'

Dr. Slanders' eyes were covering all the problems. Of course, Clara thought without thinking why that was.

'Nurse Jones is prepared to go with you and be your full-time nurse.'

'Nurse Jones?' with the voice of disdain.

'Yes,' Dr. Slanders lifted his chin. 'She is the best nurse we have in this hospital. I have asked her, and she is willing. I don't think you are in a position to be choosey.'

Dr. Slanders was right, and since she had been ill, Nurse Jones had been exemplary.

'She may not have the best bedside manner, but I can always rely on her to be efficient without losing her head. I'm sorry, Nurse Jones, but we are dealing with someone's life here.'

'Don't worry, Dr. Slanders,' said Nurse Jones, casting down her head as if she had been affected. 'If Miss Tinder will have me to nurse her, then I will willingly accompany her.'

'There you are, Miss Tinder, you cannot ask for better help than that. You will need every assistance you can get to help save your life. I shall also look in and keep an eye on you.'

'Thank you,' muttered Clara, aware she had sounded ungrateful.

The process now had begun. A private ambulance would take Clara to the commune, and Nurse Jones was to collect her things together and behave in every way as if she was a servant. Tomorrow, Dr. Slanders would bring the documents to the commune for Clara to sign.

Clara's fears came with her impatience, while Dr. Slanders was talking impossibly slowly, as were his movements. She watched as he took his time to stand and then looked at Nurse Jones with another one of his nods as if they were agreeing on something, a silent communication going on between a doctor and his head nurse.

How slowly he crept to the door. Was it her imagination they were moving so slowly? Nurse Jones watched Dr. Slanders leave the room, her eyes as a hawk looked at him as if she were mesmerized. Then she went back to her work, caught in thoughts.

What was she thinking? At a guess, Clara knew that Nurse Jones' reflections were not anchored around her; there was something else on her mind. But if she should ask, Nurse Jones would stop what she was doing to answer her. There was no time to delay.

But why such peculiar thoughts should come to Clara's head right now? Why jeopardize her life with curiosity? Time was the most critical factor now for Clara. Everything depended on time. Already her time was running out, and yet?

'What happened to the soft toy?'

Nurse Jones had her back to Clara, but she heard her because she stopped.

'Is this question directed at me?' asked Nurse Jones, her back stiffened by Clara's question.

'I see no other person who it could be directed at.'

'Do you wish me to carry on packing your cases?'

'Yes, but I would also like to know what happened to Argenta's soft toy. Did you give it to her?'

'No,' said Nurse Jones, without turning around. 'I didn't

return it to her. I gave it to Dr. Slanders; he gave it back to her.'

'So, if I were to ask Dr. Slanders about the toy—'

'Why would you do something like that?' and still Nurse Jones' back faced Clara.

'Because the soft toy was special to Argenta, and it would please me to know she had it.'

'Sometimes, you behave foolishly. Everyone is going out of their way to help you, yet you persist in finding information about someone else. Why do you have to be so awkward?'

'I don't see there is anything problematic about asking a trivial question like that?'

'Exactly, it is trivial. You are dying, and yet you want to know if someone got their toy. Argenta is a young woman, and she has finished with her toys. Returning an old memory like that will only upset her.'

'So, you didn't return it to her when you said you did?'

'Yes, I lied to you. That's what adults do sometimes to protect people from the truth. She didn't want that toy anymore, which is why she left it behind.'

Absurdly arrogant, Nurse Jones' spine stood straight without turning around.

'I have just remembered I need to collect your list of medications you had from us.'

And then she left stiffly without shutting the door behind her.

How did Nurse Jones know for sure that Argenta didn't want her silly old soft toy? She didn't, did she? Clara lay calm and curiously tranquil, as if she were in the middle of receiving the answers. It must be something to do with the weight loss that gave her this feeling of being connected to another ether.

Now diagnosed with leukemia and the possibility of only so long to live, her sensitivity grew to her bodily functions. She could feel her blood, that important material, keeping her alive and healthy. Like a swimming army of heroes, it was on the attack to keep her alive. She could feel this movement traveling through her arms, the beautiful sea of red. If she thought deeply, could she issue her orders? Kill the corrupt invaders. I want to live. I want to be well.

Was it because she now knew she was on the journey to death that she was sensitive to the fight? When her body took that turn towards destruction, it had kept this knowledge from her. It had decided to die, and in her mind, that parasite had nothing to say about it.

'I have been unkind to you,' Clara whispered to this body of flesh, blood, and the factory of organs. 'I didn't respect you, as someone should have been respected. My mind was too arrogant to give any scope to you. And now you are taking your vengeance on me.'

The sobering thought made her look at her wasted arms. She had lost a great deal of weight, which she hadn't noticed before. Of course, if you don't eat, it's obvious this will show itself. But exhaustion encompassed everything without mercy.

Oddly enough, she didn't feel so tired now. It must be the medication Dr. Slanders had been giving her. But today, he had forgotten to give this to her. It was nice and even pleasant not to be so tired.

By the open door, a face was watching, peering through at her, and then moving in. Headfirst, curious and puzzled as now, Emma's full-body stood there looking at her as if she didn't trust Clara.

'Hello Emma,' smiled Clara, also puzzled by this expression of disbelief. 'What is it?'

'You are here?'

'Yes, I am.'

'But they said that you had gone.'

'Who said that?'

'When we asked Dr. Slanders and the nurses, they said you finished with your treatment here and you didn't get anything out of it.'

Now Clara understood why she didn't have any visitors.

'No, I have been here all the time.'

'You didn't go then?'

A smile again for this was becoming ludicrous and funny.

'Obviously not. I thought everyone had abandoned me.'

'We didn't check to see. I suppose we should have. But why would they lie to us?'

'I don't know,' but then Clara suddenly realized.

Her change of health had to be kept secret. Dr. Slanders and the rest of the hospital didn't want others to know she was dying. It could bring them right down when they were already vulnerable.

'What are you doing in bed, then? You've lost a great deal of weight.'

'A bit of a fever, but I am on the mend now.'

This was becoming awkward. Emma was coming forward and looking critically at her.

'What's happened to you?'

'Just a bug, that's all.'

Necessary to distract Emma because the conversation was becoming too uncomfortable. She couldn't tell Emma she was fighting for her life, although she was sure she would win. Even so, there was a possibility of her dying. This thought made her terrified.

'A bug did that to you?' Emma was frowning hard.

'Surely, I don't look that bad? Anyhow, what does it matter? I am getting better. How is everyone? How are you, and what about Joanne and Lulu? How are they doing?'

'Oh, Lulu left over a week ago. She went to the commune and said she would let us know how she was, but I guess out of sight, out of mind. Anyhow, I hope she is happy. But why would they keep your existence away from us?'

'Perhaps because I asked them to,' Clara shrugged at the still frowning face of Emma.

'Oh—I thought we were friends.'

'We are, but I guess I was embarrassed.'

Clara lied for the clinic, even though she didn't completely understand why they had kept her presence from her friends. But even more so, why she was defending their actions? Would it be wrong to tell Emma she, too, was going to the commune?

'The fact is, I have been terribly ill—'

'Yes, I can see that. You look awful.'

'Thanks. Dr. Slanders suggested I spend my recovery at the commune.'

'You're going to the commune as well?'

'Yes, why not? They said they would help, and I need a great deal of help at the moment, but it won't be forever.'

'I guess you will disappear as well. So, I suppose I had better say goodbye to you before you also vanish forever.'

'I promise I won't disappear. I promise I will get back to you.'

'It doesn't matter because I also will be going there. It seems inevitable. Everyone goes to the commune when they have a lot of money.'

'And how's Joanna?'

'She's talking about going there as well. We are all being

programmed by Dr. Slanders about the benefits of living in a communal setting. I wish they had told me before I took drugs I would end up living with others. This was not how I saw my life. Anyhow, I had better go, so you can start getting better. There have been a lot of strange things happening in this hospital just lately. Everyone is disappearing, including some of the staff. Nurse Ryan said nothing to us about leaving.'

Emma left Clara's room aggrieved, as if she had been personally offended. Emma was right in that this had been a strange and extraordinary time. Weird, because she had started this journey so differently from the way it was now turning out. How life does backflips. Clara wanted to laugh at the bizarre way her life had been affected.

Yet, she didn't feel she would die, but Dr. Slanders had given her the death sentence. She didn't want to believe him, yet it was normal to have these doubts of denial.

She was in shock. Anyone would be in distress to find out they would be dead in less than six months. But how can someone predict another person's death? Do they take into the calculation a person's spirit and their desire to fight this parasite growing from within? And the other question was, how was it going to be? Was it going to be painful? These are the things she should know about. Naturally, any type of persuasion about a predicted death was something to be avoided, but it's better to know who your enemy is than not.

'An ambulance will be here in an hour.'

Nurse Jones walked back into the room and now with a different attitude, as if she had refreshed herself with a smile. Whatever she had gone for was forgotten. A quick look at Clara held the thought she wasn't prepared to share. Clara looked at her busy back, collecting her possessions.

The underwear, which had always been personal, was not so anymore.

'How long have I got?'

Again, Nurse Jones jerked upwards as if caught by this sudden, indelicate question.

'How long?'

'Yes, how long? I would like to know how long I have so I can plan things. That way, nothing is going to happen to me too suddenly without me being prepared.'

'This is a conversation you should have had with Dr. Slanders. Hasn't he told you how long you have?'

Ridiculous, but no, he hadn't. Absurdly, for if he had, she would plan to die at that given point in life? Not without a fight. Humor is humanity's salvation, and it was now for Clara. Imagine laughing at the ultimate event in life, one's own death. But there again, you don't have to do what others tell you to do. So, she would not die.

Smiling at this awful sentence, it then occurred that she was not a quitter, but a fighter. And it could all be down to changing her name. Yet, if she kept her old name Cecelia, would this death sentence have happened to her?

Speculation can often send you crazy, like contemplating parallel universes and what could have happened when the other newly created alternative universe went its own way.

'What do you think is going to happen to me?'

Clara couldn't help staring at the back of this very busy woman who didn't want to talk because she asked too many questions.

'I don't understand what you mean by that question?'

'Do you think I am going to die?'

'Well, we hope you aren't,' said Nurse Jones. 'We can only do the best we can.'

'Would you say I have a good chance—to live?'

'Miss Tinder, these are questions which I can't answer. A lot of it depends on you.'

'I don't want to die,' Clara muttered unhappily to herself.

Now because she was in a strange mood that if she were going to die, she would not die without letting the world know she had lived.

'I want to go downstairs to the communal room before we go. I want to say goodbye to everyone. I'm not ashamed of what is happening to me—'

'You are clearly in a bizarre mood,' said Nurse Jones, at last showing her face.

The zip to her suitcase angrily buzzed to a halt. The packing was finished. It was Clara's turn to go.

'I shall mention the mood you are in to Dr. Slanders; I am sure he will give you something to help you.'

Was she not allowed to be upset? It isn't every day you find out you don't have long to live. Of course, if it were a road accident, then you would have no warning at all. So, what was better? Not knowing you're going to die and be dead in an instance or live with a death sentence? Neither of these was on her bucket list.

'In truth, I feel perfectly well. Some people know me here and would want to see me if only for the last time. I don't need to tell them I might die, but I would like to say farewell.'

'You are being very selfish,' sparked Nurse Jones.

She picked up the suitcase from the bed and took it to the door, where she slammed it down. Someone had lost their temper, and it wasn't Clara.

'Why?'

Full faced, Nurse Jones turned.

'People are going out of their way for you, and look how you're behaving—'

'But I am paying for the service. If I pay for it, I should get what I want.'

'Selfish, that's what I call you.'

Nurse Jones moved to the door and left the room in an uncontrollable rage. Clara, though, still couldn't see what she had done wrong. Nothing. She had said and done nothing wrong. Why couldn't she say goodbye to the others? They had wondered where she was and perhaps missed her like she would have missed anyone of them. Normal to be interested in someone who had problems and to wonder what happened to them.

Oh dear, she had upset Nurse Jones, which now meant she was selfish. This was the woman who was going to accompany her to the commune and take care of her. Perhaps this was not such a good idea. Maybe Dr. Slanders was volunteering her services when she preferred to stay by the big man's side, for clearly, she worshiped the ground he walked on.

13

———

Sometimes, it felt she had become a spectator in her own life.

Now minding her own business and sitting in the large cozy armchair with an execution date over her head, Clara reminded herself she had come here to do a job. Still, that strange thought of death was awaiting her. Yet, today without the medication, she felt better than she had for some time, as if she were clawing back her wellbeing.

Bogeys filled her body. Those terrorists and invaders were going out of their way to destroy her body. Odd for a parasite to kill what it depends on.

Nurse Jones was right about her being in a strange mood.

Then Dr. Slanders came into her room with that developing look of a school headmaster. It was time to prepare herself as behind him stood Nurse Jones. Everyone knew she had done something wrong. Put out your hand and be prepared to receive the punishment.

'Miss Tinder,' he said in his reasonable voice. 'I understand you think you are fit enough to go downstairs to the communal room.'

'I didn't say I thought I was fit enough to go down there. I made it my wish to say goodbye to my friends.'

'Your friends?' he smiled, as he knew this was absolutely untrue. 'The friends who never visited you.'

She was about to mention the fabrication going on instigated by himself to say she had left the hospital. But testing the water didn't seem to be a good idea.

'I would still like to say goodbye to them myself, even if they haven't proved to be my friends.'

'We can't let you do that.'

He came into her room and, seeing the spare chair which Nurse Ryan had sat in, took the seat and crossed his legs.

'We are only thinking about your best interests. It's all right, Nurse Jones,' the doctor looked at the nurse. 'I will deal with this. Please leave us now.'

Astonishingly, this order received by Nurse Jones had taken some digesting because she wasn't sure if she wanted to go. But Dr. Slanders wasn't going to say anything more until she had left the room. He watched her, determined for the nurse to close the door quietly behind her.

'Now,' he said, uncrossing his legs and moving closer before crossing them again. 'I think we need to talk about your future and be very grownup about it.'

Clara knew she was going to be in for a very rocky ride.

'No one likes the idea you might die. We are trying to come to terms with it ourselves.'

Yes, she could agree with that.

'We have to face it like adults, and work out how best we can help you. This is going to be a tough time for everyone.'

'Especially me.'

'Yes, especially you, but it affects other people. I have to confess I hurt for you, particularly now because no one has been to see you.'

This was astounding.

'So, we are thinking of your best interest, and by this, I mean, to take you out quietly. Nurse Jones has been excellent about everything; she is an outstanding nurse; she is prepared to do everything for you to make certain you will be comfortable.'

'Yes, I understand, and thank you for that, but do you think she actually wants to come with me?'

'I don't understand what you mean. Nurse Jones has been distraught. She thinks you are against her. Please be kinder to her.'

This was now baffling.

'But I am the one who is supposed to be dying. How long do I have?'

'Three months without treatment. If it doesn't work.'

It was out and real. Now she knew in black and white how long she had. But it was not rewarding news.

'Is there any chance you have it wrong?'

'I wish I had. You do not know how much I wish for that. And because time is short for you, we need to make rapid arrangements for your treatment, otherwise—'

'My funeral?'

'Yes, that as well. But there are other things. Have you ever heard of power of attorney?'

'Yes, I have.'

'Good,' he looked relieved; he didn't need to do any more work. 'I understand you are completely alone in the world.'

Not entirely, there was Tina, her mother, but she could stay buried; she didn't want anything to do with her.

'Yes, I am completely alone.'

'No aunties or uncles? No cousins, no one whatsoever?'

'That's me, unfortunately.'

He regarded her for a few seconds.

'And what do you propose to do with your sizeable fortune?'

'I haven't thought about it. I'm still young. I never thought I would have to decide on this question so soon.'

'I know, and I understand, but the time has come for you to think about such matters.'

She wanted to cry, and for now, it had become very real. Her own death was fast approaching.

'Please, I don't want to talk about it now.'

'Yes, I understand, but at least you can keep it in your mind. Three months is not a long time, and the treatment is not guaranteed.'

'Yes, I know, but I am hoping I will get better with it.'

'Of course you are. You know with money as you have, you could do a great deal of good. A lot of research could be done in your name, and although you may not be saved, you could save the lives of others.'

'Yes.' Her lips were trembling.

She had only just come into this fortune and hadn't had time to spend any, and now it looked like she was going to leave it to someone else. It was so unfair.

'Think about it, Miss Tinder. I can see it upsets you, but I am trying to help you. Research programs are going on even now. Every one of those that are saved will remember your name.'

'I would sooner save my own life than people I don't know.'

Even while she was saying this, she knew she sounded mean. Mean that she wanted to live—would other people willingly give their lives away if they had the chance of saving their own?

'I understand you are going through a hard time. I will leave you to think about it. I will ask Nurse Jones to return.'

And then he turned to face her at the door with a redeeming thought for her selfishness.

'You know, Miss Tinder; this is your opportunity to make something great out of your life. By giving to others, you will make a wonderful sacrifice.'

With that, he left.

If she had the strength, she would get herself dressed and leave this clinic. What was happening to her didn't feel right. Wouldn't there be some inner instruction transmitted by her body, telling her to prepare herself for death? It should not have come as a shock.

Feeling she had unfairly criticized and flourished that look of anger, Nurse Jones returned. Neither Clara nor Nurse Jones liked each other, but had been forced together because of Dr. Slanders.

Why couldn't Nurse Ryan have been her nurse instead of this one? Where was Nurse Ryan? She had left. And when they go, they would prefer to forget the past, which meant the argument with Dr. Slanders. Where were all those grand words that had been threatened?

'Where's Nurse Ryan?' meddled Clara, watching how this would affect Nurse Jones.

The muted nurse's shrewd eyes cast suspiciously at Clara. Where were these questions leading?

'Nurse Ryan's has been dismissed. Her conduct was found very wanting, and Dr. Slanders had no other choice but to let her go.'

'I liked her.'

'Yes, people like you would like people like her. You

two are one of a kind. Rebellious and awkward, and refusing to follow rules which are for the good of everyone.'

Oh dear, she had upset her.

'What did she do wrong? She was kind, and at least she showed she tried to understand.'

'Whereas I suppose I don't?'

'She was easier to talk to, and she gave me the idea she cared.'

How sharply did Nurse Jones feel got at?

'There are many things you don't know about Nurse Ryan. She is not the person she paints herself to be.'

'Such as what? What was she fired for?'

Seething with buried temper, Nurse Jones left the room. For goodness' sake, what was the point of giving her a nurse who didn't like her? The feeling was mutual. There was no way she could have a nurse like this one caring for her. Can you imagine the last face you would ever want to see—is the face staring at you on your deathbed, waiting and willing you to die? She would have to tell Dr. Slanders this. This situation was impossible.

'Miss Tinder,' Dr. Slanders appeared once again, trying his best to be tolerable. 'I have just spoken to a very distressed Nurse Jones.'

'Yes,' smiled Clara, still more determined than ever not to have this nurse take care of her.

'I cannot be the go-between for you two ladies. She feels you don't like her.'

'What do you want me to say to that? Do you want me to say I like her when I don't?'

'You could be more considerate towards her; she is a very fine nurse.'

'I don't like her.'

For the first time, Dr. Slanders smiled as if he found the entire saga ridiculous and silly.

'Personality should not come into it when it comes to caring.'

'For me, it does. Especially as I will be the one paying for it. I would sooner have someone like Nurse Ryan than a cold-blooded fish like Nurse Jones.'

'Nurse Ryan has, unfortunately, left us. I had to let her go—'

'Why? She has more heart than Nurse Jones. I could talk to her.'

'I expect you could, but what you didn't know about Nurse Ryan is that she had been stealing from us. She has been helping herself to the hospital drugs. We had our suspicions, which were proved right. It was a shock to find someone we thought we could trust and who had been in our service for over five years was stealing our drugs, not only to sell but also to take herself.'

'I don't believe you.'

'That is because you do not wish to believe me, but it remains the truth. This entire experience has been an embarrassment. After an internal investigation, we understand she had been selling them to some of the patients. We wondered what was going on—'

'Who are we?'

'Dr. Barnet and myself.'

There was a challenge going on between them, as if he dared her to ask those specific questions. He was enjoying this difficult conversation. Was his life so boring?

'Dr. Barnet is in charge of the commune. We work together for the interests of our patients. Our goal is to enhance people's lives, and for those with problems that are, unfortunately, also on their own. We provide them with a family. The community is a family; it is the security that they need—'

Yes, she had heard all this before.

'And for a while, you will be part of this community and its family.'

He finished his piece, pleased with himself, a neatly tied up life.

'It was also our idea not to get in touch with the police about Nurse Ryan. We considered she had enough on her plate. You see, our ideology is based on family. Each of us has a position in this large family, and although Nurse Ryan betrayed us, we still tried to stretch out and help her. Unfortunately, she would not be helped.'

'I do not believe you. I don't believe Nurse Ryan was a drug addict.'

'That is your choice. In life, we make choices about what we want to do and what we want to believe. But with these choices comes responsibility.'

'I don't want Nurse Jones to accompany me,' Clara sulked.

'I am afraid I have no one else more qualified than Nurse Jones.'

He mused, she must see it his way. It was so sensible.

'Don't you think you are a little hard on her?' continued Dr. Slanders. 'It's unkind—you are going to need a great deal of competent nursing in the next three months. You will need someone who knows what they are doing. A friendly face and someone who is jokey as well, and someone who can make you feel secure.'

She wasn't going to die; she could feel she wasn't going to die, so please don't keep telling me I am. Clara's lips started trembling. There was only so much bravery she had inside.

'To have a nurse like Nurse Jones is an asset. You will feel safe with her. Please be counseled by my long years in the medical profession. I am thinking of you.'

She couldn't fight anymore. If she was the only one to believe there was nothing wrong with her, then she stood no chance. The power of feelings cannot be underestimated. Tears that came from the sorrow of being oneself began peeling from her eyes. It wasn't fair, no it wasn't fair, she heard herself moan while giving in to her unhappiness.

And so there she was, waiting, as Nurse Jones returned to the room, arrogantly offering her commiserations, knowing she had won. She was to accompany Clara to the commune. By degrees came the humiliation of losing personal desires, then her rights. Neither was Clara's wish granted that she could say goodbye to the other residents. She was to be taken out of the hospital surreptitiously, as if she had done something evil. The ailment of ill-health starts with these little losses. How many times can Clara say to herself she wasn't ill when they were all backing each other up and telling her she was? It was one of the worse days in her life to die as an unknown. Even when she arrived at her new temporary home, she was received in the commune when there was no one around.

Dr. Barnet was a tallish man of about five-ten with steel-gray hair. Slimmer than Dr. Slanders with better dress sense, and he was more aware of himself. Once upon a time, he could have been considered attractive in a very cool way. But he was not as chilled a personality as Dr. Slanders, and he readily smiled as if life had been kinder to him.

When Clara entered her new room, he was there to greet her. His piercing eyes looked at Dr. Slanders, who nodded politely and took a step backward. Dr. Barnet was going to be in charge from now on.

'We shall do everything we can to make your stay with us as comfortable as possible, although Miss Tinder. I must say I expected to see someone who was not very well, but you seem to look to be in the very flow of good health.'

With bright and encouraging eyes, Dr. Barnet once more turned to Dr. Slanders.

'I don't see Miss Tinder is very sick?' he said to his colleague, almost mockingly. 'What I see is a young lady who has recently lost some weight.'

And to Clara, he returned an inspiring grin.

'But I understand the validity of these findings. And you shall be treated as if you were a princess, Miss Tinder. Yes, we shall take great care of you.'

Clara had been placed on the bed to rest while Dr. Barnet came to inspect her with familiarity, pulled up a chair, he sat beside her.

'Are you certain of your findings?' he asked Dr. Slanders, showing himself to be more in command of the conversation than the other.

Was there some teasing going on?

'Absolutely. The blood analysis was done several times.'

'Oh, what a pity, nevertheless, it's not the be-all and end-all of it. You look like a fighter, Miss Tinder. Are you? Can we rely on you in this part of the game?'

'Yes, yes.'

Did this mean he thought she had a chance? Oh, how she loved this man.

'Well, Dr. Slanders, I think you can safely leave Miss Tinder in our hands. Already you can see she has great faith in me.'

The exchange between the two doctors had the peculiarity of an old friendship. It was easy to see who the boss of this relationship was, the one with the charm, while the other was exceedingly reticent. Dr. Slanders looked very uncomfortable. The self-assurance which he had shown before melted like a wallflower against this rose. Dr. Barnet not only revealed more confidence, but had more in the company of good looks. He might wear spectacles, but he didn't need to wear them all the time.

'Very well, I shall go,' said Dr. Slanders, almost as if he felt shy of this grand friend.

'Just give me a minute, and I will be out presently to talk to you,' said Dr. Barnet with a possession which said with authority. 'Wait in my office. You too, Nurse Jones, I want to have a couple of minutes with this young lady.'

The two were uncomfortable at having been dismissed this way. When the door closed, Dr. Barnet took up Clara's hand.

'We are going to look after you here. I know Dr. Slanders means well, but he is not the warmest cat in the alley. I think you must agree with me on that. That's what I like to see, a smile on a pretty face. This has not been an easy time for you.'

Dr. Barnet was indeed truly likable, and she was glad. It was made up for having Nurse Jones as her nurse. At least she had someone she could now confide in.

'Do you think I am going to live?'

'I have every confidence you are going to live. So don't give up on your life. It's yours to keep, so don't let it slip through your fingers.'

'No, I want to live. There is so much I want to do. I have been so afraid—'

'Yes, I can imagine,' Dr. Barnet jumped in, putting his hand comfortingly over hers. 'But I must go now and have a word with my old friend. He is a nice man when you get him on the right subject. Believe me; he's been anxious about you. Unfortunately, he doesn't possess a pleasant bedside manner. I will be back soon, Miss Tinder. Be at ease with your new world.'

Giving Clara one final and firm look, he left smartly and swiftly from the room.

Yes, what a relief to have this man as her doctor and her guide.

14

––––––

An hour later, Dr. Barnet had not, as promised, returned. Instead, a younger woman came to see her. She was dressed in a lemon and white uniform, similar but not quite the same as the hospital style.

'Hello,' said the young nurse, whose long brown hair was tied in a high ponytail that bounced as she walked.

Clara looked up with expectations of hope, and she was not disappointed. Walking towards her was someone she felt she could connect with.

'My name's Bess. I am a highly trained nurse in psychology and critical care, and I am very much in demand by hospitals because of my skills and dedication to my vocation. So, I can assure you're getting the best treatment.'

She smiled at that moment as if she parted the curtains and peeped through. Not only was she a professional, but she also had a personality.

'Have you been assigned to me?'

Pretty eyes, but she had just missed being attractive because her nose and mouth were too big. But what she aesthetically lacked, Bess made up in personality, her bubbly nature trapped in the supposed merriment of her eyes.

Holding out her hand, Clara reluctantly shook it, for she was not a person who enjoyed quick friendships—determining people who became your friend too speedily and easily always disappeared. Some people would say this was refreshing in the hope they weren't called old-fashioned. But when someone makes a generous offer like this, it wouldn't only be rude to refuse. It would also be stupid.

'I hope we can be friends, but I shall understand perfectly well if you would prefer someone else.'

'No, no. You will do perfectly.'

'Good. I believe in honesty because it's the only way to get the best treatment. I need you to trust me.'

Bess gushed. Her speed was too fast to be anything but false.

'I consider we are a team. There is no messing with a team; no disease or illness can get through us if we work together. What do you say to that?'

'I say that's wonderful. You've given me such hope. I am so glad I don't have to deal with Nurse Jones.'

Who was this person replying to this optimistic, enthusiastic nurse? This wasn't Cecelia. This was Clara, remember? You adapt and change as the circumstances call for it.

'Yes, you have to deal with Nurse Jones, because she is excellent in her field. I understand what you mean, but don't let her manner get to you. Have you noticed how much she dotes on Dr. Slanders?'

Bess' unique freshness proved why she was popular and why many hospitals wanted her. Brains, as well as skill, were clear in her confidence and delivery. She was the sort of girl who would always be the top of the class and the most popular cheerleader. Her too larger nose and rapid lips didn't matter once she started talking—what a wonderful gift to have a personality like hers.

'It is rather obvious,' smiled Clara shyly.

Sharp blue eyes gave Clara a quick look over and considered she was far too slim to be healthy in noticing the darkness under her eyes and the sadness within them. Was it then she decided she liked Clara? They were roughly the same age and born into the same world.

'Nurse Jones will do the majority of caring. I will be here three times a day to see how you're getting on. You are going to receive stem cell transplantation?' back to being professional.

Clara nodded.

'Good. There have been such excellent results with that.'

'Do you think so? Dr. Slanders told me it has gone to my brain.'

'You are not to worry about things like that. Miracles occur every day. Besides, with all my experience, I don't believe you are in the advanced stage yet. And, with any luck, we will catch it in time. But the thing you must do is not give up.'

'I won't, I promise you.'

Everything seemed to work differently here, or perhaps because Clara felt more optimism from Dr. Barnet and Bess. Things were done differently here.

Someone decided to build her up before she had the blood cell transplantation. She was to do everything Bess told her to do, which meant she must start eating.

Liking people wasn't easy for Clara. She envied people who could so easily trust, who walked through life afraid of nothing. Clara had come to understand her nature was critical, analytical, and nothing passed from her eyes without giving it full attention and interpretation. Everything had a meaning to it, which meant life was hard work. To be like Bess would be a wonderful thing. Perhaps she might even try being like her just out of interest and curiosity.

This life, though, was becoming stranger and stranger, as well as very frightening.

Dr. Barnet looked in on Clara that evening to see how she was faring. He took Bess to one side to speak to her quietly before having a word with Nurse Jones. Nurse Jones's body language showed she did not think as highly of him as she did of Dr. Slanders. There were a few awkward understandings that Dr. Barnet brushed aside as something that would wash away in the laundry.

The desire to get healthy was immense now Clara had decided she would eat whatever she was given.

'You understand,' began Nurse Jones, the bringer of evil. 'That there is an extreme possibility you are going to die?'

'I believe being afraid causes more harm. If I chose to feel positive about getting better, I would have more chance of survival.'

'I'm afraid Dr. Barnet and the care nurse are not being realistic. They don't accept how significantly ill you are.'

It was a shock to hear Nurse Jones talk this way. It was as if she wanted Clara to cave in and die just because it suited her way of thinking. She was one of those wicked witches that exist in life to make others unhappy. She might be professional, but she was also spiteful.

'I want to get well, and if I believe this, then I will be well.'

'We all want that for you,' Nurse Jones said, frowning. 'But you also need to be prepared. And living with false hopes is wrong.'

'I don't see it as wrong. Besides, I don't want to talk about it anymore.'

Shaking her head, Nurse Jones walked away. When a patient knew better than she, it was unprofessional. But it didn't matter what she thought about Clara because she had a friend and someone she could talk to in Bess. It was to Bess she turned when she did her second check of the day. She had just given Clara her booster of vitamins.

'When can I meet the others in the commune?'

There was a polite smile, which didn't show any hope.

'We can't allow you to mix with the others for the time being. Your immune system is fragile, which would make you intolerant to life-threatening infections. It probably seems hard on you—'

'I feel so much better,' Clara interrupted.

'Yes, I understand, but we still need to protect you. You will be given the stem cells in a couple of days, so we want you to be strong and healthy to receive them.'

'Will I notice any difference?'

'Yes, you'll notice some difference on the first day. But it can take up to a year for the full improvement to take effect.'

Bess was busy recording these last notes on Clara's chart. Quietly yet thoughtfully, waiting until these had been done, Clara then had her chance.

'I would like to see Argenta. Do you think I can have at least one guest?'

'Oh dear,' said Bess, turning on Clara with a look of regret. 'That won't be possible.'

'Why not?'

Would she always be told no to everything?

'Argenta wasn't with us for long. I didn't have time to get to know her, poor child. She was too weak to survive the weight loss. It was inevitable she was going to die, but you still hold on to hope and fight for her.'

'She's dead?'

What an incredible thing to hear. It came like a lightning bolt striking her head. An awful storm cloud eradicated her daylight for a few seconds. In the background, Clara could hear Bess still talking and explaining what exactly had happened. She was sorry she was the bringer of such bad news.

'We did everything we could for her, but she was too weak. Dr. Barnet was dreadfully upset. He insisted on doing the autopsy himself to find out exactly what happened to her.'

'What did she die of?' Clara asked in a low voice, still shocked at receiving the news.

'A heart attack. Her heart just gave out.'

It was so matter of fact, how Bess said it, it was as if Argenta was another statistic.

Argenta had been scalped of all identity, as if she had never been and had never mattered.

'So, it wasn't drugs then?'

'Drugs?' Bess looked surprised. 'Why should it be drugs? I nursed her myself. I could see there wasn't much chance for her. I tried—we all tried. It was a sorrowful and dreadful time for everyone here at the commune. Poor Dr. Barnet didn't want to let go of her, so he had her ashes scattered on the grounds.'

For those few seconds, Clara didn't know what to say. Was that the reason Nurse Jones didn't want her to know about the soft toy, because she already knew Argenta was dead? No, this couldn't be right. Things weren't adding up.

'How long has she been dead?'

'Nearly two weeks ago now,' Bess said after thinking about it. 'That's not too long before you came.'

Making it a point of smiling at her, Bess put the chart away.

'What do you think of Dr. Barnet?'

'I think he's a wonderful man.'

The answer was already on Clara's lips. She didn't have to think about it because the other alternative was Dr. Slanders.

'Yes, he is, isn't he? I think of him as a father figure. You can talk to him about everything, and he always gives good advice. He really is a wonderful man. And while I think about it, I should help you refresh; Dr. Barnet needs to talk to you about something.'

'About what?' Clara said to the passing figure heading to her private bathroom.

'I do not know.'

With a sponge in a bowl of warm water, Bess washed Clara's face. It made her feel like a baby because she was sure she was now strong enough to get to the washbasin herself. When anyone else did this for her, she never felt she was clean enough.

'Bess?'

She was happily wiping Clara's hands.

'How long have you been working here?'

'How long?' Bess breathed in a deep breath. 'About ten months now, and I love it. Why?'

'I just wondered.' Clara frowned. 'Did you know someone called Charisse?'

Bess thought about this name, and because of how close she was to Clara, the recognition in her eye clarified her answer.

'No, I never met anyone by that name. Why?'

'I heard she came to this commune.'

Now the shift of focus was on Clara.

'Yes, we get many people saying they are going to come here. But being here is a commitment, and there is one thing

I have noticed about people with mental illness, and that is their inability to commit. It sounds great to tell your friends you are joining a commune. Doing something like this sounds almost Bohemian, but in reality there is a great deal of hard work involved. No one sits around smoking joints and strumming guitars and waiting to be fed the best of food.'

'Hard work, in what way?'

'You can't be selfish when you live in a community. It's the community that matters and not the individual. The problem with most people is that the greater society survives on capitalism. Which means it is all about their wants. Sometimes, they don't think of the community's need as a whole. Do you follow?'

'I think I do.'

'Good. When you come here, you must stop thinking about yourself. It doesn't matter how you feel. What matters is the wants of the many and not of the individual.'

'I don't understand that. How do you know what the wants of the many are when you are not supposed to know what you want yourself?'

'This is the beautiful part of this philosophy. For the first year, you have to keep quiet and follow the rules of the community. It's almost like imbibing the commune's feelings. It really is a time cleansing by getting rid of the bacteria from an ugly way of life. Statements like we want reparations because you owe us are ridiculous and show the individual's selfish side. I beg the question, what do we owe you for? It could be asked, what do you owe us?'

'This was not what Dr. Slanders was telling us in his twice-weekly sessions.'

'I cannot comment on that.'

Clara watched Bess carry the bowl back to the bathroom

with the ears and eyes of the sensitive. When she came out, it was clear Bess, too, had been thinking.

'Communes—communities only work when they forget about themselves as individuals,' Bess started again as soon as she walked out.

'Yes,' Clara listened, preparing to be educated.

'The very essence of a community is sharing.'

'I can go along with that.'

While still thinking to herself, this is not for everyone, and certainly not for her. There would be some people who would be prepared to work. But with every abuse, there would be some people who wanted a free ride. They would defend this right by giving themselves a different and perhaps more fashionable title.

It was apparent that Bess believed in the communal way of life. There was nothing wrong with that as long as she didn't impose it on others. Everyone has a right to believe what feels comfortable for them; it's their lives as long as they don't go preaching it to others.

Bess had flashed Clara one of those looks, which suggested she found Clara to be glib, especially about something she felt so passionate about. Clara was almost inclined to say she was sorry when she wasn't. Her apology would have been that she didn't want to upset this skilled nurse whose friendship she valued.

'If everyone must think the same thing, then—who was the first to have this original idea?'

'Every society, there has to be someone who reads the mood of the people, who understands what his people want, and tries to give them what he believes is best for them.'

Isn't this what's called dictatorship or fascism? But Clara had to listen and be educated to understand. Without knowledge, there is ignorance.

'You like Dr. Barnet?'

This was a direct question.

'Yes.'

'You trust him?'

But now Clara wasn't sure. Nothing is black and white. But Bess was waiting for her answer, so in order to proceed, Clara had to agree.

'Yes.'

'Good.' Bess was relieved. 'He is looking out for every-one's good. He really is wonderful and even a saintly man. I would trust him with my life.'

'I understand.'

'Dr. Barnet is looking after the community's good, which is why it works and will carry on working.' She smiled. 'And now you're presentable enough to see Dr. Barnet.'

In her smart starched yellow uniform trimmed in white, Bess looked the epitome of efficiency. Not a hair out of place with a face scrubbed clean; she looked fresh and optimistic, like the face of the future. And when she left, she looked happy and fulfilled, as if she had completed her part of the session.

When you are away from home, you know you are in someone else's territory. This wasn't her world yet, not until Clara became better. It had to be her world, but it left her vulnerable. There are times when we have to do things without knowing completely why.

Before Clara left her home for the clinic, she made an unusual purchase. It was so incredibly out of character, yet it had caught her attention as something that felt lucky. Clara bought herself a pencil case in the shape of Mickey Mouse. It made her smile, and now she was glad she bought it for it sat on the table next to her bed. Sometimes, when Nurse Jones and even Dr. Slanders and Dr. Barnet came to see her for whatever reason, they picked up her case, fingered it before replacing it. She watched them and wondered if they only knew what it was. This thought also made her smile.

If they had been curious or nosy, they might have suspected the other contents inside. There weren't only pens and pencils in there but added to it were the tablets which she had been given. Why she was refusing to take her medication bordered on suicide, but that instinct, the one we are born with but learn to shake off by the fashions of modern life, had warned her not to swallow these pills. This came from her mystical self.

Again came that question. Should she have taken these tablets? Was she risking her life by being suspicious? There is no safe path through life unless you are determined not to do anything with it. Once, living by rules had been her safe option, but not anymore.

15

─────────

It was when Dr. Barnet came into her room. This time, he looked more dapper than usually. It was as if he, too, had been spruced up for the meeting. The steel blue suit suited him; a good fit, and his neatly buttoned waistcoat showed he didn't have an ounce of unwanted flesh. His gray hair would be the envy of most men, thick and lustrous and in excellent condition. It was easy to see why Bess admired him.

'Miss Tinder,' he smiled.

A big and broad smile made his deep blue eyes twinkle and suggested that Dr. Barnet should have been a movie star. Unlike Dr. Slanders, who slumped his shoulders as if depressed and didn't have the energy or the enthusiasm, showed no comparison. But Dr. Barnet was a man who showed he liked everybody.

'You are looking well and happy. How are you? I take it I'm right in saying your world is looking good?'

Sitting down on the chair nearest to her bedside, Dr. Barnet, with a smile, looked pleased with himself. The expectation was that she should return his smile, and so she did. Everything was well with the world.

'Now tell me honestly, how do you feel?'

He really wanted to know.

'I am feeling very good, considering.'

'Yes,' he nodded, still smiling.

He understood the considering.

'Now, as much as I don't want to, we must think of and consider an alternate future. It grieves me to have to put this to you, but I would fail in my responsibilities if I didn't. Do you understand what I am attempting to tell you?'

He raised his eyebrow with a face of believable seriousness. She lowered her eyebrows; he was about to enter a subject where she didn't want to go and certainly didn't want to talk about.

'Yes, I know,' he took hold of her hand and patted it gently. 'If only I could turn back the clock and make this world magical for you. But I can't, but I can be there for you, every step of the way. If you need a person to fall on, someone who can be that father figure which everyone needs in times like these, think of me.'

Tears of weakness now ran down Clara's cheeks. These admissions of failure made Clara think of her father, and again, how much she missed him.

'I understand Clara, I understand.'

He carried on tapping her hand, intensifying the comfort he passed on to her. In times like these, everyone needs a friend. And he waited patiently for her as she cried, understanding the process and the unfairness of life.

The flow of tears stopped. Clara looked up, blinking off the last of the tears, and now grateful to him for his kindness.

'You are a courageous young lady, Clara, who I am very honored and proud to have met.'

He smiled again. This time, the emphasis was on kindness.

'I must tell you I once had a young brother who I loved very much. It was my role, as I saw it, to always take care of him. He was a small child for his age and terrified of life. I knew he loved me and looked up to me. No one picked on him; I think everyone had guessed except me he wasn't long for this life. I would have done anything I could have possibly done for him. I would have even given my own life. But it was not to be. Look—'

Dr. Barnet pulled out a gold chain from around his neck; there was a little locket.

'In this locket is a lock of his hair. It is one of my proudest possessions. I carry him with me everywhere. Do you understand what I am saying to you?'

She didn't, but she couldn't say this to him. He smiled kindly.

'You, my dear, will never be forgotten, especially by me. I shall always remember the true hero you are and how you have struggled to deal with your fight. I shall talk about you to others. I shall have a photograph of you on my wall, and I shall ask these others to say a prayer for you. Yes, I believe in God. I believe in the goodness of God, and I trust Him, although there are times when I struggle with that.'

He smiled to himself before looking once more at Clara.

'Clara, you are going to have to do something about the future which you might not see.'

This sudden order startled her. For those following few seconds, she couldn't look at him, and in her distress, she pulled her hand away.

'I know, Clara, but we have to talk about it. You see, once

we face the issue and get it over and done with, we don't have to think about it again. You will be free of this problem and able to get on with your life.'

'I don't want to—'

'I know you don't, and to be honest, neither do I, but you owe it to the people around you. Unfinished business is something we should not leave to anyone else. Clara, I understand from Dr. Slanders that you have inherited a vast fortune; do you really want to let it go to people who do not deserve it?'

Tina walked into her mind, the mother who was never there for her and who certainly didn't care. No, she did not want Tina to have anything, not even a burned-out matchstick. Clara shook her head.

'Good,' Dr. Barnet muttered. 'I understand you have no one in your life. You have never been married; you have no children?'

He waited for her answer. The probing eye was expecting him to negate this supposition. But no, she had no one, absolutely no one in the world.

'What a sad state of being. Is there anyone you would like to leave your money to?'

Phoebe now appeared and smiled at her, but she was in another dimension whose borders, for now, barred Clara from entering.

'No,' she whispered.

It was like she was admitting she was going to die. One concession—one admittance in agreement with your enemy, and you are on the deadly path down to losing all your rights to exist. He retook charge of her hand, the one we need when walking in the dark.

'Now, I am going to suggest something to you which I hope will ease your mind. It would be a wonderful gesture and a great help to a special selection of people from you. You might tell me to take a hike, I will understand, but the gratitude would be immense, and the appreciation would be overwhelming if everything should fail for you.'

Say it, say what you want me to do?

'This is a great embarrassment for me. I feel I am being very indelicate, my child, but man was put here to help one another.'

She knew what he was going to ask. That inquisitive side of her mind was now watching and listening to how he would put this delicate matter.

'We are good people living and working here. People who have come from all avenues of life, to find that sharing fellowship of common ground we have all suffered.'

Clara listened and then dipped her eyes. He is after my money. Even dressed up in his finery, it's my money he is after.

Why did she suddenly feel so sane? She had looked into the abyss of death and seen what life was about.

'We want you to live, and we are all rooting for you.'

She had heard this before.

'Have you considered leaving your money to the community, us the commune?'

'Dr. Slanders suggested this as well.'

'Yes, and what did you say?'

How surprisingly unattractive he looked; she could almost picture the reflection of her money in his eyes.

'He also suggested I should leave my money to research,' she smiled gently.

The first sign of discomfort as the smile remained still on his face.

'Well, I suppose I will just have to sell myself.'

The smile lit up; he would not give up without a fight.

'You know, Miss Tinder; charities are notorious for robbing people. If you want to make money, start up a charity. Oh dear, I seem to have shot myself in the foot. What I am trying to say is wherever you leave your money, there is no guarantee what it will be used for. Administration takes the biggest slice of the cake, which means in plain English that the people who run this charity always believe they should get the biggest cut.'

He regarded her with merry eyes.

'And you are going to ask me if we are any different? Well, we are. I take it you've spoken to Bess?'

He was waiting.

'Yes, I have.'

'And what did you think of her?'

'She comes across as being a nice person and very sincere.'

'Good, I'm glad you like her because she also likes you. She told me you want to meet the community. It is understandable you would like to talk to people and make friends. We have been very hard on you by restricting you from interacting with the people in this community. But you know why, don't you?'

'Because of my immunity.'

'Yes, exactly. But I'll tell you what. Once you've started your treatment for stem cell transplantation, we will allow three of the community to come and see you. You can talk to them and hopefully get to like them. See what the people of this place are made of and get to appreciate our work. You know, Miss Tinder, personally, I don't believe you are going to die. I can see you living. Oh dear, have I upset you again?'

The tears had started once more. Everything just lately had been such a shock, and to be taken out of the everyday environment and often left on her own for hours was too awful to bear. She didn't want to acknowledge what was going on inside her.

'I don't want to die.'

'Of course, you don't want to die. And I don't want you to die, either. But don't think of this as dying. Everyone who has money has to make a will. Who was it that left you all his money, someone I hear called Peter?'

'Yes.'

'Can you imagine if Peter hadn't made out a will? You wouldn't be sitting here, would you? Where do you think you would be?'

'I would probably be in a hospital. Or if not, walking around not knowing what is happening inside of me.'

'Yes. But you have been grateful for his forward-looking enterprise.'

'Yes.'

'Now, I will take a bit of a liberty, and you can say no to me if you wish. That is your prerogative. I have some papers with me. I had taken it you would be pleased to sign, but I had it wrong. Anyhow, this is my proposal that you leave everything in your will to the commune.'

He brought out some papers from his inside jacket pocket.

'If you would like to read through them before you sign, then we can forget everything about this very distasteful affair.'

Passing the papers across to her, Clara felt herself spinning when she took them. For a second, her eyes could not focus on what the contents of the papers said. But then the words stood as large and as awful as troubled reality.

This is the Last Will and Testament of Clara Tinder of 100, The Commune.

She stopped there; it was too awful to read.

'I know how you feel. When I had to sign my own Will, I felt my life in some way was over instead of beginning. Anyhow, I will tell you basically what it says. It outlines your assets. Although I we don't know exactly what your fortune entails. Perhaps you could get a copy of your inheritance; it would make this process so much easier. We can fill in that part of your will later. Now, if you don't mind signing.'

The papers sat frozen in her hands.

'Shall I show you where to sign? If you like to pass the papers back.'

She didn't think she could move, but she did. Her hands had a life of their own, or were they as repulsed as herself to see how she was being orchestrated into doing something she didn't want to do. She was dying, and they were trying to get at her money even before her death.

'Here I have a pen. If you would like to sign, just here and print your name.'

Dr. Barnet gave Clara a pen, smiled, then waited anxiously. Just sign—it's easy. Put the pen on the page and sign your name. You know how to do that, don't you?

But with this spear of destiny in her clasp, she failed to put her blood on this, her last testament. She could hear his heavy breathing, an orchestra to the buildup of pressure.

Seconds ached in passing, but nothing moved across the dotted line. One will over another. Such a simple task that she felt she should sign just to get it over and done with. But no amount of bullying would get her to move her fingers across and sign her new name, Clara Tinder; I release all my possessions to you.

'I can't do it. I'm sorry I can't do it.'

Her eyes, which had been on the document, now looked to the good doctor.

'Yes, you can. I know you can,' he continued to smile.

'Once you have made your mind up, you can do anything you like. Just sign your name, Clara, and then it will all be over and done with.'

'But I know as soon as I do it, I will be worth more to you dead than I am alive.'

'Now that's nonsense.' How hard he was trying not to lose his temper. 'I am getting you to do this now to get it out of the way, and that's when you can start living. Just sign the document, Clara, just make your impression on the paper—'

'But doesn't my signing have to be witnessed?' she desperately tried to gain time.

'It's a formality which can be done afterward. Just sign the damn paper.'

'I can't,' Clara said, dropping the pen. 'I don't like what is happening here. I want to leave and take my chances somewhere else.'

'Hang on there, Clara,' Dr. Barnet's redden face was puffing out an exasperated smile. 'You've got this all wrong. Of course, it doesn't matter if you don't. You have misunderstood me, my dear. I would not harm you for all the gold in China. I was just trying to get a very uncomfortable matter out of the way.'

He stopped to look at her so she could see how much this had grieved him.

'Now what's this you wanting to go somewhere else? We are your family. You wouldn't want to desert your own family, would you? You're staying with us so we can take care of you.'

He took the pen and then the document out of her hand to erase the evidence. Folding the paper quickly, he put it inside his jacket where it would be safe.

'I was thinking of leaving my money, should I die to—'

'We will not talk about this anymore. You must do things in your own time. Doing it this way has always suited the others, but everyone is different.'

She now lay back, so grateful to Dr. Barnet for removing the pressure. If she were going to die, she would die, but please, not like this.

'You're not angry at me, are you?'

'No, not angry. I just misunderstood you and the situation.' And then he laughed as if the pressure was off him too. 'Sometimes, I try to be too good, but I am far from being an angel. But. I'll leave you alone to rest.'

When he left the room, she heard him laughing.

Nothing more was said about this extraordinary incident. Clara watched for signs of temper when Bess came to check the curtains and other unnecessary tasks. She watched Bess moving with a purpose and looking very efficient and official while attending to absolutely nothing. It was Bess' eyes which Clara was waiting to see, for in them she knew her feelings lay. Was she angry with her?

Checking the bedcovers, patting the arms on the armchair, and then finding an infinite molecule on the armchair's head, she took it to the bathroom, but still no eye contact.

'I spoke with Dr. Barnet.'

'Did you? That's good.'

'You said I could talk to you about anything,' struggled Clara.

'Yes, of course you can.'

'I don't know why I couldn't sign the will he brought with him.'

'That was your choice,' said Bess, her eyes now steady on her chart. 'We each have to do what we feel is best for us.

There was no pressure, absolutely no pressure. Dr. Barnet was trying to do what he thought was best for you.'

'I know, I'm sorry.'

'There is no need for you to be sorry.'

Now Bess' eyes met Clara as she came across to her.

'Forget about this for now and concentrate on getting well. Nothing will come of the papers because you are going to get well. In two days, you will receive the first of the stem cells, and you need to be well for that.'

She smiled; it was a smile of forgiveness.

This was a hell of a time.

16

To be at the mercy of others, no matter how kind they are, always produces worries that you have done something wrong and will be punished. Being strong and in control of your life was swept out of the way. She was vulnerable, and Clara knew she depended on the mercy of those who were now in control, which made her weak and even tearful. She was doing everything she could to please Dr. Barnet and now Bess. It was an awful situation to be in.

But there were now only twenty-four hours before she would receive the first treatment of those beautiful cells that would thrive inside her to rescue and fight off the cancer. Get well, body, please get well; Saturday couldn't come quick enough. And then she would meet new people and talk to them to find out what it was like to be here. And be reassured by them that her imagined fears of this commune were all wrong.

Was Lulu here as she said she would be, or had she, too, decided this wasn't the place for her?

It would have been nice to leave here as she threatened.

It was wrong that they should pressure her into signing. She was sure this wasn't legal. Just because all the others had signed willingly, it did not mean she should do the same. Besides, they were probably younger than herself and, therefore, easier to manage.

Did the commune rely solely on legacies left to them? Why not? There were a lot of organizations that depended on death inheritances, including universities. Even now, she had been bugged by letters of remember us in your will.

A strange world: it would be a good idea for everyone in this world to experience psychoanalysis. Was she the only sane one on this planet?

The weight she had lost was reappearing. When she was helped to change for bed, Clara got up as soon as her lights were out. She had been doing this for the last three nights and exercising. Nothing too exhausting. A little walking about the room. Sitting down and standing up. A few bends and breathing, and already she was feeling the benefits.

Was she really as ill as she had been told she was? What is it that tells you that you are dying? Is it just pain? Well, she hadn't had any pain yet, and the only time she was exhausted was when she was on their medication.

Taking up her pencil case still on the side table of her bed, Clara unzipped it and looked inside. There was quite a collection of her prescribed tablets in this innocent container. Again, was the idea she was being silly to herself by not taking her medication? Bess had noticed she wasn't as tired as she had been when she first arrived at the commune. Was this a good thing for Bess to remark on? Should she now pretend she was sleeping when Nurse Jones or Bess came into her room and show signs of exhaustion throughout the day? Perhaps it might be a good idea if she pretended. It would be safer.

Previous conversations had greater significance for Clara because she was continuously left on her own. There was no television in her room as the commune didn't believe in outside influences bringing in their problems and dramatizing them out of all proportion.

And as for books. The library of books in the commune was mostly to do with God and the benefits of giving. She tried to read a couple but found them difficult because they went against her beliefs and principles. If you work hard and gain from your efforts, then you should be allowed to keep it. And not have to give it away because other people needed it.

How Clara missed so much contact with the real world. The pace and noise, and the constant changing from one topic to another were exciting. It was life. The long hours of loneliness and waiting were crippling, but now her world had gone silent. It was just filled with thoughts about herself, and mainly about her death.

These previous conversations would take on another dimension of life. Clara would replay these talks, emphasizing different things. Sometimes the traffic in her head became so loud it was driving her out of her mind.

The boredom of doing nothing was the most significant problem for the rich. They spend their lives filled with idle complaints. Inconceivable that her life had now also become trivial.

But even if she was dying, shouldn't she fill her life with something worthwhile? Wasn't she supposed to find out what had happened to Charisse? She was here in the place where the Lamonts last heard from her.

Start thinking, Clara. You may or may not have leukemia, but this shouldn't be making you dense. There would be an office in this place, even if it was a commune.

Too much trouble to change into her day clothes. It was late, so what was the point? Gone eleven at night, and most of the day staff would be gone, although as a commune, why would there be many staff, anyway?

The fear Clara had when taking hold of the door handle was that it would be locked. She was wrong; it wasn't. But when she turned the handle to leave her room, she felt she was treading on forbidden territory.

Like the hospital, the commune had the same layout. Seeing a staircase in the middle of the hallway, Clara went creeping softly and barefooted along the stairs. Exaggerated footsteps to make as little noise as possible, Clara listened out for signs of anyone else. Passing doors, she heard voices coming from within. It was comforting to know other people were living in this building.

It would be nice to know what had happened to Lulu and if she were here. It would be more rewarding if she came across Charisse to ask her for an explanation. Now Clara held that imaginary conversation, which she supposed would go something like this. 'I wanted to get away from my father and his family. They only want me for one thing, and that was my money.' A conversation that Clara would entirely agree with.

A peek down the stairs told her no one else was anywhere to be seen; she might as well take this opportunity and run down them. Not easy for Clara to do because going too fast now made her wobble. She was just in time to catch the handrail to prevent herself from falling. Was this the first start of the symptoms? Cancer? Whatever. She had to keep herself busy. Please don't dwell on it, don't allow it to take a bigger shape and grow. Tomorrow, she was going to receive stem cell transplantation.

This place was a replica of the hospital. It was as if she

hadn't moved at all, but had remained there all the time. Something not to dwell upon. It was just another peculiarity between these two doctors and didn't need her wasting her time. If this place had the same layout, then the office should be in the same place as the other one.

And it was, but the door was going to be locked. She tried it, and it wasn't—another fair bit of luck. Yet to do anything was tiring.

Switching on the lights, Clara took a quick look around the office to see where the best place was to start. Filing cabinets and a table. Nothing to entertain the imagination. But there was another door on the other side of the room. What was in there? A room full of secrets. The first room would be in constant use by everyone, but what about the second room?

This door wasn't locked either. How wonderful!

The signs were on her side, giving Clara the feeling she had won something. Here was a smaller and much darker room. This must be where the crown jewels of the operation were stashed. Pushing the door gently, she hit the light switch. An odd rectangle room held gray filing cabinets; this furniture stood back from the walls. The hard-false lighting of the fluorescent tubes drilled its interest in why she was here—none of its business. Clean and tidy, the room was coated with seediness. No matter how much scrubbing was done, this room would never feel clean.

To the filing system, she found the drawers were coherently marked up alphabetically. But of course, they would be, Clara smiled, knowing instinctively that these men were professionals. The art of making money had been taken seriously. But trying one drawer, it would not give itself away. It remained as it was supposed to remain, locked.

'Damn it.'

All that effort, and it went for nothing. She felt like hitting the cabinet for thwarting her efforts.

'I don't know why she was upset—' a voice had entered the first part of the office.

Clara hit the light switch and dropped herself into the camouflage of darkness to stay hidden.

'I told Dr. Barnet she was overtired, but he wasn't interested in what I said. It's how he likes it. But that's not my problem; it's not what I am getting paid for.'

Peeping between the doorway, Clara thought she recognized that voice; it belonged to Bess. She saw her in zigzags as she moved across the room.

'I feel sorry for her. She is new to this place; it takes a while for them to get used to the routine.'

'What are you going to do?' it was the other voice.

'I'm going to give her a course of Modafinil; it will keep her awake for at least twelve hours.'

'And then what happens when the effects wear off?'

'Then I'll give her another dose. She will be all right. Trust me. It's better than the other alternative.'

With a large keyring, Bess went to the cabinet. There was a rattling and jangling of keys until she took the key she wanted.

'It will be all right,' said Bess as if to confirm her action. 'I've done it before. Who left the light on? I thought I switched it off when I left earlier.'

'It wasn't me, but it could have been one of those spontaneous reactions. I've done it many times, left the light on and the door unlocked.'

'Yes, me too. And isn't the doctor mad when you do that?'

They both laughed, sharing a nervous joke before leaving the room. Was that the lock turning shut from the other side? A minute passed before the action was confirmed. The door was locked when Clara tried it. Damn. Now she had really put herself into an awkward situation. She was trapped inside this office with no way of getting out.

There was a telephone, but who was she going to call? Certainly not the police, not yet, because she didn't have any proof except suspicions.

What an idiot. It was all going so well, and now she had put herself into a perilous position. When they opened the door, they would find her there. Questions would be asked, and explaining would be difficult. Oh Clara, you had better make up some decent answers.

She had been sleep-walking. She imagined that someone was calling her and telling her to come here. Dr. Barnet would never buy it. Nurse Jones would say she knew it all along that bad things were going on with her.

Going to the window, she looked out at the moon and cursed herself softly again.

Like the other house, it had the same old type sash windows, and they were not locked. Turning the metal catch, Clara hoped the painter hadn't applied his paint too liberally to the window frame, as this often happened. With a hope and a prayer, she lifted the window; it growled out grievances while being pushed up. A veranda going around this part of the building meant that it was safe for her to climb out without a drop.

The night was chilly, but not too much of a shock. Now Clara stood outside padding the wooden boards. How would she get back in? Walking along the wooden veranda, she wished for another window to have been left open.

Voices were coming from inside. Not all the residents had gone to bed. Should she wait until they did and hope they would leave a French door open?

'Why don't you go to bed instead of lying down on the sofa? You know you'll sleep better in your bed.'

'Yes, I will, but I want to think.'

'Think about what?'

'I don't know. Sometimes, I wonder, I question if this is right.'

'God makes it right. You have to trust Him and devote your life to Him. He is merciful if you allow Him to be. Go to bed and pray for your sins. We are all born sinners.'

'Yes, I know.'

'You are the biggest sinner because you are rich, which is why you must pray harder. It's easier for a camel to go through the eye of a needle than it is for a rich man to enter heaven.'

'Unless he has a good lawyer, then he can do anything he wants. But I'm not rich anymore.'

'Really? I'm pleased for you. I am going to bed and so should you. You had better close that door first before you go to bed. Do you want me to do it for you?'

'No. I want to breathe some fresh air instead of those car exhaust fumes.'

The other female laughed, finding this funny.

'Good night,' said the first voice.

'Good night,' replied the one still struggling.

Pressing herself against the wall next to the French doors, Clara waited for the sound of the doors being locked. And for herself to be stranded outside.

What were her choices? To reveal herself and then see where she stood or to remain outside for the rest of the night. It wasn't too cold now, but she might think differently in the early hours of the morning.

Already she had decided when she moved to the French doors. Looking inside the room, she could see the owner of the other voice lying on a large sofa and staring up at the ceiling. Would this young woman hear her open the door and enter this way into the house? There was only one way to find this out, and that was to try the door.

It rattled when Clara pulled it. A squeak sounded from the poorly fitted door. Immediately, the person on the sofa sat up, on hearing this.

'I'm sorry to enter the house from this entrance,' said Clara, already with an explanation.

'Who are you? What are you doing here?'

The young woman of about twenty-five was all eyes and full of fear.

'I've come from upstairs. I'm a guest here,' Clara said, as if this would make it entirely all right.

'Guest? I have never seen you before. You're a robber.'

'Do you think I would rob this house dressed in my nightclothes?'

'I don't know. I don't know how thieves dress.'

'My room is on the right side of the staircase as you approach from the lower floor.' Clara moved cautiously towards her, still smiling. 'My name is Clara. I don't know how long I have been here, but I guess it's been over a week. I haven't been well; I've lost a great deal of weight.'

She held out her still thin arm to the woman with shoulder-length brown hair and impassive green eyes.

'If I believe your story, what were you doing outside?'

Ah, now that was a good question. What was she doing outside in her nightclothes and sneaking around? Information was required. What was she going to tell this suspicious mind?

'Do you mind if I sit down?'

The young woman lying down on the sofa hurried to sit

up as if she didn't want this strange-looking ghoul next to her.

'First, can I ask your name?'

'My name is Lori.'

She was staring, terrified.

'How did you get here?'

Clara smiled.

'Who are you? What are you doing here?'

Lori panicked. Her voice was fast, quick, and angry, yet her eyes confessed she was terrified.

'I don't believe anything you tell me. This is another trick. The outside had come stalking in. You have everything I have. What more do you want from me?'

Such was the force of her fear that Clara pulled back.

'I'm sorry. I didn't mean to upset you. You see, I've been confined to my room, and I am only guessing at how long I've been here. I have been so ill. You are not the only one that feels that games have been played. I've been treated as if I was a prisoner.'

Her head jerked back, and she stared at Clara as if she recognized a common denominator between them.

'It's not right what they are doing to us,' Lori said in a much more sober voice. 'I've been told so many things about myself which have upset me. I've tried to be good and to understand, but it's not easy.'

Clara sighed. 'You should leave here.'

'Leave here. I can't leave here. There is so much to learn. I am a bad person.'

'Bad?' she frowned. 'This is how they gain power over you by making you feel bad about yourself. That is when they take control of you and your life.'

'You don't understand, but perhaps you will be made to know the evil or your ways. I am trying so very hard to be good. To obey all the rules and work for the benefit of others. All I have I have given.'

Slavery at its worst. First, make them feel guilty about being the person they are. Then use religion and reeducation to change them.

'Why don't you leave here?' Clara asked. It seemed the most sensible idea to do.

'I can't.'

Again, Lori's sad eyes filled with terror. The mind games these people made up and used had been thought out carefully. How to subdue and take over is all about changing ideas. Intelligent and cunning people like this target and work under the tidal lines of manipulation.

'Why can't you?' Clara frowned. Surely people still had a right to be who they are. To feel good about themselves doesn't do anyone else any harm. Or it shouldn't. 'It seems from where I sit, your leaving is very easy to me.'

'I fear my parents, that's why. They are my enemy, and they want to harm me. They don't want me to live, and they want me to go mad. I've got to keep out of their way. Being here is the only safe place for me to be. Dr. Barnet said he would protect me from them.'

The stress had been too much, and it came with pain. Lori broke down in tears of rage and anger, but also of self-pity. How on earth had she got to this place? There must have been a time when she was happy. Yet that seemed so far away now. There must have been another world, in another time, where people had been kind to her. She hadn't known she was such a dreadful person.

'Although I don't know you, I sense you are a good person. You've been convinced that you are bad, and the reason I think this is so these people can gain something from this.'

'Don't you understand? Everything I believe is wrong and bad. I was born inherently bad, which is why I need educating.'

'Do you believe that—do you really believe that?'

'I don't know. I never thought I was a bad person, and it seems there is nothing I can do to get rid of my sins except work. And it's made worse because I don't believe in God. I was rich, and I didn't need to believe in anything. Oh, I don't know what's happening to me; why am I so evil?'

'You've got it all wrong, Lori. It would be best if you didn't think like this. If you were to look at it from a different angle, you would see what I mean. I just need you to walk over to my side. Come on now—'

Lori walked over and joined Clara.

'Once you accept the seed they have planted in your mind, then you are lost. There is no going back. There is no compromise. They have you. The next step is to make you feel guilty about who you are and where you came from. They attack you as a person, and the privilege you have been born into.'

These two doctors were insidious in what they had done. They had sold an idea and made it work.

17

The first thing to be done was for Clara to think of her own wellbeing. She couldn't help anyone if while she was vulnerable. Lori was someone who she could have on her side, someone who was more confused than herself. But first, she had to gain her trust. And that had to be done carefully, by being friendly with an invitation to take this very nervous but angry young woman up to her room to prove who she said she was. But she couldn't share with Lori that she was supposed to be dying, not yet.

Lori looked about the room, noting Clara's possessions, clothes, a few books, and her famous pencil case.

'I'm a writer by profession,' said Clara, taking the pencil case out of Lori's hands.

'A writer. Really—what do you write?'

'Stories mainly. Little bits and pieces. One day, I would like to write a book—a good book, something that people would want to read over and over again. Perhaps one day I will. But I guess this book will be about me and the life I have led. The most wonderful story we have is about ourselves and the circumstances that made us the person we have become. What about you? What do you do?'

'I studied fashion. It was interesting, but I didn't need to work. I was what you would call rich and lucky, although it's really my parents' money. They were the ones that made it. What I want now is to be good and do good things in life.'

Lori was not a beauty, and with a better-than-average education for someone from such a wealthy family, it wasn't necessary to be too bright. Hers had served her for a lifetime of enjoyment. If her education had been better, Lori would not have ended up here.

'This is my second breakdown,' smiled Clara. 'I had a breakdown over someone I thought I loved. His name was Thomas. Very handsome and very vain. What I didn't know was that he was already married. Anyhow, that's all in the past now. I made a fool of myself, so enough said.'

'|Do you still feel the same about him?'

Lori, now sitting in the other chair, looked relaxed.

'Yes, my feelings haven't changed.' Clara nodded goofily. 'It doesn't matter what I tell myself or the sermons I go through; if he were to leave his wife now and come to me, I would take him back in a second. I have no morals or scruples.'

Lori laughed at this; she thought it was amusing. In this significant instance, and under the guise of friendship, she liked Clara. This moment was important because it also showed trust.

'Ten years ago, now when this happened. I have wished for him to grow old and ugly and fat. But he probably hasn't. Sometimes, I think I must have fallen in love with the idea of love. When I was in love with him, I felt so beautiful— stupid, isn't it?'

'But you are beautiful.'

Clara laughed. She hadn't told Lori this to receive a compliment, but it was nice and made her feel good.

'What is wrong with you?' asked Lori, now looking more interested in Clara. The fear had slipped away.

How could she tell Lori what it was when she didn't believe it herself, but she owed something to her because she was curious? The other thing was that she needed Lori's help.

'They say I am seriously ill.' Clara smiled gently, waiting for Lori's shocked response, but there was none or nothing dramatic.

'I wish you well,' Lori said after a few seconds of absence. 'It makes you appreciate good health.'

'Yes, I suppose so. I have been terrified.'

This wasn't what she imagined would happen. Clara expected this would produce some reaction, but there was nothing except acceptance.

'I am going to fight for my life.'

'Of course you are. I would expect nothing else.'

No sympathy came forward, no outpouring of emotion to say how shocked and sorry she was for her.

'I will say a prayer for you.'

'Thank you,' Clara muttered.

The world went very flat, for without realizing she was seeking compassion from one of her kind. Should she ask her why Lori didn't seem surprised to hear that she was seriously ill? It couldn't be that she didn't care.

'Why are you here in this commune?' Clara asked, trying to swallow those silly emotions just because she felt Lori didn't care.

'I'm an alcoholic.'

'You didn't go to rehab hospital; I would have seen you there if you did.'

'Well, I did. I was there about six months ago. I haven't touched a drink since, although sometimes I feel the need to have that one glass. But one glass will turn into two. I went back home, and then I did drugs. It was my parents who pushed me to come here. I didn't want to. I wish I had never come, although it's probably the best thing I have ever done.'

'You were in the hospital six months ago?'

'Yes,' Lori frowned at Clara's tone of voice.

'Did you know Charisse from the rehab hospital?'

'Yes—I did.'

She looked at Clara suddenly, as if she didn't trust her.

'I was her friend.' But this was followed by an expression of defense. She didn't want Clara to ask any more questions about her.

'I knew her family.'

'What family? She had none. No one cared about her as much as I did.'

'Do you know where she is now?'

If Charisse were well and healthy, then Clara would pass this news back to the family. As much as she didn't like them, her father had the right to know how his daughter was.

'Charisse is safe now from her father. The only reason he cares about Charisse is for her money. All parents are evil.'

Thoughtfully, Clara looked at Lori; she was losing some of her trust. How to gain it back?

'The truth is, I don't like her father that much, and as for her stepmother, even less.'

'That woman is not her stepmother,' Lori vehemently stabbed out her thoughts in an angry tirade. 'She is the woman that Charisse's father married after Natasha died.

He killed his first wife from neglect, by bringing his whore and showing her off. Natasha died from heartbreak. Though they say that people don't die from heartbreak, they do.'

'I agree with you,' Clara added anxiously.

Because, without warning, Lori's anger flared to an unreasonable passion.

'It was also what killed Charisse. People don't just break one person's heart in a family, they break the hearts of those who love them.'

'Is Charisse dead?'

A startled look of shock crept across Lori's face until it became incomprehensible.

'Yes, she died. She had cancer, bone cancer, and she was in a great deal of pain. I loved Charisse. She had a sweet and pure heart, but her father wouldn't know anything about that. What he saw of his daughter was a cash cow, and as long as he kept milking her, he could pretend he cared.'

'No one thought to tell her father, Raphael, that his daughter was dead,' said Clara, more shocked than she imagined she would be.

'Probably because she didn't want them to know. As long as they could draw Charisse's money from her, that was all they cared about.'

And Lori was right. The only time the Lamonts missed Charisse was when the money dried up.

'I was there for her. I sat with her. Wiping her brow, she was in a great deal of pain, but she never complained. It broke my heart to see how much she suffered. She was such a good person, and she was always concerned about me,' said Lori, looking back into the past. 'She said to me I should leave her side as it wasn't right for me to witness her sufferings.'

Lori's eyes were dry, as if she had already wept a lifetime of injustice.

'I never knew her,' mumbled Clara, feeling a great sense of regret that now she would never have the chance.

'She was terrified of death. And at first, it looked like she would survive. She started to improve and gain weight. I was so happy for her. We had made plans. We were going to leave here and live together. It was just a nasty virus, Dr. Slanders had told her. She had been ill with a fever. Dr. Slanders wondered what it was and if it was contagious, and then when the blood test came back, it was a shock to everyone.'

'Why weren't her parents informed she was seriously ill?'

'Didn't you hear a word of what I've been saying? Charisse didn't want her father to know. She prevented the hospital from telling him.'

Lori was staring at Clara with a month full of angry words.

'I was the one she trusted. She didn't trust anyone else— and who could blame her? And then, as soon as she found out she was seriously ill, she went downhill quickly. The pain she was in was diabolical, worse than the devil's touch. It was only me who she relied on to take care of her—not Dr. Slanders or Dr. Barnet. I was the one she trusted to give her medication for her pain. I don't trust anyone, Lori said. They all want her dead so they can get at her money. But she was ill or otherwise, she wouldn't have been saying things like this.'

Lori looked at Clara to see if she was still listening.

'It was me who gave her the painkillers, the Oramorph, and she wouldn't accept it from anyone else. And I am proud of the fact it was always me she turned to. She would look at me and say that she didn't know if she could take this pain anymore. I would smile at her and tell her I know— you do not know how much I suffered and how brave I had to be for her.'

She took a deep breath to remember those trying times.

'I had never liked Dr. Slanders until then. I never trusted him, as I know Charisse didn't. He would wait outside her room for me to go to him. So, Charisse didn't see him. He always stood out of the way. He would wait patiently, sometimes for an hour or two. He never complained. He knew Charisse was dying and it would be painful, but he had all the time and the patience in the world for her. I never knew he could be so kind.'

Tears were now coursing from Lori's eyes.

'I have been so mixed up about this entire world and my part in it. Dr. Slanders wanted her to come to the commune because he said she would be more comfortable, but Charisse was too scared to go. She believed her father had something to do with it. As she became more ill, she lost a great deal of weight, and her eyesight deteriorated because her body was packing up. It was a dreadful thing to witness.'

She stopped short and stared into that vast chasm of horror.

'What are our lives all about if we are to be punished like that? What did Charisse do wrong? It was not her fault she inherited so much wealth. It became a curse, and she felt everyone hated her for it.'

Again, Lori stared at Clara as if she were seeking the answer to all of life's horrors.

'I would not have been able to do what I did for Charisse if it weren't for Dr. Slanders. He offered someone else to sit with Charisse to give me some rest. But I couldn't do that to her when she was struggling in such a way. She would cry and ask me, why so much pain? I wanted to cry with her, but I couldn't allow myself to do this. Someone had to be strong, and it had to be me.'

They had talked about Charisse and the person she was, other than her illness. She was nothing like the person Clara had constructed in her imagination of a young woman who was born to be rich. Charisse had an understanding far greater than her age. She remembered her mother, who cried for the husband she loved, knowing he was in someone else's bed.

Charisse's need for a father was great, but again, and like her mother, she also knew she would take second place to her half-siblings. Then she understood it was only for her money that her father took her into his family.

'She was a beautiful person,' said Lori. 'But in the end, the hurts and pain corrupted internally. She had cancer because of her heartbreak.'

It was a story of tragedy.

When Lori had left after making promises she wouldn't talk about Clara leaving her room, Clara felt a mutual understanding between them. Sitting on her bed, Clara pondered over what Lori had told her. Charisse had suffered cancer because of the unhappiness she carried. The poison and the hurt had corrupted her body. Is this what had happened to her? Her father and the guilt she carried, and then Thomas. The pain and the hatred growing inside of her, and then Peter. These thoughts were terrifying. Is this why people in terror turn to God?

Hideous thoughts were banging on Clara's door. Did she really have cancer? Being in denial was not helpful; it was not canceling the illness out. What was the world all about if it was only repentance and pain?

A horrible depression Clara had been slumped into.

When Bess returned in the morning, she found Clara crying and asking for help. And Bess, the best there was, knew exactly what to do. It was just as well Clara had found this place, for the commune's mission was to help those who were dying.

'The people who have led a depraved and vain life have been able to turn themselves around to help others,' said Bess, her face now radiant. 'You have come to the best place there is for that. Put your faith in them, and they will see you through it.'

Clara's tear-stained face now smiled. She would now be the best person she could. She would do everything possible to be good. Her regret and need to improve herself were real; she was grateful by realizing how lucky she was to be here.

It was then, in that moment of divine inspiration, that Bess offered to say prayers with Clara. She prayed over Clara for God to be merciful, and if he thought it was right to save Clara, please let her be saved. And thank you to the wonderful doctors, Dr. Slanders and Dr. Barnet, for being there for Clara.

With closed eyes, Clara listened, feeling her heart-lifting. She almost felt godly, and in that inspirational moment, she opened her eyes. Standing next to her was Bess' matronly waistline, moving and shifting in the adoration of her praise. Ringing like the call of angels was a chain full of keys. It caught Clara's eyes.

The numbers on the key tags quivered and shivered one by one. The door to the staffroom, one to the games room, one to the office, and then the one Clara had been trying to gain entrance to—the gold room.

The bunch of keys were dangling from a hook on her

waistband, silly really and precarious because they could easily fall off.

'Thank you, Bess,' said Clara, her eyes still trembling with the dew of fear.

'That's fine, my dear. I am so glad you have seen the light and you are now following the right road. It happens to us all. I was bitter with resentment before I came here. My life was put on hold, and I had been passed over in my work by someone who I thought to be less deserving than me. We are here to serve one another. There is no better work in life than to work for each other. And those who sit on golden thrones and spout their mouths off about how hard they are done by while knowing nothing about life, get it all.'

Her eyes quickly filled with anger and raw emotion, which Bess had managed to keep away. But now, the ugliness and bitterness showed itself in all its glory. And that gentle face which had just missed out on being attractive, with her posed smile and Los Angeles accent, had concealed like a tissue of lies how she truly felt.

Now was not the time for Clara to take her opportunity, but maybe tonight would be better.

'It's not long now before you begin the stem cell transplantation. You must be very excited.'

A quick shift from one subject to another for something slipped into Bess' mind, which made her feel happy. Life can't always continue to be bad.

'Are you excited?'

'Oh yes, of course. It feels like the beginning of the end.'

'Why do you say that?' Bess frowned, unhappy about this comment.

'I don't know. It was just the way it came into my head. Perhaps I am just tired.'

'If you want it to work, you must believe in it. You must

do half of the work to convince God that what you have to offer is worthy it.'

'I keep on asking myself, why me? Why should it be me? And then I think about Charisse—she was much younger than me. How awful it was to have happened to her. She must have asked the same questions as me and said it's not fair.'

'Yes,' Bess nodded. 'The ways of the world and God's influence on it all appear to be unfair. But that's because we do not know what God's Masterplan is for us.'

'Yes,' whispered Clara to herself. 'We shall never understand.'

But what she now understood when Bess left her room was that she had lied to her. On the first day when Bess introduced herself and Clara had asked her about Charisse, Bess told her she had never heard of Charisse. And there it was out. Bess lied. She dabbled in the truth, which meant she couldn't be trusted.

This knowledge, which came as a disappointment, couldn't be taken personally. Yet had to be stored and savored as something else added to her list of growing suspicions.

But there was no proof that Charisse was dead. Evidence came in the forms of graves and documented information. The way she died, the time and date, and then the last one of all, her grave. Even so, there was no actual evidence.

Two young people, Argenta and Charisse, had followed the same tragic course. With Argenta, though, it had been a heart attack. Another yet explainable happening.

Was this a commune of death?

18

That evening, when Bess walked about Clara's room looking smart and efficient. Her upright frame, poised with confidence, reminded Clara of Dr. Barnet. He relied very much on Bess. Earlier in the afternoon, the two were in her room talking about how they would carry out the stem cell treatment. Bess could have been his second in command, and she was undoubtedly obedient to his every word. Nodding and blinking as if these snapshots of data she received and stored perfectly in her mind were the most important things in the world.

And all this for me, Clara thought, watching from her armchair view. It was awe-inspiring, but then, of course, she was paying for this privilege. A satisfactory performance they displayed to her with looks of confidence and authority placed firmly on their shoulders. A great responsibility. It made them feel grand, and they were determined to get it right while Clara felt herself being squeezed out of the picture.

'Right, Miss Tinder,' said Dr. Barnet, his blue eyes very

blue without spectacles. 'It looks like it is going to happen tomorrow. Are you excited about it?'

'Nervous. I want so much from it. I want it to work.'

'Yes, that is understandable. It should work. No—it will work. Prayers have been said for you by all.'

And then he regarded her significantly.

'You know, you need a friend—other than Bess, that is. Although we know Bess is the best, she is also a member of staff, aren't you, Bess?'

Nodding slowly, Bess didn't smile. She was taking everything Dr. Barnet said seriously.

'I have been thinking a great deal about your wellbeing. You are going on a grand journey, Miss Tinder, the journey of your life. You need your own friend, someone who can be there for you. Would you mind if I suggest someone who I think would be fitting?'

He lowered his head on this very sobering point.

A new and frightening episode for Clara, now stepping into the future. Clara stared at Bess. Finding out that Bess had lied had toppled her, but the journey she was doing still demanded that she should trust her.

'You need a friend, Miss Tinder; this is obvious. Now I'm going to suggest someone for you. She's here in this commune, and I think you will like her,' smiled Dr. Barnet. 'We are very proud of her. Shall I get her for you?'

Another friend? After finding out that Bess had lied to her, it didn't feel like it was possible to trust anyone here.

'Yes. It would be nice to have a friend.'

'Good.' He smiled with pleasure. 'I hope you would say that. I'll fetch her; she's waiting outside to meet you. Lori, would you like to come in, and I'll introduce you to Clara?'

Creeping around the corner, Lori smiled at Clara. They

had a shared secret already, which she appeared to hold close to her chest.

'Please to meet you,' said Lori, now walking towards Clara.

Clara stared at Lori. Was she going to keep their secret, or was she going to blurt out that they had already met?

'Pleased to meet you.'

Their two hands met in friendship.

'From what Dr. Barnet has been telling me, we have many things in common,' smiled Lori.

'I don't know what he has been telling you about me, so I can't make any comment except that I hope it's all good.'

'Clara is going to start her treatment tomorrow for stem cell transplantation,' began Dr. Barnet. 'We are hoping for a great deal of success, and this is where you come in, Lori, as the morale booster. It's something I know you are good at.'

Lori quickly glanced at Dr. Barnet; it was something she wasn't sure of.

'Well, I'll let you two young ladies get to know each other better.'

Nodding to them both, Dr. Barnet relaxed. Followed by Bess, he cheerfully left the room, leaving the two of them on their own. They waited until the door had closed upon them before they sighed with relief.

'You never told me you had cancer.'

'No. I think it's because I still can't believe it myself. But I guess that's how Charisse felt about her health.'

'Charisse didn't want to die, and yet she also accepted it. In some ways, it was a relief for her to stop all the fighting going on in her life.'

'What about her will?' asked Clara, the multi-million-dollar question. 'Who did she leave her money to?'

If Charisse didn't leave it to her father, or her half-sisters and brother. Who did she leave her fortune to?

'I don't know about that; it was something we didn't discuss. I was caring for her, and it wasn't easy. But she didn't leave it to me. I wouldn't want any of her money, anyway.' Lori lowered her head, sneering. 'I've given all my inheritance away since I've been here. What do I need money for? It destroys lives. I would rather my life be worthwhile than going to the shops every day to buy clothes I would never wear.'

The one question Clara should have asked Lori but didn't; was who had she left her money to? Why give all your money away when you are still alive? Perhaps it was because she had just inherited it and didn't understand the disadvantages of not having it? Crazy, though, how people spend their lifetime amassing a fortune and then just give it away at the end. Peter had acquired properties and beautiful works of art, but spent little time enjoying it. Such a shame. Now, this wealth had fallen on her shoulders, and then her own was suddenly reduced. Was this an irony?

Clara yawned, suddenly tired. Life had lost its luster. It had been a shock to find out Charisse was dead and to die in such a shabby way without relatives, except for this one friend.

Seeing her yawn, Lori said she would return later.

Her light doze in the armchair was disturbed by the efficient Bess, who was delighted to see she was resting as if everything she wanted was going to plan.

It was the keys on Bess' waistband, which attracted Clara, but what also seemed such an effort. Again, that thought came that this was the courtship of her illness taking her ever closer to death.

'If you don't mind,' said Clara, trying to keep her eyes

from the keys. 'Would you help me to my bed? I feel exhausted.'

'No, I don't mind.' Bess was smiling.

Was it because she was pleased to be of use or was it because Clara showed signs of illness? Hard to speculate on what Bess was thinking.

'Take hold of me,' said Bess, seeing Clara was suddenly too weary to help herself.

Clara had her arm around Bess' neck and held on for dear life; now she was panting.

'Oh dear, I feel like I'm falling.'

Clara slipped; her hands ran down Bess' back. She was afraid and trying to hang on, but she was losing this fight.

'I have you, don't worry. You'll be safe with me,' cried Bess with confidence. 'I am a lot stronger than I look.'

'I feel dizzy,' Clara softly moaned, her hand catching on to Bess' waist for support.

'We are nearly there. Just a moment, and I'll lift you onto the bed. You are safe now, Clara, don't you worry.'

Bess was right; Clara was now completely on her bed with her head laid on the pillow.

'I'll help you take your housecoat off and tuck you in so that you can have a proper sleep. It would help if you ate, Clara. You haven't been eating as much as you should, which is why you are so weak.'

'I just haven't had the appetite for anything. I've been feeling sick.'

'You've got to fight, Clara, for this is how it is. It would be best if you did everything the doctor tells you. I know it's hard, but this cancer raging through your body is determined to take your life.'

Feebly opening her eyes, Clara saw that expression on Bess' face. She looked pale while her now pinched face revealed she really meant what she said. Why then had Clara doubted her? Was it because of the lie? Many strange things were happening here, and it all added up to certain people making a fortune.

But she had what she wanted in her hand, gripping them tight so they wouldn't rattle or drop into her housecoat pocket.

'You would be more comfortable when I help you out of this,' Bess' worried eyes resisted the smile which was pinned tenuously on Clara's lips.

'No, no, please, not now. I don't feel like being pulled around.' Clara held up her hand to ban the unwanted help. 'Please, just give me a little while to recover.'

With a mixture of hurt and offense, Bess backed off. She was just trying to help; this showed in her face.

'What is happening to me? I felt I was getting stronger and on the road to recovery. Is this how it's going to be until one day when I awake, I won't want to battle anymore?'

'No, don't say things like that.' Her dark blue eyes, which had once shown detachment, became alarmed. 'You're going to get better, remember that. Tomorrow, you're going to start your course of stem cell treatment. You've got to fight, Clara.'

'Yes, I will, but when things like this happen, it terrifies me. You must have worked with lots of people who have been at this selfsame doorstep just like me.'

Taking a step backward as if Bess were reminded of something, a trail of remembered faces who wanted to make it but had not, even though their spirit fought for their lives. What was it about Clara that made her more courageous than the others in the battle for life? Hesitating, Bess reminded herself of her professionalism.

'I'll come back later to see how you are.'

The bobbing ponytail with the unsmiling face, Bess had once again distanced herself.

'No, please. I'm sorry about what happened. But now I feel I just want to sleep. You really are a wonderful person, Bess. You are always here every day, seeing to and caring for me. I'm sure I can't be the only one. Don't you have any time off? Your dedication is remarkable, but you must have a life of your own.'

The face which Clara was talking to remained unfixed. Unlike before, she allowed no expression of compassion to reveal itself, but something was going on beneath her eyes.

'I enjoy my work. My work is my life, and I am good at it.'

'But you should get married, have children and enjoy all those things which satisfy people,' pleaded Clara.

Clara, too, was making her own observations. Two sets of eyes regarding each other. What were they thinking?

'But you aren't married,' said Bess as if this was an implication of fault.

'But I was engaged.'

'But you didn't marry him. Did you ever intend to commit?'

Such an intimate question took Clara by surprise. These two women, who were roughly the same age, were not so different?

Smiling, Clara pulled the sheet up to her nose. She was not going to say. And Bess, who had now looked at Clara coolly, nodded before leaving the room. She stopped at the door as if there was something else she wanted to say. This relationship had gone past being professional. Was it possible she was interested in Clara? She may even like her? One thing for certain about Bess is she couldn't easily dismiss Clara as being just another patient.

Now glad Bess had left her room, as in three hours, when everything was quiet and with the keys to the filing cabinet in her grasp. She could enter the forbidden territory even if it is locked. But was she really dying? Being told she was did not justify the way she felt. An impossible idea to accept this death sentence. But of the evidence. She had been ill and exhausted, but much of that had passed since she had stopped taking those tablets and started eating.

Tomorrow, though, she was going to start the stem cell transplantation. This was a strange world, but this was a world which she understood far better than the usual run of life.

Three hours passed when she awoke. She hadn't meant to sleep so long, but tiredness had come like a heavy blanket pulling her down when it settled itself on her.

Someone had entered her room and helped her out of her housecoat; the only one Clara suspected was Bess. When did Bess ever go home? Didn't she have another life other than this commune? Yes, they were both very similar in lots of things, but perhaps not their motives.

At one o'clock in the morning, no one should be downstairs wandering about. It was her turn to walk the night. Yet, opening the door and stepping out didn't come without that degree of apprehension. Like what would she find when she turned around the corner?

A couple of lights to guide her way illuminated the stairs, one at the top and bottom. Perhaps they had been left on by mistake or by one of the residents going to their rooms.

Did Dr. Barnet live on the premises? These thoughts filled her mind while listening to her heartbeat as she went quietly and carefully down the stairs. Step by step. What was his private life like? Did he have a wife and children?

But somehow, judging by his manner and other things about him, suggested he didn't. Impeccably dressed, his etiquette was without blemish, but this hinted that this was nothing other than a veneer covering many secrets.

The deep red of the thick staircase carpet set off against the dark oak stained paneling gave the hallway a plush and opulent feel. A different story was told to those living in this house. The grandness was just a façade of the unhappiness within.

How incredibly sensitive one becomes when doing things one shouldn't or be expected to do, but there again, no one had identified the rules. When everything is securely hidden away under lock and key, this spoke that something was wrong and secrets were being kept.

So far, so good. Moving toward the office, the world remained silent. Selecting the key clearly inscribed with the word *office,* she held it ready to insert. Would it work? This thought hit Clara as she pushed the key in to the lock and turned. Then the door opened with a click, and Clara swiftly moved into the room. Closing the door behind her, she felt the tension of excitement and uneasiness. Her next step was the other door. But first, the wicked schemes of fear and intuition poked at Clara to lock the door behind her. Another key, another lock, and this opened pleasantly as well.

The filing cabinet stood guard, stiff, quiet, and forbidding. This gray metal box with all its shadowy foreboding was not enough to prevent Clara from accessing its secrets. Stabbing the smallest key into the lock, the guard and all its secrets surrendered—she was in.

Standing straight in the top draw were a couple of dozen neatly placed buff-colored folders. Sometimes, it is possible to know precisely what you are looking for. Though most of the time, such secrets have a disturbing aftermath. Although there were many folders, there were fewer than Clara assumed there would be, but there again, what was it she was looking for?

It didn't make any sense to Clara when turning over the papers in the file. A list of numbers and what looked like names that had to be in code. Nervous, Clara wiped her hands on her housecoat to ensure her fingermarks did not mark the crisp white paper.

What was this all about? It looked like a game and didn't seem significant enough to hide away, and yet, it must be of great importance. The problem was, she just didn't know enough to figure out the riddle of the code.

Moving to the lower drawer, and now she had to be quick. She opened it and discovered about twenty or more other folders. Only this time, the folders were colored green. A very exotic and vibrant green, like that of tropical plant leaves.

Inside each of these folders were similar sets of numbers and coded names, none of which made any sense. She held up one of the folders. At the top numbers were grouped and ringed as a code, with an extra set of numbers at the right end side. Staring at them, it was evident that these were all part of a code. These numbers had meaning, but how was she to break the cipher?

In each folder, there were different colored sets of files, and all had names, although not the real names of whoever they were meant to be. The names were peculiar, like North Ride, Sweetie, and True Blue. Clara leafed through them, puzzled and thoughtful. Office work, that's what it felt like. Then she came to the last filing cabinet.

Most startling for Clara when she pulled out the drawer was to find a group of black-colored folders, standing like tombstones in the ground. For over ten seconds, Clara held back from touching them. Black could only mean one thing. Her thoughts shocked her as she looked on. But if she was going to get anywhere with her investigation, she had better do something, which became almost an impossible thing to do.

Fighting back, she picked up the first folder. On looking inside was another one of these names. Going Steady was the first name on this file. She wished she had her cell phone, but these things were prohibited. Number one rule, residents weren't allowed to contact the outside world. Her entire world was now contained within the commune. The significance of this rule stood out brightly. This was how Dr. Barnet and Dr. Slanders could keep full control over its people.

But none of these names made any sense until Clara picked up the last folder. Silver, it said. Silver, not gold? Who were they writing about? Looking at the name, Clara had a funny feeling that she knew this person.

It must be a woman with a name like that. Of course, this wouldn't make any difference to the people who named this folder. They were naming it for a reason, so what reason could it be? It must be something to do with money.

Didn't argent in French mean money? It also meant silver. The person who Clara was thinking of came out from the shadows to stand in front of her. Argenta, but she was dead. Yes, this folder was named after Argenta. Such a shock that the folder nearly jumped out of her hands. The folder remembered this death, which was why it was black.

Fear collected together. Standing boldly in unison to be worshipped, Clara, now horrified, opened the document of the dead. Would she find the cause of Argenta's death? Did they come with omens punishable by death? Should she look inside the secrets of the deceased? No, that was silly. Superstitions. What was happening in this commune was manmade.

Like all the other colored folders, another list of permutations had also been entered. Another list that didn't make any sense. Except for one. A date. The day that Argenta died with a question mark after this record. There were also two words: cardiac glycosides. Cardiac was obviously to do with the heart, but the other word was not familiar. She knew that glycol meant plant sugar. Clara thought about it. Was she possibly diabetic? People who have problems with food usually have strange diets. Argenta could have existed on candy. She could, but somehow Clara didn't think so.

On the righthand side was another name just as enigmatic as the rest, Good Queen. Who could be called a Good Queen? Did she know of this person? Clara rattled off the list of people she knew here. And there it was, another figure coming out from the dreamy shadows of thought. A figure barely recognizable but asking questions.

What are you doing here?

You called me.

What are you doing in this affair?

That is for you to find out. And then she smiled and walked back into the hazy glow of suspicion.

What on earth was going on?

Sharp, how her ears ranged out listening for danger. The clicking of a door handle, the lock being tried, came from the other room. How quickly still one can become. Click, click, convinced that someone was inside her. Dropping the folder, Clara zipped lightly with toes of fire to escape to the other room.

'I thought I saw light coming from under the door,' a woman's voice said.

The door handle triggered again.

'The door's locked,' another woman's voice said. 'Who would be in there at this time of night? Bess has gone to her room, and the others are off duty.'

The door handle moved again.

'It's locked said the second voice walking away. Come on, let's finish the rest of the checks, and then I am going to get myself a hot drink and off to bed. I had a dreadful night's sleep last night. She just wouldn't shut up.'

'What was wrong with her?' the first voice was now following. 'No one is forcing her to be—'

The rest of this conversation died out of earshot—just silent words on the wind in passing.

Clara was still alive, but how long for, especially in this type of panic? For her heartbeat ran like a racehorse coming to the final sprint, faster and faster yet dragging. Putting her hand to her chest, she could feel her heart pounding on its way to the end.

Just keep going, she mused to herself, returning to the other side of the office. Yet really, there was no mystery to this. She was humming to herself the chants of reason. People have basic needs in life to appease their desires: family, self-satisfaction as in careers to feel that their lives have been worthy. In contrast, the most elementary of them all, which canceled the rest, is money. Yes, Clara nodded.

There is no need to worry about the other two, love or careers, for the love of money. Money mounts and grows and sits in the bank, saying how well I have done.

A fantasy was being built surrounding the myth of the two doctors. What did they do at the end of the day? Were they even human? How had they met? Two opposites. Both had gone down the same route in science. And at that juncture in their life, when roads had crossed, did they find each other interesting and exciting? Or was this an exercise of trying to persuade the other about what they thought life was all about?

Codes and ciphers. Would you, when planning something illegal, write down what you were doing? No, never, not even in code. As code in the written word can easily be cracked.

These two men, both doctors, were not of the familial kind. They wanted to be astonishing, known in their chosen field, but it never arrived. They would never write that revolutionary paper to obtain that accolade. Be another Freud lining the history books. So, what else was left them? Money, only money.

When all else fails, the only friend of the disenchanted has to be money.

So, you didn't make it in life. You were the greatest support to your husband. You took the back seat so that he could shine. How wonderful he is, yet he walks the walk and talks the talk, but it's all emptiness; nothing came of it. And yet, and yet, he is called wondrous.

That strange and almost misshaped profile took to the world as beautiful. Everything he touched became golden and true. But look inside the bag of glories, and there is nothing to be found—just promises and hooks for empty dreams. If you could see what I can see, you would see the future in your own carving.

Disappointment had brought these two together. The only conciliatory substance was regret. To have missed that target by a fraction is the same as a mile.

Their own wants fool everyone. While the truth is cloudy, it's there.

So, what are you going to do to claim your share of the accolade? You married the man, and he told you he would make it; this is the promotional story. You married him. You must have seen something special about him.

That promise doesn't matter if it is empty. A promise is beautiful, and a promise is whatever you want to make it. Clara hoped she would pull through this sickness, which she didn't feel she had. At the same time, everyone said she was too sick to live. Health is so intoxicating. To love life is to want to live life.

19

———

Today was the day of her stem cell transplantation. All hopes were based on this simple procedure that was to correct whatever was going wrong in her. She would get well and then happy, but what else comes after that? Maybe the truth?

Dr. Barnet, ever handsome in his maturity, came with the glorious elixir. Smiling in his pale purple suit now and wearing glasses. He held up the case which sat the answer. Was this the antidote to the invading poison? And Bess was there, walking behind Dr. Barnet, taking her position with the glazed eyes of a Madonna.

'Miss Tinder, this must be the most exciting day of your life.'

Was this the promise?

'How do you feel?'

'Nervous.'

'Nervous or excited. I hazard a guess that it's excitement you feel. Bess, would you do the honors? Now I want you to relax and rest and let the cure do its work for you. Remember, from now on; you are recovering. Bess, would you get the syringe out of its case?'

Bess had been watching Clara, and then she glanced over to Dr. Barnet, almost as if to say,—I thought you were going to do it. Dr. Barnet chose not to see this look. So, she came forward, took the case, and undid the catch.

The day that Clara had been looking forward to had arrived, yet a fear held Clara back. Needles were not her thing; she passed out as a child, seeing the needle pierce into her flesh. A little blood spat out, red. Those eyes looked at Bess, who was almost as fearful as Clara's.

'What's the matter with you, Bess? You haven't tied the tourniquet,' said Dr. Barnet, whose voice tipped in annoyance. 'Can't you get anything right?'

'I'm sorry, I forgot.'

'Here, let me. Do I have to do everything? Remember what this is all about.'

He took the syringe out of her hand.

'Now put on the tourniquet and make sure it is tight. Do I have to do your job for you?'

'I twisted my wrist this morning,' Bess held on to her wrist with a grimace of pain. 'I can't do it.'

'Then if I have to do this. Stand out of the way,' he sighed. 'So suddenly, to become a coward. How can I ever rely on you?' Dr. Barnet's anger came with frowns, while his words came without thought. 'It's what we agreed on. Do I have to remind you?'

Stepping back and turning her head as if Bess, too, didn't like the sight of a needle.

'Just once, that's all it's been, just the once,' murmured Bess.

Yet, it didn't hurt when the needle punctured Clara's flesh, cold metal against flesh, while pumping in the serum.

'There now,' smiled Dr. Barnet. 'It's all over and done with.' And then he considered Clara with a knowing eye. 'Don't suddenly expect to feel better straight away; in fact, you could actually feel worse, but that means it's doing its job. In fact, the worse you feel, the better it's working.' Now turning to Bess. 'You see, it is all over and done with.'

Bess lowered her eyes, now unable to look at anyone.

'I have never let you down before,' she muttered under her breath.

'Remember,' said Dr. Barnet. 'We are all working for the same thing.'

Lying on her bed after the two had left, Clara waited to feel the strangeness of the serum. Where was it going? What was it doing? She could only imagine what was happening as it coursed through her blood vessels.

Oh God, please make it work.

Crazy, but since she had been at the commune, every day had brought improvements in strength and her desire to eat. At the hospital, the desire to eat had left her, but now it had returned. In the mirror, she could see a fuller face, softer and now with less gray pallor.

How was it possible to feel any healthier than she already was in body and mind?

But there had been changes in someone else, Bess; she was not so confident in her approach as she had been before. She now hesitated in everything she did. This morning, Bess had come in earlier looking worried, as if something disastrous was about to go wrong. She looked about Clara's room in a sort of desperation.

'Are you all right, Bess?' Clara was concerned. 'Oh, that reminds me, I saw your keys on the floor last night. I must have dislodged them when I fainted. I put them in my drawer for safekeeping. It's in the top drawer of my cabinet. I'll get them for you.'

While passing across the keys, their eyes met. Without hesitation, Clara smiled reassuringly.

'You must have been worried about them. I saw them last night when I was in bed. I wondered what they were at first, when I saw the reflection from the silver in the moonlight.'

'Thank you,' muttered Bess.

'You know Bess. You have been so good to me, supportive and reassuring, and I don't know where I would be without your care. I never went very much on the mental health nurses in the last hospital, but you are exceptional. You treat me like a human being with kindness and respect. If there is anything I can do for you, please think of me as a friend.'

A smile that Clara had never tried out before now came easily. Well-meaning and appreciative of the other person's worth, made though as a way of defense. Yet, it worked, for Bess looked uncomfortable, as if she were guilty about something.

'You know that when you confront death as I have—or are still having to.' Clara picked her words, choosing them with delicacy while smiling and engaging throughout. 'It makes you wonder about life and its meaning. Each of us takes different roads to get to what we want. I'm afraid that for most of my existence, I haven't taken my life seriously. You never do until you come up against something like this.'

Bess listened.

'With Peter, the man who left me everything. You know you were right. I was never in love with him. I was flattered, although, in the beginning, I found him interesting and yet difficult. He traveled all over the world; it was his job. I wished I had got to know him better. I wished he told me what he intended to do about his money. Sorry, am I keeping you?'

'No,' the practical and robust voice was drained of energy.

'I feel guilty he had left me everything because I wasn't the friend he needed. And he needed friends. Friends— don't we all need friends? I know I need friends. And yes, the gift of the money was wonderful, but in the end, it isn't there for you in the way of friendship.'

What was going on with Bess?

'But the odd thing is, now I have it, I would never part with it. Perhaps I can make some good use of it. What do you think?'

Nothing was coming from Bess.

'Do you think we could become friends?' smiled Clara. 'To be honest, I have never had a friendship with anyone. I've always been a bit of a loner, but this last episode has taught me a great deal. There is more to life than money and prestige. I don't want to be forgotten tomorrow like Argenta and Charisse. What were their lives all about? Money.'

'I'll come back and see how you are in two hours. Try to get some rest,' said Bess hurrying out of Clara's room.

'Bess, is everything all right?'

'Yes, of course. I am afraid I have other duties to do.' she was nervous.

'Is everything going to be all right?'

Bess had caught the door handle; she stopped and turned around.

'What do you mean?'

'I am afraid—I don't want to die. Not now, not when I have just realized what life is all about.'

'Then think positively. Think like a fighter.'

'What are my chances?'

With strained eyes, Bess wanted to get out of the room.

'I would say they are good, but a lot of it is up to you. You have to fight—and you must be determined you want to live.'

'Do you know of anyone that has got through this? Now tell me truthfully, I trust you, I don't for some reason completely trust Dr. Barnet even though I like him. It's impossible not to like him; he is always so upbeat and happy. I wonder what his secret is. What are my chances, truthfully?'

'I don't know. You are asking me an impossible question.'

And with that, she managed her escape...

So, the stem cells were now racing around her system.

It was three-thirty-five in the afternoon when something attacked Clara's stomach. She had been lying on her bed when the pain made her leap up in agony—clutching her stomach, she groaned and fell to the floor. It couldn't have been something she had eaten because she only had a bowl of oatmeal with a few nuts sprinkled on top for breakfast.

Massaging her stomach alleviated the pain just as quickly as it came. A touch of indigestion, hopefully, but this only happened when she was stressed. She hadn't been worrying, but she was worried now.

Bang, another pain hit her intestines, and this time much worse. A sharp pain in the depths became excruciating. Sitting up and still clutching her stomach, what was happening to her? This couldn't be an attack of stomach cramps. It was different.

Not now. Clara tried to catch her breath. After the last stab, she was panting. God help me. Her body roared with heat while sweat gathered together in beads of perspiration.

No more pain. Please, no more.

'Bess,' cried Clara, seeing her door open and Bess standing there. 'Please help me. Something is happening to me. I'm afraid.'

'What is it?' she frowned while coming almost apprehensively towards Clara.

'It's my stomach. It feels like someone has taken a knife to me and cut me up from the inside. I am not going to die, am I?'

'Lay flat, don't try to fight it. It will pass; just lay back.'

Bam! Another punch was taken to Clara's stomach. She leaped up as if she were animated, jerking into life like a puppet. This time, Clara screamed.

'Please, Bess, you've got to help me. Please stop it. I don't want this pain. What is happening inside of me?'

'Don't panic. I'll get you a cold compress.'

Bess hurried away, eager to be out of sight.

But the pain wouldn't go away. It stabbed again and then again until Clara didn't know if she could breathe or gasp for help. Now she was writhing, curled up in the fetal position on her bed while trickles of sweat poured out of her pores while she groaned.

Bess, now with the cold compress, was trying to apply it to Clara's fevered brow while she moaned with her mouth wide open.

Pain, the worst enemy of health, was telling her something was very wrong.

'Just try to relax and stay still,' said Bess. 'Try not to fight it. Clara, stay with me.'

The room spun around, going up and down. Clara was hardly in this world while consciousness slid in and out, yet she still kept returning to await the next attack of pain.

Through the warped eyes of agony, Clara's landscape took on a different dimension. The air became bullets attacking her. She couldn't think what was happening to her, and then she felt herself breaking up. Was she real anymore? Something was keeping her mind alive but not functioning as if she was suffering from the worst fate of all —dementia.

Afraid, Bess watched. This was worse than she had remembered.

'You've got to stay with us, Clara.'

'Argenta,' whispered Clara, staring at some unholy shape that appeared to her. 'Have you come to help me? I don't understand what you are trying to tell me. Please help me. This pain.'

'Clara, you've got to stay with us. You will be all right, I promise you. This will pass.'

Bess ran her cool hand over Clara's profusely sweaty brow, which soaked her hand.

'Clara, do you hear me? Everything is going to be all right. Try to keep a hold of it. I won't be long.'

The ghost of an unreal Bess hurried out of the room and left Clara to her interview with death.

'Oh Argenta, please help me,' again Clara moaned, watching the form coming towards her before stepping back.

A cool breeze entered the room, and this time with another needle. Clara didn't feel it piercing her flesh, but it released her from the agonizing pain within the count of seconds. Her crippled, contorted body was now losing its tension as it unwound to give her the peace she needed.

'What did you do?'

Clara's eyes were now open, and she stared at Bess with surprise.

'I helped you. I release you from the pain,' Bess said, placing the hypodermic needle back into the container.

'What was it you gave me?'

'A relaxant. Don't you feel better?'

'Yes, I do,' Clara frowned, unable to understand what had happened. 'But have you destroyed the stem cell cancer transplantation?'

'No, I haven't. I didn't believe you should have to suffer. I don't believe anyone should suffer for any type of treatment.'

Bess was angry. Perhaps it was something to do with helping Clara out of this pain. Bess' lips were pinched together as if there was some unknown reasoning going on.

'You know you were talking about this Peter and what he had done for you?'

Clara nodded.

'From all the conversations we have about your mother and your father, take this money for what it is—a gift. Don't worry whether you cared for Peter in the way you feel you should have—just enjoy it.'

She stared hard at Clara to impress on her a kind of philosophy she had recently come across.

'Just accept the money as a gift. I am certain there is no one else he would rather have given the money to. But he must have felt that what you had to offer him was enough. So, my advice to you is to go and enjoy your life.'

'Thank you, Bess. I really appreciate that. I have been feeling so bad about how I treated him.'

'Forget about that. You were the woman he wanted to marry, even if he wasn't the man for you.'

Why was she telling her this? It was so generous of Bess that those times she had doubted her, were irritated by some things Bess had said or did, didn't matter anymore.

While Clara took in what Bess was saying, Bess was watching her.

'Do you know what I think?' said Bess on an impulse.

Clara shook her head.

'That you should leave here and get yourself to another hospital—'

'But I have just begun the treatment. I want to get well.'

'Proper hospitals, in my opinion, are more set up to look after people like you rather than in here.'

'But I am getting the best help, surely.'

'Just get yourself out of here and make good use of your life. Now take care of yourself.'

'Where are you going? You talk as if this is the last time we will meet. Have I done anything to upset you?'

'No, in fact, quite the opposite. Let's say you have put me on the right road about everything. Life can be more complicated than you think. And I have to get on with my conscience to live without guilt and regret.'

'You are a good woman,' said Clara. This made Bess smile.

'I once was, but not anymore. I am finding it hard to live with myself. And the person one has to live with twenty-four seven is oneself. When you spoke about money, let's say that you made me think.'

With a smile of relief, Bess came across and kissed Clara on her forehead.

'Take care of yourself, Clara. Now get yourself out of here—quick.'

'Is it something I've done wrong?'

'Clara, I am not stupid. My keys,' she smiled. 'But I won't say anything more. Just pull your thoughts together. I worked out what happened, but I'm not angry. It was a wake-up call that told me how much I was deluding myself. You're right, it matters if you can live with yourself. Now I've got to do some thinking and a little talking with myself.'

She hesitated again, as if she knew this would be the last time she would speak to Clara.

'I am beginning to understand life can so easily be taken away if you allow others to walk in and claim it. You got to fight for your rights to live, and you've got to have the courage to say that I'm worth it, and that I can give something back—'

Bess stopped her speech and then smiled as if she had grown shy. Out through the door, she went, closing it quietly behind her. There is a time in everyone's life when they must bow out gracefully.

Mystified, Clara watched the door closing on Bess' figure. In a hospital, Clara could see that Bess was a marvelous figure, a force for good, someone you would want with you in your battle for life. Although Clara had distrusted Bess, it didn't stop her from liking her. Her spirit was enthusiastic and joyous, and if the timing had been different, then they might have been friends. But the chances of that now happening were very low because both of them were loners.

An enigma, Bess and herself were so alike and yet so different. Then Clara noticed something shining on her bedside top, a set of keys. Looking at the door again, she knew Bess had left them for her. How much else had Bess guessed and suspected? Was Bess going now before the boat sunk? If Bess had guessed, then had the other two?

Thank goodness for Bess. The pains in her stomach had subsided, and sanity had returned. Sounds coming from the lower floor interested Clara enough to investigate. Weak yet determined, she dressed herself to find out what was going on. No one could ban her from meeting the other residents.

Daylight followed by electric reaching into the night gave a different perspective on the world and its happenings.

Each light creates another story and interpretation. The evil that Clara had felt when she went down the other night in the dark had been artlessly dusted away. All wicked thoughts drawn from frightened and creative minds dissolving into fantasy, childish games. How normal the world looked now without the chiaroscuro landscape.

Two voices were coming from the other room, beckoning Clara's curiosity with the thought of who they were and why they were so angry with each other.

'I told you to sort out your domain and not bring it into mine.' it was Dr. Barnet's voice.

'When it affects my arena, it also affects yours. You cannot blame me entirely for what has happened?' the other voice was Dr. Slanders.

'I can and do. It was you who insisted you wanted to keep Nurse Ryan.'

'Because she was an excellent nurse.'

'A nurse who doesn't obey orders but carries out what she believes in is not in our interests.'

'Which is why she isn't here anymore.'

Dr. Slanders' rather bland and monotonous voice took a tone upwards, bearing the heaviness of offense.

'And which is why we have the police on our backs. I cannot believe how badly you have dealt with this matter.'

'So, tell me, what would you have done better?' Dr. Slanders was insulted.

'For one, I would not have hired Nurse Ryan—she was far too old and too set in her ways to adapt to ours. And two, what were you thinking of by using Nurse Jones? I never took you for a fool. That was the craziest of ideas.'

'She was in love with me. That is the biggest reason of all. And love will do anything—'

'But love doesn't make one competent, does it? You should know that. You are a fool.'

Dr. Barnet was exasperated, and in a fury, his anger was reaching rational discord.

'In all my years I have known you, I never thought you were reckless and careless,' his voice dropped as if he was muttering to himself. 'Using of all things emotions.' In exasperation, Dr. Barnet had raised his voice. 'We don't do emotions; we do logic. Emotions get people to us; then we use logic to get what we want from them.'

'But she is gone now. I don't know why you are so upset,' Dr. Slanders' voice took on that familiar shade of dull. 'It's been sorted. She's in a place where no one will find her.'

'And how do you know that?'

'Because I trust Nurse Jones.'

'Oh God, when you say things like that, I feel like I should run to the highest cliff and jump.'

There was an audible groan coming from the other room. The door was ajar only a little, but enough to hear very well what was going on.

'So, why have the police come here yet again asking questions?' asked Dr. Barnet impatiently. 'It's obvious they didn't believe what you told them?'

'I can't answer for the police investigations, but unless they have a body, they can't prove anything.'

'If they get to Nurse Jones and keep on repeatedly questioning her. She will break down; I know she will break. I would bet my life on that. You've got to do something about her.'

'I've thought about that. If it comes to the worse, I'll tell her that I'll marry her.'

There was a fit of loud laughter making a ridicule of the world.

'You—marry her? Are you mad—'

The laughter carried on and then stopped as suddenly as if something had caught his attention.

'The door,' said Dr. Barnet. His voice raised while approaching, told Clara he was making his way to it. 'You didn't close the door properly.'

Clara didn't need any orders. Eyes flitting for escape, and for that moment, she was dazzled by fear—where to go, what to do? Then she ran with the spirits of hell to the first concealing corner. Scared, so scared, she could have cried. But even in fear, she needed to know if she had been spotted. Had Dr. Barnet caught the end of her legs in her escape?

Leaning up against the wall and feeling hot, Clara listened. Her heart rate swelled as her body throbbed with palpitations.

'I could swear that someone was outside listening.'

A laugh coming from the room said that Dr. Slanders was enjoying himself.

'The man who treats others for paranoia is paranoid himself.'

Dr. Slanders' voice was still legible, if only because of his glee.

'You should be worried as well—' Dr. Barnet closed the door on his voice.

It took a minute for her heart and crazy thoughts to relax before Clara could handle herself to get back to her room. She looked at the stairs and wondered how she was going to climb them again. Any second now, she was convinced the door would open and they would catch her. Where had all her calm gone, she was a riot of fears and shaking? She couldn't stop trembling. But it was exciting.

20

Something terrible had happened to Nurse Ryan. At her wildest and most desperate guess, Clara's thoughts turned to murder. Judging by what these two doctors said, Argenta had died of a heart attack while Charisse had died from a rare bone cancer. People die conveniently, especially here when there was plenty of money. And now she too had come into great wealth and was also dying, but this time from blood cancer.

'Get away from here,' Bess had warned her. 'Get yourself to a proper hospital where they can take better care of you.'

What did she mean by that? It was too awful to think about, and yet, why not? Where the power of money rules, people stand in front of what others want. This should be mine; you have always had it. Move over and give it to me; otherwise, I will just have to take it.

Sitting on her bed and trying to calm herself by breathing more regularly, Clara turned to the keys still settled on her bedside cabinet. She must hide them away. This next time might be the last time she would be able to gain entry to the inner office, the inner sanctum. Armed with more knowledge, she could make better sense of what was going on in those folders.

Something had happened to drive a wedge between these two doctors and to sour their project. The hairline fracture had started in their perfect crystal.

Lying on her bed, Clara thought about Bess with sudden warmth. First meetings didn't always dictate how people will be, but she had instantly liked Bess. It was with these thoughts that Clara fell asleep.

The rattle of her bedroom door awoke Clara as if someone had forgotten how to undo a door.

'Have you seen Bess?' demanded Dr. Barnet. For the first time, his friendly face was graphic with temper.

It took Clara a few seconds to know what was going on.

'Earlier today. Why?' she was still intoxicated with sleep.

'What did she say to you?'

'To take care of myself,' and then Clara stopped herself from going any further.

'Anything else?'

'No. Is she okay?'

His eyes were thunder as he smartly closed the door. Something was going on which concerned him greatly. Tonight, she would investigate the office again.

It seemed like she would go without dinner tonight. Oh well, never mind. Bess, who had run the ball game, had gone while Nurse Jones had progressed to the two doctors' bad books. Was this a good thing that she had been forgotten about? It was another crack in the smooth-running operation. It was then that her door opened, and Lori came in with a tray in her hands.

With a grim face, Lori glanced at Clara before looking at where to place the tray.

'Thank you,' smiled Clara, pleased to see her and

surprised that she felt hungry. 'I haven't seen you for a while. It's good to see you. Where have you been?'

'We have had the Feds here asking everyone questions. Nurse Ryan has gone missing. I thought I liked her, but then I hear she has been stealing drugs, especially morphine.'

'Are you certain about this?'

'Yes, of course I am. Dr. Barnet himself told me. I can't believe she would do such a thing. It's so low and mean of her. I hope when they catch her, they put her in prison for a hundred years or even longer. I thought she was the best nurse in the hospital. I really liked her; it feels like a betrayal. But I know now why she was so willing. No wonder pour Charisse was in so much agony. The morphine she should have had was switched by Nurse Ryan. In its place, she mixed up a cocktail of tablets, which was why Charisse died in so much pain.'

Dr. Slanders had told Clara about Nurse Ryan using a truth which she didn't want to believe. No, this couldn't be true; Nurse Ryan was the only decent and caring nurse at the hospital.

'Now I understand why she wanted to disappear, because she knew she was going to be found out,' said Lori.

'I find it very difficult to believe this of Nurse Ryan,' said Clara because she had a right to be thought innocent until she was found guilty. 'Who reported she had gone missing?'

'Her partner did. Now that was a surprise. She led everyone to believe she lived on her own. Dr. Barnet demands complete dedication to this way of life.'

'But that's ludicrous not to allow a member of staff to have a private life.'

'Why?' Lori stared at Clara. 'It's expected that everyone should have full commitment to the commune for it to work; besides, she was paid enough.'

'It sounds perverse and ridiculous.'

'Ideals are never ridiculous. Dr. Slanders and Dr. Barnet have given everything to this, and they, too, are not married. So, here we are. It's deplorable. I don't understand people like that.'

And I don't understand people like you. Clara focused her eyes on Lori, seeing her in a different light. A fanatic, an activist, a person who cannot be reasoned with, which meant she could be dangerous. Never had Clara come across a personality like this, and they existed, if only in small numbers. People like John the Baptist, whose vision thrived on madness, surviving only on wild honey and locusts, and dressed scantily in camels' hair. And then, Joan of Arc's visions were the madness of the obsessive.

Lori would defend her ideals to the end. But that wasn't Clara's problem, except to be cautious of her and play along with her.

'It must be difficult for people like Dr. Slanders and Dr. Barnet to keep their vision going. I haven't been versed completely in their ideology. It would help if you could explain it to me. I have been too ill to be educated.'

Clara's manner was gentle as her words also came as being sincere. She gave the look of a novice, willing and waiting to be indoctrinated.

'I am too small and too unimportant to appreciate the depth of their understandings, but what I can recognize is they are trying to build a beautiful world for the few.'

'Yes,' Clara nodded and smiled. 'It sounds wonderful.'

'The idea is that they are going to build a huge and beautiful house of worship to the only true god. And people such as Argenta and Charisse and me will be able to pray and feel we have been accepted.'

'But those two are dead—' said Clara, confused and astonished.

'Yes, but their souls are still with us. They will join with us in a union when we pray.'

It appeared like Lori was searching for ideas to explain all the gaps in her knowledge. She was filling those empty spaces where her teachers had failed to instruct and explain.

'It sounds wonderful.'

'Yes, it is. Have you ever wondered why you think and feel the way you do when everyone about you is happy? Have you ever wondered why you are unhappy with those thoughts entering your mind that you should kill yourself because you are undeserving? That everyone else has a right to live except you?'

Lori yearned with her voice and eyes to make Clara understand. Something so close to her heart that she needed to share with someone who could understand her world of loneliness.

What should she do? Should she lie to Lori to convince her she understood that she, too, had traveled that same route given to the lonely soul? There had been a time when the world had changed its shape for Clara by denying its peace.

'I have been there. I know what you are talking about.'

'Well then, if you do, you will want to help. Oh, Clara, I knew you had the same kindred spirit within you. I shall tell Dr. Barnet of my talk to you. And he will be grateful and happy.' Lori gushed.

'Perhaps not just yet. I don't know what my future will be. And to give him hopes and then to take them away might dispirit him.'

'You are right. I never thought about that.'

The burning masses of feelings and now torments were raging through Lori's eyes from the entanglement of her mind. For her, the two doctors were her gods. Lori believed everything they told her.

'But you can serve them in other ways.'

Clara leaned her head to one side in speculative interest.

'If you cannot give yourself, you can give in other ways, which is everything you have to them.'

'You mean my fortune?'

'Yes, there is no nobler way, and Argenta and Charisse have made this sacrifice, which is why they are worshipped.'

Clara smiled, such a simplistic understanding, yet it sounded creepy. Again, Clara's mind flew to the files in the office.

'I was asked to do that already, but it felt like I was signing my death warrant.'

'Oh, then you were foolish not to trust them. You believe that once your money is signed over to the foundation, they would kill you?'

'No, it was just superstition I had.'

'You should trust in God. God will always be there for you,' said Lori faithfully. 'You do not know how my life has been turned around since I believe in them.'

A weak smile wavered on Clara's face as she felt confronted by genuine madness.

'Well, I had better do my duty and eat the food you have brought me and get well. It was kind of you to remember me. What is this?'

'I chose vegetarian for you. It's more wholesome for the soul by allowing your spirit to reengage in its rightful place.'

'Thank you, you are right.'

Picking up the knife and fork, Clara regarded her plate with apprehension. This wasn't what she would have chosen for herself, while Lori, with hollowed eyes, realized she should leave Clara to her private communion.

'I'll come back and collect your plate later.'

After Lori left, Clara had a mind to throw this meal away, but she could not afford to be fussy. She needed all the energy she could get, and food was the only way to gain her strength.

There was nothing illegal in leaving your money to whoever you wanted to, even if it was apparent that Charisse and Argenta had done this willingly, no matter what the Lamonts had to say about this. Ralph should have taken better care of his daughter, even if Anise was against her. She was still his daughter. Oh, what a pretty web we weave when it comes to money.

Charisse's death was tragic, as was her life. To have such a substantial fortune and never to know happiness. It begs the question, what is happiness? Is it looking about you and welcoming what you see as being beautiful and joyous? If one has the eyes and knowledge to understand what you have been given, then that is a true gift.

Again, Clara thought of Peter and what he had done for her. This money had eased her up in many ways. She could do things she could never have done before. Travel and buy anything she had a fancied for. She could buy everything. This massive door has been opened to her. Perhaps one needs to be poor first to enjoy riches as like as you nearly need to lose your health to appreciate what it was to be alive.

She ate the dinner and found she enjoyed it. Again, Clara surprised herself that she had been hungry. Then, laying back on her bed, she fell asleep.

Upon opening her eyes, the world had moved back into darkness. What had happened during this time? Dancing through her head were the thoughts of persecution, feeling amassed; she had done something wrong. She had been dreaming of her father. First, she had been telling him how much she missed him and loved him, and then she changed. She was glad he was dead. He should have done this sooner. But it was when he walked away from her with the saddest expression it was then when she opened her eyes.

Over twenty years had passed since then, and yet it still held its arms out to her in remembrance. How do you own up to something which hurts so much? If he had left a letter and told her that this was his wish to die and he didn't blame her for it, then maybe she could forgive herself and move on. But he didn't leave any message or reason as to why he had killed himself. It was in her estimation that her thoughts supplied this gaping hole.

Now the night had come, it was time to make that visit to the office. It was just as creepy going down the stairs as it had been the other night. But tonight, she heard the calls of birds from an open window, unusual to find any of the windows open.

This time Clara remained dressed. There was something vulnerable in wearing nightclothes, but she felt like she had joined the human race when dressed.

Opening the first office door with the keys Bess had left her, Clara locked the door behind her as a precaution. Once again, this side of the offices held nothing of interest. It was in the other office that the true business of the commune was settled. Opening and closing, she locked this door too.

No windows in this box-shaped room. The only source of light came from the electric lights. Everything looks so normal lit this way. But now to business.

Taking out Argenta's black file, Clara flicked through the pages, now armed with more knowledge of these figures' significance. On the nineteenth of every month, fifty thousand dollars came out of her trust fund and was paid into another trust called F and G. What of Charisse? Quickly pulling out this one, another somber black folded, a tangible reminder that she was dead.

This time, the money that was drawn out was significantly greater, five hundred thousand a month. But what was to become of this money? Into a temple? Where was the proof? Money being drained away needs to be tracked.

At the back of the drawer was a flimsy folder; it lay crooked as if it had been hastily put away, and by the uncomfortable way it had been placed, called out for attention. Clara picked up the folder to look inside. It was called Heartbreak, another code name. A hundred thousand was being drawn out of this person's account from the thirtieth of next month. Yet, no money had been taken; this file had only just recently been created. A person who was new to gifting the commune. And why was that? Perhaps this person was still alive and waiting to die.

Blood was on the next page and a date. It was the same date as when Clara entered the commune. The third of August.

The coincidence leaped out at her; the folder ascribe to this person was herself. The date staring up at her with accusations was the tenth of September—this year. And to her was an example of what was going to happen to her, cremation. She was going to die on the tenth of September, and she was going to be cremated.

Her death echoed in her head. With less than ten days to live, her head spun around with dizziness. The shock shook her into a spiral of fear. She had just a few days to live. Why hadn't they told her?

Everyone wants to know if their death was inevitable so

they can do all the things they want to get done, like getting drunk, laid, or gamble away their fortune. Do all those crazy things. But hang on, she had never said she would leave all her money to this commune on her demise. But they were going to take it regardless of what she wanted.

But how did they know for sure she was going to die conveniently on this day? How did they know? Was it a guess, or had they ways of making it for certain she would do what they wanted?

Someone had entered the other part of the office with a crash.

'It was you who told me to trust her.'

Clara recognized the angry voice of Dr. Barnet.

'Yes, it was me,' the quieter tone of Dr. Slander entered behind in the tenor of reasoning. 'And she was trustworthy. We had a long talk about it. I told her, in so many words, what was expected of her. She told me she had been dissatisfied by an unequal system, working days and nights for a pittance. I showed her the type of money she could make here with us.'

'I knew you were an idiot. I just didn't know how big a one you were.'

'I understand you are upset, and you are lashing out, so I will not take what you said personally. Just try to calm down, and think before you next speak.'

'If she goes to the police, we are done for, don't you understand that? You have always been slow on the uptake—'

'I am meticulous while you go rushing in. I consider everything. I am deliberate and slow, and that is my worth.'

'Slow, yes. You are certainly slow on the uptake, all right.'

'Please, can you refrain from being vindictive?'

'Tell me, what are we going to do? How are we going to get out of this fix? We've already had to get rid of Nurse Ryan, which was only successful because it was a one-off. We cannot use the same excuse with another nurse by accusing her of also stealing the morphine to sell on, and that she too was an addict.'

'I manage to catch Bess on the telephone. I asked her what it was all about. She told me she couldn't do it anymore. I said, very well, fine, not everyone can do it. And then she asked if the people we were treating for cancer really had it—'

'What did you say?' snapped Dr. Barnet. The tension in his voice was almost breaking.

'I told her what she wanted to hear.'

This was Dr. Slanders at his best; he had everything under control, nothing was going to faze him.

'Which was?'

'That the people who were coming to us were dying. We gave them a safe place in a community somewhere they could consider as their home. The only issue which might have verged on the illegal was to be in a part of their wills. I then told her we did this so that we could help others who were suffering likewise. I tied it up neatly, and she believed me.'

'Do you really believed she fell for it?'

'George, you should know by now that people believe the things they want to hear. They will disprove everyone's version until they come across the one they want to believe.' A snort of a laugh, and in one breath, it was gone.

'She is not a stupid woman, far from it. She has worked fifteen years in first class hospitals, so she has seen plenty of life and death.'

'And has been disenchanted with it.'

'I don't know. Sometimes, I think you are purposely naïve.'

'I offered her money.'

'Oh yes, and how much?'

'Three million.'

'Three million?' Dr. Barnet's voice nearly took off. 'Are you crazy? Where will we get three million from? And why did you offer that much? Do you know what she is going to do now? She is going to ask for more. Oh, Franklin, I sometimes wondered what I am doing with you. Are you certain you didn't bribe someone to get you through med school?'

Clara was pressed up against the door devotedly listening while her eyes depicted the scene going on only a few feet away.

'Do you think bribing her with money will stop her from going to the police?' again, it was Dr. Barnet.

'Why not? Why do you always go from one extreme to the other? When the going is good, you're happy and satisfied. But when things change, you panic. Your world has gone wrong; you want to cry and stamp your feet.'

'You are not being realistic. And this is your fault, Franklin. You want to believe everything people tell you.'

'Are we into name throwing now? I am telling you now, this is going to work out all right.'

'Has she said she would take the money?'

'No, not yet. I've given her until midnight to think about it. I have reassured her that what we are doing in this commune is helping these poor sufferers. We are like a hospice—because that's what she wants to hear.'

'And what if she refuses the money?'

'She won't refuse. Why would she refuse? That would be insane.'

'There are some things in life which cannot be bought,

haven't you come to understand that, Franklin? Haven't you understood there is something far greater than money for some people?'

A thoughtful silence continued.

'Principles,' cried out an exasperated Dr. George Barnet. 'People need to live with themselves, and they do this on principle. Just because we don't appear to have principles doesn't mean that most people haven't either. She is just one of those people who has decided that they have principles. How moral and ethical she must think she is. Oh yes, I can see her now, thinking herself so much more superior to us. Perhaps even going on television to expose us.'

His voice was rising in tone and temper.

'How everyone will love her and congratulate her—she will be on every television station, courted and congratulated. And the three million you offered her will be nothing compared to what the people want to shower her with.'

'Calm down, George. You are over exciting yourself. Remember your heart—'

'And why do you think I am angry? Why do you think I am so-called upset? We will go to prison—haven't you realized that yet? Prison. Not a slap on the wrist. We will go to prison for a very long time. Goodbye to the good life. Goodbye to our dreams. You can kiss everything goodbye when she makes her telephone call to the police.'

He had become breathless with terror as he spoke faster and faster.

'Oh my God, everything we have worked for would be gone—everything would be taken away. But one thing's for sure, though; we will probably go down in history as two of the worse American criminals. I wonder what they would call us. Doctors of death, no, I think that has already been taken.'

'Calm down, George. Even if she goes to the police, she must know that she, too, is implicated. She won't come out of this lily-white either. She doesn't hold all the cards.'

Keeping his voice neat and tidy, Dr. Slanders would not allow himself to panic. He prided himself on having more control over himself, expressed by how he dressed and the distinct and monotonously controlled voice.

'So, you have come up with an original idea?' he laughed. 'Since when have you ever come up with anything remotely interesting?' Dr. Barnet had entered the arena of sarcasm.

'I won't answer that. I can see you have worked yourself up into one of your states.'

Something hit the floor violently, which jerked Clara back into fright.

'Did you have to do that?' asked Dr. Slanders. 'It was an award which I was very proud of.'

'It's not broken.' And then he sighed. 'What are we going to do?'

'Not panic for one, and I will show you the reason,' said Dr. Slanders. 'She is not so high and mighty or pure as she likes to think she is.'

His voice was coming closer to the door on which Clara had rested her ear.

'And what do you have up your magical sleeve?'

'Look, I'll show you.'

The key went into the lock near Clara's ear and turned. Jumping back in fright, she looked around—they were coming into this office. Lord God. She had to hide, and quick or they would find her, but where? There was nowhere.

The door opened, and the two men came inside.

'Did you leave the light on?' asked Dr. Slanders.

'No, I didn't?'

'I bet it was Nurse Bess, which just goes to prove that she must have been looking for something. And which also proves she doesn't have much on us except hearsay.'

'The proof of a devoted and qualified nurse who every hospital wants so much that she now veers heavily towards the law.'

'And we don't, George? Come on, snap out of it. It's not like you to jump into a shark-infested sea. You've got to get a hold of yourself.'

'I believe we seriously have something to be anxious about,' said Dr. Barnet.

'As long as we hold up our heads, we will be all right. I credit I am a lot smarter than this nurse. Tell me, what does she really know? That we help people on their way. It is her word against ours. Really, George; it is not as bad as you are trying to make out.'

The filing cabinet was not against the wall. It stood out towards the middle of the room and below a set of shelves that contained some hefty books on mental illness. Behind these filing cabinets, Clara had fled and crouched down in the shadow, making herself as small as she could.

One of the drawers was snatched out, and a thud on the cabinet top told that several folders had been extracted.

'I'll show you something.'

He had opened a folder and was taking out its documents. Licking his finger, he shuffled through the papers.

'Here, do you see this one?' said Dr. Slanders. 'Do you remember Caitlyn Walker, a shareowner of Walker Beauty products? She died nine months ago, and who do you think administered the fatal dose? Do you want to have a guess?'

'You are going to tell me it was Bess?'

'Yes. Congratulations, you have got the right answer. Top marks. But have you noticed something else?'

'Can you please cut to the chase? I don't appreciate these little games,' Dr. Barnet asked, now exasperated and mentally worn out.

'Look here,' he was pointing to something.

'Yes, I can see. It is an initial.'

'Correct again.'

'For heaven's sake, Franklin. Tell me some good news if there is any.'

'It's not my initial, and it's not yours. It's Nurse Bess.'

'That doesn't mean anything. She gave the medication instructed by one of us. This will be her argument.'

'Flip the argument on its head. We will deny we had ordered the switching of the medication. What Bess gave Caitlyn Walker was oleander. She has signed and acknowledged it; this was her first death and why she got a bonus. She never questioned about the bonus, did she?'

Dr. Slanders was almost laughing with unsuppressed pleasure.

'Why didn't you tell me about this?' Dr. Barnet was near to being annoyed.

'It was something which I was experimenting with. I wanted to see how far I could push her. When I told her about what we did in this center, I wanted to know whether she would suddenly get afraid, which was something I speculated on, and if she told the police, then the evidence would point to her.'

'Well, I am surprised.' There was a noticeable relief in Dr. Barnet's voice.

'Did you think you were the only one who could come up with good ideas?' asked Dr. Slanders, pleased with himself, yet still managing to be insulted. 'How little do you know me?'

'I guess I don't, but this has been a pleasant surprise. I wish you had told me sooner. Which now begs the question, as to Miss Clara Tinder, what are we going to do with her?'

'Lori, our faithful worshipper. She will do the passing of the offerings.'

'Yes, I have noticed how Miss Tinder has taken to her. You know, Miss Tinder is still an enigma to me. Our detective has been unable to turn up anything on the woman. It's like she appeared out of nowhere and suddenly came into a great deal of money.'

'Why don't you ask her?' suggested Dr. Slanders. 'You are the one with the charm. You can get the women to confide in you.'

'She's a clam when it comes to giving away her private life. But I suppose it doesn't matter now. By the tenth of September, she will have breathed her last. And as she doesn't conveniently have any family, no one will claim her inheritance.'

Dr. Barnet spoke confidently, as if he had done this many times before. With his tone, it was as if he had almost become blasé about it. He knew people and how they worked; this was his business and his profession. He lived a life of understanding people and their peculiarities, but he was vain to believe that he knew her.

The first terror had gone. Hiding and holding herself so tight behind the filing cabinets while listening. Knowledge made Clara bolder by correcting her thoughts on her own vulnerabilities, because now she was in on their secrets. It wasn't so much she was going against their advice anymore. She now knew the people who they were harvesting from were only the rich. By taking these people into their nest to care for, they could entrap only the most susceptible to feed off.

The desire to stand up and announce she was here was intense. As was her anger, which wasn't the best way to go about bringing them down. And how much she wanted to destroy their evil empire.

'We have just got to keep our cool,' began Dr. Barnet. 'This sort of thing was bound to happen. Now you have evidence on Bess; I feel a great deal happier about it. But we need to do something about Nurse Jones?'

'I don't know how far I can push her,' answered Dr. Slanders. 'It took it out of her with Nurse Ryan. She is not a natural killer.'

'What did she do with the body?' Dr. Barnet was curious.

'I didn't care to ask. I trusted her to take care of it.'

'We don't want it turning up as evidence. I've never found her to be the most imaginative of people. I hope she hasn't taken it back home with her. Find out what she has done with it.'

The opening and closing of the cabinet drawers suggested the folders were being returned.

'It might be appropriate,' began Dr. Barnet, 'if we hired professional people who know how to make people disappear. It will cost, of course, but these are factors which we have to weigh against the benefits.'

The last drawer slammed closed.

'Tell me,' said Dr. Barnet. 'How do you feel about Nurse Jones? Are you fond of her?'

'I led her to believe that there is something special between us. But no. She is very willing, and that is her charm. Why, what are you thinking about?'

Two or three seconds passed as if Dr. Barnet was stretching his neck in thoughtful consideration.

'You understand her affection for you is a weak spot?'

'It has passed through my mind.'

'Consider this. She could also be a liability and a danger to us.'

'If I have to do without her, I will do without her.'

'Franklin, you make me smile. Looking at your face. I would say by your expression that you not only like her, but care about her.'

'No,' Dr. Slanders was adamant. 'If I have to admit to anything, it is that she flatters my vanity. By the way she looks at me, all doe-eyed and believing everything I say. It would be impossible for anyone to be immune to her appreciation. Why, what do you have in mind for her?'

'Franklin, she knows too much about our business.'

'As does Bess,' Dr. Slanders spoke quickly in defense.

'Yes, she is definitely a problem. But leave that problem with me. I will sort something out for her. Meanwhile, I suggest you carry on speaking to her and promising whatever you have to promise. If she wants to go any higher, ask how much and then agree. In the end, it won't matter. Oh, yes.' His distancing voice proposed he was moving away towards the office door. 'I feel so much happier now about this little situation.'

And then he stopped.

'I think that September the tenth is rather too far away for us now. There isn't any reason why we should hang on until then. The will is written out and signed, and everything is ready. And this time, we should try cyanide. It is instant and very tidy. I will do the autopsy myself instead of our regular. Not that I don't trust them, but the big handouts annoy me. Such a simple job, a diagnosis, signing the form, and they demand two hundred thousand.'

'If you think this is a good idea.'

'Look, in the end, who wants to know about a nobody? They want to get on with their lives with no fuss. On the whole, people are lazy. Oh, come on, Franklin, I need a drink. It's very tiring worrying about loose ends when really there is nothing to worry about. The best thing we have got going for us is that we stick together and work as a team. When we do that, no one or nothing can part us.'

The door closed behind them, and then it was locked.

Three, four, five minutes later, Clara stayed scrunched up, until finally she unraveled herself. She ached. Was it safe now to leave the offices? Creeping to the inner door, she pressed her ear to it. No human movement or sound came from the other side while the beating of her heart kept her company.

They had gone. Gone for that much needed drink Dr. Barnet spoke about.

Creeping up the staircase exposed in the middle of the hallway made Clara aware of her slight presence compared to Dr. Barnet, whose vanity required that he kept himself fit by working out. A man who wanted to live his life well, and he would use anyone to get what he wanted. If he caught her now, there was little she could do to defend herself physically. Yet, in her fear, she still couldn't hurry to her room.

21

———

It was a night's sleep that she didn't think she would have, but Clara fell asleep with the heart and mind of an innocent. She awoke refreshed, if still a little tired. Nothing wrong with her, again Clara repeated to herself, and it was what Dr. Barnet had said. She wasn't ill. Difficult to believe she was healthy as it was just as hard to believe that she had been seriously ill. Yet nothing was completely safe or for certain.

Nurse Jones had killed Nurse Ryan and disposed of her body. The little that Clara knew of psychology told her that this was not in the nurse's natural inclinations. For nearly a week now, she hadn't seen Nurse Jones, and now Clara understood why.

She and the nurse never got off right from the start, and yet, somehow, she felt sorry for her. Sorry, this woman had fallen in love with a man who used her and wasn't worried about how he disposed of her. Just like herself in a way with Tom, but Clara couldn't worry about everyone. She had to think about herself now, which means taking up Bess' advice and getting herself out of here before it's too late. But for some reason, acting on this decision took a great deal of courage. Perhaps it was because she was still physically weak that it pulled heavily on her emotional courage to do anything. She just wanted to climb into her bed, pull the covers over, and forget everything.

The two doctors now wanted to kill Bess, who had become a problem for them from their conversation. Oh well, when you are thrown into the deep blue sea, everyone has to help themselves.

Come on, Clara, move it already. There is more to you than meets the eye. So pull it all out and show me what you can do. Believe in yourself. It's not a good idea to stay up here in this room all the time, especially with your imagination. No one was banning you from going downstairs to meet the others.

How different and reassuring everything looks in the daylight. Clara went down the red-carpeted stairs. The disturbing conversation she had overheard last night had lost some of its threats.

A couple of people she had never seen before passed by; they were so engrossed in their conversation and lives that they hadn't noticed her. She was rehearsing what she was going to say to the pair, but they weren't even aware of her.

Though they hadn't paid any attention to Clara, she had interested herself in them. Both underweight, with pale white faces and very young, somewhere in their mid-twenties, but no older. From the quick sketch she made of them, deep in thought and worried, there were already lines forming on their young brows. Too young to have such burdens on young shoulders.

On their backs were rucksacks, neatly tied tight so Clara couldn't see what they were carrying. The little conversations she caught said they would do much better in this other area. Make what you can of that.

The large entrance doors came open, which suddenly frightened Clara. They opened to a flood of late evening sunshine. From the silhouetted figure trapped in the sunbeam, the outside world appeared to be caught in another dimension. Abruptly, it threatened her world with too much life. The thought she was going to go out into it made her heart race.

When the front door closed, the world out there stayed out. From the sunlight emerged the developing figure of Nurse Jones. When these two met, they stopped to understand their enemy.

While Nurse Jones pulled off her gloves inside the doorway, her almond eyes squinted with hostility, which made her nose look pointed. It really was too hot to wear gloves.

'Hello Nurse Jones, it's good to see you,' said Clara, breaking the ice. 'How are you?'

The face which peeped at Clara was surprisingly one of fear. She had changed dramatically since the last time Clara had seen her. The beauty that Clara had first credited her with had become distorted. The soft lines of her face suffered an earthquake of emotions, and cracks had formed where none had been before. Her skin had badly ruptured in crevices. This was a face that had suffered.

'I'm busy,' said Nurse Jones. Her eyes were hanging on Clara's.

'Are you all right?'

It seemed strange for Clara to ask. It was like seeing a wild creature you had once feared and wished dead but then realized that you had no more fear of it. Because coming across it caught in a trap and finding it tortured and suffering, compassion stalks in. Surprised to see your enemy in a weakened state that contrarily Clara found herself not wanting Nurse Jones to be harmed anymore.

'That's none of your business,' said Nurse Jones, making a wide berth as she passed Clara.

'I only wanted to know if you were all right,' Clara said as Nurse Jones moved along the corridor. Idiotically, this annoyed Clara.

'You know, you should be more worried about yourself than me.'

This was enough to make Nurse Jones stop in her tracks. For a second or two, she stayed where she was before turning.

'Is that a threat?'

'No, it's a warning,' said Clara.

'And who are you to warn me?'

Wait, Clara's inner voice was telling her. You don't know for sure about anything. You overheard a conversation; you don't have any proof, and besides, she has never been a friend to you.

'Nothing. I didn't mean anything by what I said. I was speaking out of turn. I am sorry.'

But she did not move away. She stayed where she was, still staring at Clara.

'Yes, you did. What were you going to tell me? I can see it in your eyes.'

There are plans for your death being made even now as I look at you by the man you love.

'I know we haven't seen eye to eye on things, but I have also noted how dedicated you are and that you are truly devoted to your profession.'

With eyes which had seen things it should not have done, Nurse Jones stared unflinchingly at Clara. She had prepared herself for other things than this, and this wounded her more. She lowered her head and then turned to the side. It was something that Dr. Barnet had said to Clara, which reminded her.

'Everyone needs a friend. For whatever it is worth, I am offering my friendship to you.'

Nurse Jones, engulfed in some sort of torture, returned another of her horrified expressions as though reason had slipped and deserted her. She was falling into the torment of the damned. Looking from one side to another for that needed escape. Nothing was there for her. Hugging herself, she hurried away from Clara, a mess of misery stuffed with regret and overwhelmed with guilt.

So, she must have murdered Nurse Ryan. Clara watched after Nurse Jones, wrapped in anguish, which she would now never be able to shed.

Today, Clara felt weak, and she also felt shaky in herself, which led to lively thoughts about the inevitable. Did Dr. Barnet get it right that she was going to die? And then, no, she told herself; she would not die because she did not have cancer. As far as she knew, there was no cancer on either side of her family. But her family wasn't large; her father had two brothers, one of which went to Australia, which meant that correspondence died out. The other brother, the youngest, moved to South Africa, and he too disappeared.

No one except Tina and herself went to her father's funeral, making his death more tragic; the funeral directors took seats in the church with them. A man's life should be worth more than this.

But as always, these memories were in the past. This was her future, and she had to claim it as her own. Her intention now was to get to the dayroom to be with the others. It would help her feel more normal instead of this strangeness that often took over her.

'What are you doing down here?'

It was Dr. Barnet, and he spoke as if he was not surprised to see her. Nurse Jones must have told on her.

'I wanted to mix with other company; I am allowed to have some company, and besides there's no harm in me getting to know them.'

'Most of them are out for the day doing God's work. There is no point in you being down here. You might as well be resting. Remember, the stem cells are trying to do their work to get you better.'

This was the man who last night had plotted to have her die sooner. What did he think about when he looked at her? Did he see her as a walking ghost? A reliable bank account. What went on behind his glasses, that dark conventional veil which concealed his real identity?

He doesn't like me; Clara kept this thought quietly masked underneath her brow. He doesn't want me here. I am obstructing his plans. We are so different, and his pretense of liking me is false. But what he wants is something I've got, and that is my money. He just wanted my money, my properties, and the artwork. It was something to feel good about. For once in Clara's life, she felt herself to be secure. But when someone comes after it and demands it as their right, this was the time to fight back and not run away as her inclination dictated, especially since last night.

'I understand all of that.' She was not returning to her room, not without a fight.

'Good, if you understand, then you should return,' and then he sighed in exasperation. 'I am your doctor. You should pay heed to what I say. Return now before any damage is done, Miss Tinder.'

'And what about me? What about my wishes? I feel like a prisoner in that room.'

'Miss Tinder, how do I explain to you what we are trying to do for you?'

I know what your plans are for me, Clara brooded. And yet, if eyes could speak. His face became tempered with anger as if he wanted to shout at her. Leaning forward, she wasn't sure if he meant to strike. At that moment, something of his true self was released—there was another man behind this mask, cold-blooded and calculating. For over fifty years, he had traveled to be where he was, and she would not get the better of him. Rage was in his blue, spitting eyes.

It was on his lips to say something to scare her. What is it you want to tell me? Clara's staring eyes were trying to coax him to say. Isn't it better you tell me exactly how you feel about me? Wouldn't it unburden you to get a load off your chest, and then perhaps it will help you even more when you ask how much I can give you? You know, as a donation for this strange and awful game you have been playing. Because if anything, it has been entertaining, I would agree to that. But I am afraid you have gone too deep for my liking.

But whatever was happening between them suddenly broke with a snap. The wicked wizard had broken the spell because it was no longer working for him.

'Of course, Miss Tinder, if you want to meet the others. Who am I to stop you? I am afraid you will not find them as entertaining as you hoped. They are quite a motley crowd of your average twenty-something-year-old's.'

He smiled. Being charming suited him better, as he obviously felt better because of it. He didn't like being thought of as a monster, mostly by himself. With Dr. Slanders, it was different; it suited him to be the objectionable one.

'You see, Miss Tinder, I was only thinking of you. But we are as we are, and you can decide for yourself if these people are interesting. If there is anyone there to see at this time of day… Lori,' he hailed a figure that had been standing out of sight, a willing servant. 'Come here and take Miss Tinder into the dayroom.'

Here comes the fanatic, thought Clara as Lori stepped out from the shadows. The person who would willingly die or kill for a cause.

Nerves make one smile; this is what Clara whispered to herself because she thought she liked Lori. But now, after getting to know her, and after listening to her and what Dr. Barnet had said, Clara now drew a new conclusion—this person was not safe. She was dangerous.

With a meaningful look, Lori stepped forward.

'You want to see the dayroom?' she smirked. 'But why? You've seen it before. You know there is not much to look at.'

'What? You mean Miss Tinder has already seen the dayroom?' asked Dr. Barnet, still smiling but now caught by surprise.

'Yes,' answered Clara vaguely for herself. 'The first night I came here. I was excited and curious. I wanted to know what was going on.'

'You never said.' Puzzled filled thoughts turned to frowns.

'Clara was on the outside and looking in. I thought she was a burglar,' said Lori.

'Hardly a burglar,' Clara laughed, for this was not funny. 'I was attracted by the smells coming from the garden and wondered what flowers there were. I thought I could smell jasmine, although it could have been honeysuckle. Then I saw some beautiful oleanders in the flowerbed.'

The smile soured on Dr. Barnet's face.

'Yes, we grow them. They are my favorite plants. But I

am surprised you could smell their perfume. They rarely release their fragrance late at night.'

'Oh well, it must have been the honeysuckle or just me trying to imagine there was a smell. It doesn't matter anyhow. Is this the way to the dayroom?'

Clara walked ahead, nervous and annoyed, taking short, sharp, jerky steps. The next thing she had to do was to get out of this place, and quickly.

'You see,' said Lori, following Clara into the dayroom. 'There are no other people except you and me here.'

She swept around almost in a dance as she alluded to the emptiness with her hand. And then she went over to the window, absent-mindedly Lori gazed out. Looking at Lori, Clara didn't trust her, not anymore. She couldn't believe anything Lori said. The spy in the camp of disciples.

'Why did you come to this commune?' Clara asked Lori, still looking into the garden.

'You asked me that question before—' she turned. 'And like before, I told you that in my life, I had been a bad person. I got into drugs and lost my way. But being here has re-educated me. I understand now where I went wrong, and I want to make it up to the world. My true vocation is to follow the lord, and I can do so by making an offering of myself to him.'

And then she swirled around.

'You should consider it as well. You don't have much longer to live. You should think about donating your money and possessions to the commune for what good is it to you?'

She stared hard at Clara while coming closer.

'Look how unhappy you are. How worried and thin you have become. Evil is eating you up inside. You have lost your way. Poor little rich girl. Why don't you try to save your soul?'

Stopping in front of Clara, Lori bared her thoughts. It was hypnotic. Clara couldn't move her eyes. Hatred and even scorn manifested in Lori's eyes. She was one of the chosen that if anyone crossed her, she had the right to do whatever she wanted to get back at them. And then Lori smiled as if this had been a timed expression. Was Lori really crazy?

'I have actually been thinking about leaving my money to a worthy cause. And you're right, the outside way of living has poisoned me.' Every word Clara uttered was taken with extreme attention, carefully, thoughtfully. 'I had hoped that I would survive with this treatment, isn't that the idea of this place? To be well and happy, and to serve others, as you do? I, too, would like to change the error of my ways. Perhaps I should go back to my room.'

Lori continued to watch Clara. The smile was gone, but not the ugliness in her eyes.

'No,' Clara held up her hand. 'I can make my own way back. I am not as weak as I look yet.'

'I'll bring you up something to eat and your medication. Dr. Barnet told me he had prescribed something to help you with nausea.'

'But I don't have any nausea.'

Lori walked behind, dogging Clara's footsteps. Her closeness was intimidating.

'It is better to follow the advice which Dr. Barnet has set out for you,' said Lori, determinedly following Clara.

Did she know what the two doctors were up to? Clara thought now as she mounted the stairs. Lori was becoming freakier and scarier as time passed. It would not surprise her if Lori knew what was going on in this commune. Perhaps she had worked it out herself. The deaths and how everyone left their possessions to the commune. And yet, Lori had declared how much she cared about Argenta and witnessed how greatly she had suffered. If she knew it was from her hand Argenta had received the poison, would this be enough to send her out of her mind?

Not five minutes later, Lori knocked before entering. On a tray, she had a plate of salad.

'You need to eat,' she said, placing the tray on a table and pushing it towards Clara's bed.

At the whim of another, Clara felt she was being treated like a naughty child who needed discipline and then punishment. This female was at least ten years her junior.

'And you are to take this.'

She put a small plastic cup on the table with a see-through capsule inside.

'I'll have it when I'm ready,' said Clara, looking away from the dishes feeling her temper peaking.

'Ok, then you must take your medication now while I'm here.'

'What?' how insulting and how dare she. 'I am not to be trusted?'

'I didn't say that. I was told to watch you take your medication. There isn't a problem with that, is there?'

'I'll have to remind you I am not a charity case. I pay to be here.'

The anger was out.

'And look at you. You are so privileged you can afford to forget those who need help. You have never suffered as others have suffered. You take your education as it's your right as you take everything as your right.'

Shot with fear, Clara stared at Lori, almost paralyzed by what she was hearing.

'You are so ungrateful, complaining and whining all the

time about how badly life has treated you. What have you ever done for others except to look after yourself?'

'How dare you talk to me like that?'

Finally, that anger came crashing through.

'How dare I? I have all the rights in the world. I speak as I see it, and what I see is nothing of worth. And you have had so much.'

Swiftly on target, Lori crossed to Clara, and kneeled on her bed to look down at her with gripping black eyes. It was threatening, and it was meant to be. Hatred poured from this strange woman. The mentality and personality of a fanatic.

'Well, thank you, Lori, for reminding me,' Clara smiled, hoping to disperse the spell of this spinning madness. 'Like you, I have been fortunate and lucky as it is, but at least I am trying to help myself now.'

'You could help much more. The world needs a temple so that our God can appear to us.'

Her eyes sparkled with inner zeal. There was a vision unraveling itself to her.

'But surely God doesn't need a temple to appear in. He was, I understand, a humble man who despised false grandeur and false gods.'

'Do you dare to say that you know the mind of God?'

'No, I never said that. It's in the Bible.'

Fury raised itself in Lori. Too late, Clara reminded herself that her opinions were not others' opinions, and that she was already on unstable ground. But the need to speak and be heard for what she knew to be right was demanded. She could not keep quiet or cap her silence and remain hidden away for what she felt. It would be like denying herself not only the right to speak and express herself, but also it would erase her identity.

'I can see who you are now,' Lori's voice was rising. 'You are the devil. You have taken the form of a vulnerable woman to gain sympathy. And now I know what I am up against, and I despise you. You are now trapped in your mortal form and shall die in this body. And I shall not pray for you or beg for the peace of your soul. You have no soul—'

'I am sorry I have upset you,' broke in Clara. 'But you have also upset me.'

Lori grabbed hold of the plastic cup and held it to Clara's face.

'Take it,' she said, shaking it in front of Clara's quick blinking eyes.

'I said that I would take it when I am ready. But I will certainly not be ordered to take it by you.'

Violently. Out tumbled the tablet into Lori's hand. Her hands were on Clara's face, clawing away at her mouth to open it while Clara's arms were thrashing to stop the attack.

'You will take it now.'

Lori's determined voice was pulling at Clara's face. If Clara opened her mouth, she could so easily have bitten Lori. And then what would have happened? It would not be Lori, who was found to be at fault. Clara knew with certainty that the blame would be hers. She could feel her mouth being stretched and the pain of Lori's nails cutting into her cheeks, but she was losing this fight. If she opened her mouth to call out for mercy, she knew this would give Lori her opportunity to drop the tablet into her mouth.

There was only one option left for Clara to prevent this violence, so she held up her hand like the white flag. Seeing this waving hand, Lori relaxed her grip. But she still held on to Clara's face.

'What is it? What do you want to tell me?'

Clara nodded, then crossed her fingers as a sign of submission. Then those hands left her face while Lori's eyes continued to hold on to Clara's.

'Yes, what is it?'

'Okay, I will take the tablet, but please take your hands away from my face.'

Blood had run down Clara's cheeks to pool in her mouth. This was pure madness; it was difficult to distinguish Lori from a demon.

'You are going to take it now?' Lori insisted.

'Yes. I was always going to take it. I know it is to help me. I just wanted to do things in my own time. You frightened me, Lori.'

'You had to be frightened. You said some wicked things from your mouth. I knew the devil possessed you. The devil is in you now.'

The devil, Clara thought, has possession of you. But this time, she would say nothing for or against. Like one cannot reason with a drunk, it can also be said that madness cannot be reasoned with either. Their rules are not the same as the sane.

'I will take the tablet with some water. I can't take it dry. I will choke on it if I try.'

'Very well, I will get you some water.'

Taking the plastic cup with her, Lori went to the bathroom to draw Clara some water.

There was no way that Clara could take this capsule, and now she was more certain than she had been before that it was a carrier of poison. Argenta died of a heart attack, but that was because she was given a dose of cardiac glycosides from the oleander plants.

Everything was falling into place. No one here died a natural death.

'Here,' said Lori aggressively as she passed the glass. 'Open your hand.'

Clara obeyed and dropped the capsule into her palm, a brownish powdery substance inside the capsule.

'What is it?' Clara was taking all the time to delay.

'Vitamins. Put it into your mouth, otherwise.'

'Yes, I know.'

She went to drop the capsule into her mouth.

'How do you know it's vitamins?'

She bent her head to the cup; it was one question that Clara suddenly wanted to know.

'Dr. Barnet told me, of course.'

'And you believe him?'

'Why should I not believe him? He never lies. But you are asking all these things to delay taking the tablet.'

'I was just curious. I was curious to know how much you trusted him.'

'Take the tablet. Now.'

Clara smiled. Holding the tablet in her hand, she dropped it into her mouth. From the glass, she sipped some water and then swallowed. It was all so easy and so quick. But still, suspicion lit Lori's face.

'Open your mouth. I want to see if the tablet has gone.'

Still smiling, Clara opened her mouth obligingly while Lori looked inside. She turned Clara's head this and that way. There was nothing to be seen behind teeth healthy with veneers. Standing back, still with her suspicious eyes on Clara, there was a torrent of thoughts silently speaking to Clara.

'Now, I should ask you for an apology for not trusting me. But I won't. Tell Dr. Barnet that I have taken his vitamin tablet.' Clara eyed Lori. This was a deadly game.

Without saying anything else and now uninterested,

Lori left the room. Clara watched the door and listened to the footsteps taking themselves away. Then, with eyes and wits bright with fear, she sprinted to the bathroom, fell onto her knees, and then put her fingers down her throat to heave.

Oh God, let it be in time. Let not what was in that capsule dissolve yet. Let me get to it out before it gets to me. I don't want to die, not the way Charisse had. Please Charisse, Argenta, help me, please help me. These terrifying thoughts pumped through Clara's petrified mind.

Stretching her fingers deep into her throat as if to catch hold of the vessel, she pushed them further and further down. This action's brutality met with violence to her gullet as it recognized Clara's hand as an alien instrument set to harm it. She heaved and wrenched, but nothing was coming. The small sacred tomb was aiming itself into the softer recesses of her stomach, and there it was, determined to do its work.

Oh God, I am going to die.

A little fluid came out, a spit of saliva, nothing more.

Up off her knees, she ran for the glass. Please don't use any energy body, not this time. Don't work to produce power. Don't look at that small and harmless capsule and wonder what use it can do for you. It will do no good to you except to injure you by taking away your use and purpose, and you and I shall be no more.

Grabbing the glass, Clara drank the contents. This should swill out her stomach with fluid and drowned that little bomb of evil.

Back to the bathroom again and in the missionary position, fingers thrust down into her mouth. She heaved and wrenched and then heaved again. The water she had only seconds before drank was now back up, swilling out into the basin.

Dizziness, her eyes everywhere, but there was no pill to be seen in the toilet basin. Again, she had to repeat this awful procedure. This time, her fingers rammed further until her stomach heaved at this unwanted intervention, and then suddenly, like a fountain, it all sprayed out. Green bile, along with the now warm fluid. And it was there, floating on top. Bobbing up and down cheerfully at her terror.

Picking it up for examination. It was almost complete, but not entirely. In its middle, there was a hemorrhage. Dabbing at it, some of the brown content was drawing itself out and breathing life. Her eager digestive juices had examined it.

Clara stared incomprehensibly at it. Was this the taker of lives?

22

If there was any actual harm to this capsule, such a small amount of leakage could not be significant. So much energy had been spent trying to get rid of this poison that she now needed to replace it. She could not afford to be weak, not now. She needed to eat her salad, but if she ate it now, would this work against her and make her ill? Argenta's words were in her mind, pulled from a distant conversation they had. Be careful of the food. They drug it.

Poor Argenta, how right she was and how late she found out. Clara must learn from this poignant lesson; it was dangerous to stay here any longer. She now knew the truth of this place and had seen the evidence. But even escaping this place could not be done in haste. It was not as simple as packing her bags and walking out of the front entrance. She would immediately be stopped and questioned and then kindly coaxed back with gentle reminders she was ill.

Ill, what was their proof? The only evidence she had was what they told her. Her weakened state of health was caused by what Dr. Barnet had prescribed to her. Her sudden decline was rapid and frightening, but then so was her recovery, which began when she didn't take their deadly medications.

Clouds of confusion had prevented Clara from making any interpretation of what was happening to her, but the answers were now coming thick and fast out of the haze. You are not lost. You are here. You are finding your bearings within this maze, intended to obscure your vision and direction.

Finding out these secrets was becoming exciting, as it was also becoming more dangerous.

Now Clara was understanding what the symbols meant in the dead people's files. CN- for cyanide. Then there was 11541511, a number which meant nothing on its own until she had searched in the commune's gardens for that incredible perfume. Next to these beautiful and exotic flowering shrubs had been this number staked to the earth. The commune had been harvesting its own toxic solution for their rich and exotic guests.

Oleander, one of the deadliest flowers, and Clara knew about it because of Phoebe.

'They are lovely, but be careful. Treat them with respect, Cecelia.' Phoebe, the best friend that Clara ever had. She cherished this short-lived friendship, the awkward English woman who added to Clara's personality by showing her it was all right to be herself. Like a ship that had dropped its anchor and could not move on, Clara still missed Phoebe. But now she had to move on with life and do the best and be the best; she owed this to her friend.

Thank you, Phoebe.

The lines of the battle were forming in front of Clara's vision. Her best survival was to leave here as soon as possible. To achieve this, she had to take them by surprise when the two doctors weren't prepared for her rebellion. The only time this could be done safely was to sneak out at night.

Once she was out and free, she would go straight to the police and report what she knew about this commune and the mental hospital. She was sure they would be interested in the excellent little business they were running, these conveyers of death.

Should she risk eating this salad? Probably not if she feared it, and yet Clara was tempted. It looked so innocent.

Tonight, she must leave. Lying on her side in bed to prevent her from looking at temptation, she felt so hungry she wanted to cry. Life was so precious. Next time, if there were a next time working as an investigative journalist, she would be more cautious, and this was a very definite promise. She would get out of here and live.

But for now, she should be more assertive in her actions. Take a leaf out of Peter's book. Why not? He never gave up hunting down the people he needed to kill, a contract killer, a cleaner. Her mission was not too different. These doctors were also unwanted and unneeded people who feathered their nests, stealing from others. Grown men—society's dropouts who didn't want to work with honesty. Yet, they still wanted to live off society's benefits.

To the future, which was always present, Clara looked out through the window. Nature was still so remarkable, holding a wealth of secrets. For every poison, there is always a cure. Humanity just needs to listen to nature to unlock it.

Clara's physical weakness came in kindness this time by making her fall innocently to sleep.

An icy hand on her arm aroused her eyes to awaken, but Clara did not move. She did not show that this touch had awoken her. There was someone else in her room.

'I watched her take the tablet,' it was Lori's voice. 'I made certain she swallowed it.'

'You understand what we are doing, Lori?' it was the voice of Dr. Barnet.

'Yes, sir, I do,' came Lori's voice steeped in respect and loyalty. She trusted him and believed in him; Lori worshiped him.

'So, you understand she is poisonous to our cause?'

'Yes, sir.'

'She will try to destroy everything we have created.'

'Yes, sir.'

'Do we risk saving one lamb for the sake of the flock?'

'No, sir.'

'We have tried for Clara. We have done everything we can to save her. But there is something evil within her. She is like a corrupt bacterium, that if we allow it to get out, it will destroy everything it comes into contact with. We cannot allow that, can we?'

'No sir, absolutely not, sir.'

'You know how important my vision is, Lori?'

'Oh yes, sir.'

'You are the only one who understands me best. It is meant to be. That is why our paths have crossed. Every prophet needs faithful disciples, and you are one of the best. You will always be remembered even when your fleshly being comes to an end. Do you know how I see you, Lori?'

'No sir, how do you see me?'

'I see you like Simon of Cyrene, who picked up Jesus' cross. You are that strength when mine is lacking. I see you as the Virgin Mary who never deserted her son on the night of his death. I see you as Saint Paul the Apostle who carried the word of Jesus to keep the Lord's memory. You are a good and faithful servant, Lori. But I also see you as the

Archangel Michael, who destroys those whose evil mission is to ruin us.'

'Oh yes,' said Lori proudly. 'I will do anything for you.'

'And that is good because my word is good. I am a being who is even now being misunderstood. All my energy is being focused on my vision—our vision—but I am also constantly fighting against evil. Why does this woman see me as evil, Lori? I ask you because she is one of your sex? Do you understand why this woman hates me so much when I have only tried to help her and do everything that is good for her?'

'No sir, I do not understand her. I do not understand why she doesn't see you as I do. God has chosen you amongst all others, but the devil must be in her eyes. I knew when I first met her she was corrupted by evil.'

'You did, my child. I wanted to believe she was lost and now is found.'

'Amen,' murmured Lori.

'But we are being challenged here,' said Dr. Barnet, now more up spirited. '*The hope of the righteous brings joy, but the expectation of the wicked will perish.* Proverbs 10:28. And we will find it within ourselves to resolve the problem of this evil.'

'Yes,' again, Lori murmured faithfully.

'And I put my trust in you.'

'Thank you, sir.'

'You knew I needed to get rid of this evil within the next ten days?'

'Yes, sir.'

'Well, I have changed my mind. This evil has become so big and corrupt; it must be removed now before the world comes rushing in while we are still unprepared. We are not ready for these people yet.'

'Only tell me what I have to do, sir, and I will do it.'

'I knew I could place my faith in you. I don't care how you do it. But I want you to do it tonight, now. As soon as I leave the room, perhaps the forces of good will move into you. To help inspire you with the desires of our Holy Spirit.'

'Yes, sir, I will. I feel that even now, the Holy Spirit has been awoken in me. I feel good and strong. Oh, just give me this one chance, and I will serve you.'

'You know, I always wanted to have someone to stand by my side. That rare woman I could rely on who I know loves me. Perhaps now I have found this other one. What do you think, Lori?'

'I would weep with joy for you to do that. But I am not worthy; surely I am not worthy, sir.'

'God will make you worthy when he has seen what you have done for him. I shall kiss you on your forehead, my child, and say my blessings over you. Stay still while I do this.'

'You make me so happy, so humble. Forgive my tears. I never thought this honor would be given to me.'

'God is merciful,' Dr. Barnet said after the touch of his lips passed over her head with the mutterings of a few incoherent words. 'And now, I am going to leave you and let it be for the last time that I have to deal with this ugly evil.'

Clara's ears pricked with shattering fear. Every movement which entered the space behind her was recorded with an icy definition. Each movement was charted as to where each of them was. And then Clara's eyes. The scavengers of fighters ran here and there looking for an escape, searching for how she could help herself.

Could it be true she was going to die at the hands of Lori? It could be true, but only if she allowed it. Those hands that not so long ago had smothered her face and dug its claws into her flesh. She had been too weak to compete against this fanatics' strength, especially when Lori's belief told her she was the victor and on the side of good. But this time, Clara would now fight for her life.

The door closed softly on Dr. Barnet. He didn't want to see what his champion was going to do. A smile closed on his lips once the door shut. Everything for him was going to be nicely sorted out.

The next minute would show what would come of this man's wishes.

Chest heaving visibly. Was she about to die? If she were, she would not go without a fight.

Now, she had to move with the essence of surprise when Lori approached, believing that Clara was sleeping in the depth of unconsciousness.

Her dinner was still on the tray, cold and waiting to be taken away and with it the curtesy of elegant living. A napkin, some flowers, and silver cutlery.

Leaping from her bed, surprise was on Lori's face as Lori tumbled backward. One, two steps. Naïve of Lori to have taken it for granted that Clara was asleep. In her hands was the Mickey Mouse pencil case; Lori had opened it and had looked inside. In Clara's surprise dash, Lori couldn't say anything.

Quick, targeting the tray, Clara ran long-legged madly to it to grab anything that came to her hands, the silver spoon.

What was she doing—Lori's eyes said? Was she going to eat her dinner now? Pure confusion on Lori's part, but she was also quick to understand, and dropping the Mickey Mouse case, she too ran to attack.

Clara's breath beat in her ears. She had to win. This time, she could not afford to cave in. But with a spoon, what was she going to do? She should have considered her options instead of diving into the pool of chance.

Bodies met instantly. Clara jumped on Lori, her legs wrapped around Lori's waist while grabbing and holding on to Lori's head.

Muted grunts, power breathing, ejections of feminine pains. Clara pulled Lori's hair; it was instinctive, the power of killing comes when it is taught, but this wasn't enough to kill her tormentor.

Next, a pair of fangs sunk itself into Clara's leg. The pain. She grabbed Lori's hand, which was trying to pull Clara off. Clara's enemy caught this hand. And blood, blood was drawn.

There were no cries for help or admittance of hurt. This was a proper fight, and they both meant business.

Short, sharp sounds of exasperation. Lori had Clara's hand, and she was now pushing her fingers back. Clara couldn't get her hand free, so she leaned down still on Lori's back and bit hard on her ear.

Whizz, a stinging resound around Clara's face, informed her that Lori had retaliated. A nuisance, because Clara still had the spoon in her hand while Lori was trying to bend over to get Clara off her back.

They were staggering from one side of the room, back to the other. Neither of them would give in while Clara was trying to avoid Lori's spiteful hands. An assault of one will over the other. Then Clara found her back was under attack. Lori was running backward into the wall with Clara still on her. It was one way that she could hurt her. This also hurt her elbow, and now she was going to receive an enormous bruise, thanks to Lori's passion.

Back towards the table, they fought. There, Clara's tray

sat waiting for these wrestlers. Turning her head, Clara could see what Lori was up to. There lay the knife on her tray that Clara mistook for the spoon.

If she picked up this knife and plunged it into her back, it would be sharp enough to do the job. But the fight was nearly over when Clara realized she would not be the victor, and she still had this worthless spoon in her hand, the one used for soup.

She was screaming. Clara could hear herself yelling with temper. She was not going to die—she did not want to die. She wanted to live. And then suddenly, she was on the floor, rolling over with Lori. From Lori's face, blood spurted out to cover them both.

Her hands had been released; Lori had let go of Clara. The spoon was still in Clara's hand, but it was covered in blood. And between the gaps where Lori shielded her hands, there was an eye hanging. Without realizing it, Clara had gouged out Lori's eye.

What she had done made Clara roll over and wrench, heaving up her stomach in revulsion and unaware of any dangerous threat that Lori might want as revenge.

But Lori was also involved in her pain. Hugging her face, she ran as if she wanted to escape. Backward and forward, she was running across the room. Into the walls, she took no notice and crashed into the window in flight. Moaning and crying as she held her face. The first time Lori had run into the window, the glass had fractured. The second time, the glass shattered, and out she went in a cascade of glass. A second later arrived the thud and then silence.

It was all over. Lori was not attacking her anymore. Getting up from the floor covered in Lori's blood, Clara went apprehensively to the window and peered out. Lori was lying there on the ground, her head up and one eye missing. The other eye looking upward while through her chest was a large shard of glass.

To the side, a few feet from Lori, two faces looking up at her, Dr. Slanders and Dr. Barnet.

23

———

'You can't kill her.'

The voice came from the other room, Dr. Slanders.

'I am certainly not going to kill her. Do you remember? We always get someone else to give the lethal dose just in case, you know, just in case.'

'Well, it's not working, is it?' this was the voice of Dr. Barnet.

'You have made too many mistakes—I told you that you were becoming too greedy. But you wouldn't listen, would you? You always thought you knew right. Well, look at us now. A body in the garden which, incidentally, we have got to dispose of. And putting covers over her won't make her go away, especially when the sun hits on her. It won't be too long before she stinks.'

'Just shut up, Franklin. The trouble with you is that you are weak. You wouldn't be the rich man you are today if it weren't for me.'

'And if it weren't for you, I wouldn't be facing prison either.'

'You are never grateful, are you?'

'Grateful about what? I had enough money—more than enough until you came along with your wild ideas about making not just one billion, but the start of many. How much money do we need to feel rich? The joke is that I spend most of my life here. I never have the time to even think about spending it.'

'Are you saying now you wished we never began this exercise?'

'Yes, I am.' Dr. Slanders was adamant.

'And there was never a time when you thought this was enough and we have got everything we wanted?'

'Yes, I told you a long time ago, I said, George, we have done very well. Let's quit while we are ahead.'

'Liar, you said no such thing.'

'Are you calling me a liar?'

'Yes, right to your face. You were thrilled when we were making money. Everything was great when the honey was running into our cups. The smiles and grins on your face told me so. But just because something went wrong, you want to abandon the ship. I know your sort. I have always despised that attitude in you.'

The argument came to a sudden halt when reckless words turned with a vengeance.

'Do you know what I despise about you?' yelled Dr. Slanders bitterly.

'Oh, here it comes. Retaliation from an expert. I rue the day I stretched out my hand and pulled you on board. You know, I felt sorry for you, and I thought I could use you. You never had much going for you.'

A laugh of scorn.

'Funny, because that is what I thought about you.' Dr. Slanders' voice now turned waspish. 'I thought, this man, this dandy, a man who can't hold relationships, a narcissist who can't stop looking in the mirror to see if he still exists. I know what you have been doing with the money. I stole into your office and looked for myself. You see, I didn't quite believe what you were telling me. The money comes trickling in every month while I haven't even got a paltry million yet. Why is this?'

'Overheads.'

'Oh yes, the overheads. I forgot about that. I tell you what, if it is too much for you, I'll take over the financial side, and I'm sure for my trouble, I will give myself a bonus.'

'Stop,' snapped Dr. Barnet. 'Do you see what we are doing? We are panicking, and because of that, we are attacking each other. The situation is bad now, okay, I agree, but it is not something we can't sort out together. And I mean together. We can still contain this situation, but we must keep calm, cool heads. And together, we will get through this. Look, Franklin, I'll give you my hand on it.'

He chuckled; they should be good friends instead of the enemies which they were fast becoming.

'Come on, Franklin, give me your hand. You said as many nasty things and more about me than I have about you.'

Male bonding was happening.

'Isn't this what we tell our patients to put it all behind them and move on?'

A begrudging murmur of yes came from Dr. Slanders.

'Let's work towards the future. And if you like as proof of goodwill, you can take over the accounts. If you have seen some disparity in the accounts, then I have been negligent, and I am sorry. I will not say that I have had a lot on my mind just lately because I think that is a lousy excuse. There is more than enough money for us both. As you say, the money is more than trickling through. Would you like to take over the accounts?'

'Yes, I would,' Dr. Slanders said with suspicion.

'Then you shall have them. I shall send the books over to you later. What I can't understand is why you don't have a million yet. That is strange. I have nearly twelve million.'

'Yes, I know.'

'We must sort this out straight away. Meanwhile, we have something more pressing waiting for us in the other room.'

It was only a matter of time before the business would be on her. Clara had been dumped on a chair in the other office. Effervescent molecules of fear triggered inside Clara; she smelled danger. Wherever she looked, the threat of danger had formed a real shape.

The door opened, and Dr. Barnet's eyes were the first to fall on Clara. Behind him was Dr. Slanders, who was still white with infused anger. But for the moment, the target of their rage was safely directed at her.

'Well, Miss Tinder, for the first time, we finally meet. This is what is called denouement—do you know the meaning of denouement?' asked Dr. Barnet too politely.

'Yes, I do, thank you.' Terse and annoyed with her wrists bound too tightly, Clara was angry.

'Tell me exactly who you are and why you are here?'

'I had a breakdown...'

'Forget about that cover story. You will die whatever happens, so you might as well make a clean breast of it all and have some courage to tell us who you are? Are you an undercover police officer?'

No, she shook her head, which brought a smile and a look of relief to Dr. Barnet in particular. So, this is what Dr. Barnet thought and feared. Clara wished she had been sharper and had been given something more to go on than fear.

'Perhaps you are from one newspaper or television stations, oh how they loved to be involved in making world breaking stories.'

'No,' Clara said, still staring at Dr. Barnet's merry blue and sparkling eyes.

'I will not accept your story about heartbreak. I have been checking around on you. I understand you have been best friends with one Cecelia Clark, a fascinating lady. But since you arrived on the scene, she has unfortunately disappeared.'

'I am an investigative journalist, and I am working for the Lamonts. Raphael Lamont is the father of Charisse.'

'Oh yes, I remember now,' begun Dr. Barnet, now smiling. 'She was a distraught young lady. Her father, she felt, had abused her, and he was, how did she put it, under the thumb of his gorgeous wife. I have seen her picture; she is beautiful and someone who should be treated like a real princess. The problem with women is that they always want more money.'

Although Dr. Slanders' eyes were on Clara, his thoughts though were a hundred years away. The occupation of listening to Dr. Barnet had glazed his eyes into thoughtful consideration. They had made up and shook hands as friends, but the hornets' nest had been dropped with a likely reprise.

'Why is it always the pretty women who have all the money? Am I missing out on something here? Oh, I don't object to sharing wealth and fortune with our species' attractive partners, but they, I am afraid, are not so generous the other way around. Once it's in their greedy but beautiful hands, they insist it should always be theirs.'

Dr. Barnet lifted his chin as if he were about to embark on a sermon or a history lesson.

'These days, women want to keep men submissive to their will by holding on to their fortunes, and society agrees with them. They argue that this is their time and that we have had our way for centuries. Do you think this is fair? I don't. I have had to work for my fortune. I put myself through medical school and paid every one of my bills. And yet now, I am being told I have always had it so good. My argument and the facts of my life are that I have not. But women, our beautiful ladies, are trying to heel us into the ground, are trying to tame us like domesticated animals, and then they become disappointed with us. Where are all the real men these days? You find that clearly imprinted on their lips. Madam, I say to them; you have unmanned me, and now you complain.'

He shrugged and detailed his eye on Clara.

'Do you think, Miss Tinder, that women have climbed too high and, in their hefty derision, have thrown us poor males away? We would do anything to keep you happy.'

Dr. Slanders sighed.

'What is the matter, Franklin? Do I bore you?'

'No, I was just thinking.'

'Then tell me what you are thinking,' demanded Dr. Barnet, who's patience had already been tested too much.

'It was nothing.'

'Nothing—I can't imagine you will ever think of nothing. An intelligent man as you are. Tell me what you are thinking about?'

'Very well, I was thinking if you are going to dispose of Miss Tinder, then who are you going to get to do it?'

'Well, let's see.'

Dr. Barnet raised his eyes skywards.

'First, though, we have to do something about Bess. Are you still in talks with her?'

'Yes, she is very interested in more money.'

'Then promise her everything she wants. Just to give us more time. Who says that no one has a price?'

Such an engaging and mischievous smile twinkled from Dr. Barnet's eyes as if his plans were running smoothly and not by the mess they were in.

'I have someone lined up for Bess,' smiled Dr. Barnet merrily. 'Is there any hope that Nurse Jones could finish off Miss Tinder?'

'When I last saw Nurse Jones, I had to send her home. She told me she found it difficult to eliminate Nurse Ryan, so it appears it came at a cost, her conscience. She has all the symptoms of someone going mad.'

'Mad people are prone to talk. It's not looking good, Franklin.'

'I know it's not,' snapped Dr. Slanders.

'It looks bad,' Clara had been listening.

Both eyes went straight to this oracle who spoke.

'I would be worried if I were you—' even in terror, Clara could still smile.

Psychological weapons could be enough to unsettle their apple cart. Perhaps not for Dr. Barnet, who was loved by his vanity, but Clara's observations were affecting Dr. Slanders. Although the calmest of the two, his face had frozen with concern.

'Look, you see what Miss Tinder is trying to do?' began Dr. Barnet. 'Her intentions are malignant. She is getting us to worry and then to turn on each other. A good try, Miss Tinder,' smiled Dr. Barnet warmly. 'But we will deal with you later. Do not listen to Miss Tinder, Franklin. The lady has a lot to gain with us at loggerheads. And now we had better do something about the body in the garden before the others return. It is a shame about Lori. She would have been good as a trained killer; she has that psychopathic makeup.'

'You deal with the body,' said Dr. Slanders. 'I will not sully my hands with it.'

Dr. Barnet stopped and regarded Dr. Slanders with something like puzzlement. The words which were playing around in his mind remained where they were. Upon leaving the room, Dr. Barnet looked thoughtful.

Something disturbing was playing on Dr. Slanders' mind. He was in the room where all the evidence lay. He had dismissed Clara as if she weren't there, for something more was troubling him. Clara's concern was centered on what Dr. Slanders was doing. Something was bothering him.

With the first drawer pulled open, Dr. Slanders was searching for something. Running his fingers across the top of the folders, he knew what he was looking for. Completely fascinated by his probing, Clara wanted to ask what his problem was; she desperately wanted to know because it could involve her.

Another drawer was pulled open. Again, the search progressed faster with each drawer he opened. His obsession was a kind of madness; whatever he was looking for was just out of sight. And then Clara remembered that first night when she entered this office that something had caught her eye even if it had not registered at the time.

F. S. was, of course, Dr. Slanders' first mort, following by an ironic smile to the side of this entry. Dr. Barnet had all the proof he needed to keep Dr. Slanders obedient.

'It's gone, isn't it?' Clara's calm voice raised in humorous accusation.

He stopped and turned immediately with eyes almost rabid with terror.

'I know what you are looking for. I didn't understand at first what it meant. Once you look enough at the code, it simply falls apart.'

'You've looked at these files?'

'Yes, I told you. I am an investigative journalist. Three people know where I am, apart from the Lamonts. At the end of August, in a couple of days. I have to check in with them. If I don't, they might decide to get in touch with the police.'

'I don't believe you,' his eyes were caught haunted by the light of Clara's confidence.

'I guess you don't because it all sounds very convenient. But it's true. That's why I'm not too worried except, of course, that I would rather not die. But I don't have to die, do I? I mean, you were innocent about what was happening here in this commune? A place where certain people find they have cancer and then, conveniently, they die.'

Still bound, Clara managed to shrug her shoulders with significant effect.

'I don't understand what you are talking about,' Dr. Slanders frowned hard.

'What I can see is that you are not the murderer in this business; it's your comrade, Dr. Barnet. He's the one gaining from this interesting venture. All the wills are in the commune's name, but not the hospital. Wills from which Dr. Barnet profits from.'

'How did you manage to get into this office?'

'Bess gave me her keys. Bess told me she saw what was going on and that everything was linked to Dr. Barnet's name. She wanted to expose him, not you. You are, as far as she could see, the innocent one. Isn't that true?'

Aghast, his mouth was open, Dr. Slanders quickly nodded to this happier scenario.

'I am afraid it's all going downhill with this business. Did you really have a hand in what happened to Elizabeth Grain?'

'It was an accident. When she came here, she was dying. She was twenty-seven with breast cancer. It was too late for her. She said she didn't care about life until it was too late. I did my best to save her. Dr. Barnet didn't know about her until I told him what she intended to do. She wanted to leave all her money to me. Elizabeth said I was the only real friend she had. She had a couple of million to leave.'

He was suddenly earnest and thirsty to tell Clara all about what had happened. His worried eyes were casting back over the past, trying to explain how this awful situation came about.

'When Dr. Barnet found out that Elizabeth was dying, he was excited. He said my reputation would look bad if she left everything to me. Very superstitious, his very words. I had to admit, I was worried. "We have to protect you, Franklin," he said. "Listen to my idea. If Elizabeth Grain left everything to the commune; no one could object about that."'

'Brilliant idea,' smiled Clara.

'I asked Elizabeth to change her will. I explained why, and she agreed. In those last few days, she had lost a significant amount of weight, and she was in terrible pain. The drugs we had at the clinic were not strong enough. She needed morphine. I told her I would get her some morphine to give her the relief she needed.'

He shook his head at the memory.

'Dr. Barnet, the man I thought was my friend and comrade, cheated on me. He primed the hypodermic needle with what I thought was the new batch of morphine just recently arrived, but instead, he had prepared a dose of oleandrin. Elizabeth died in agony. I shall never forgive him for that—never.'

His sigh was deep as he looked into the past. Whether it was a faithful recital of the past depended on Dr. Slanders' conscience. But it was as probably as near to the truth as one could get.

'And that's how it started?' she asked innocently yet artfully.

'Yes,' he nodded, only too willingly.

'Then you have nothing to worry about,' she smiled. 'It doesn't matter what Dr. Barnet says. He is trying to frighten you. Evidence can be faked. You have nothing to worry about.'

24

'So, now you show your true colors.'

Dr. Barnet returned to the room, his face grim. He had not disposed of Lori's body, but stayed outside the room to listen.

'It was her,' Dr. Slanders, who had been leaning over the cabinet, turned around, shocked that he had been caught out. 'I was playing to her. I was trying to find out what she knew about the set-up, and as you said, she knew a great deal.'

'You know, I have had enough of your whining and lying and the way you don't accept responsibility for your actions. You really have become a great hindrance to me. Spying on me and always with so much distrust. Bess didn't like you. It was she who told me not to trust you. But I ignored her, as I thought you and I were friends. I was prepared to forgive all the minor faults you had. The way you hid behind me and always distrusting me. I have been watching you for quite a while now. And I've concluded perhaps a little late that I don't need you. You are always pulling me back.'

'What are you going to do?' Dr. Slanders was now backing away from his rival.

'What I should have done nearly five months ago when Charisse Lamont died. I know you have been keeping evidence against me. You are not the only one who is into distrust. I have a grand little portfolio on you, too.'

Dr. Barnet was walking towards Dr. Slanders. He had something behind his back.

'If anything should happen to me.'

He was trying to edge away from Dr. Barnet, eyes terrified at what he intended to do to him.

'If anything should happen to you, then I have the proof that you had gone mad. That it was you who killed Nurse Jones.'

'Killed Nurse Jones? Is she dead?' asked Dr. Slanders.

'You tried to help her, and you wanted to calm her down, so you gave her a lethal injection of morphine. You didn't mean to, but she was blackmailing you.'

'George, look, I'm sorry.'

Dr. Slanders was backing away and holding up his hands. Moving closer, Clara looked on horrified; it was a scene from a diabolical play except that this was not theater but real life.

Now Dr. Slanders had backed himself into a corner, which served Dr. Barnet very well.

'I'm sorry, George, please don't do anything to me. Look, let's start all over again. You know we have had our minor differences. As you said, this can be worked out. It's nothing which is out of our control.'

'Franklin, just drop it. I have made my mind up about this. It's for the best you'll see. And it won't be painful. You'll fall asleep, and that will be it. You see, I'm still looking out for you.'

From behind Dr. Barnet's back, he pulled out a hypodermic syringe.

'George,' Dr. Slanders was rightly terrified. 'This doesn't make any sense. Think of the consequences of you trying to get rid of me. There will be an investigation—you'll be found out.'

'They will find the suicide note telling all about the people you had murdered. And also detailing how you poisoned Argenta.'

'What are you talking about?' he had managed to back out behind the filing cabinets.

'Oh, you haven't heard the latest? Argenta has two cousins who want her death looked into. The suspicion is on the hospital, which, of course, is you. These people don't like the families' money to go out of the circle. They claim that this is not characteristic of her to bequeath everything she has to a charity. You know, of course, this means a lawsuit.'

Dr. Barnet's now calm composure suggested he had been thinking about this problem for a while. Seeking all the likely avenues of investigation of where it would leave him, and now he had decided on a solution. For him, this had come as a relief. Taking a horse to save the king was worthwhile. Everyone has to compromise. Such a relief when a resolution is made.

For that few seconds of successful congratulation, Dr. Barnet left the planet and the time zone to see himself in the future. Applauding himself for covering his back that he didn't see Dr. Slanders had taken this opportunity to escape.

'Of course, I shall be magnanimous. I shall offer to return half of what Argenta had bequeathed. I would say I was being very decent. Then I shall produce the last will and testament. There will be no argument with this document.'

But this was an argument which Dr. Slanders couldn't help replying to because of its untested ludicrousness. He stopped on his approach to the door.

'Don't you understand that if you do this, then everyone will ask for their money to be returned?'

'That is a point I have had taken into consideration. Instead of sharing half of everything with you, I'll happily share it with the late departed's family.' He smiled with satisfaction. 'So, you see, everything is going to work out fine. I believe the late departed's family would sooner have half than none at all. A long legal battle would result in most of the money disappearing into the greedy hands of lawyers. And now all I have to do is kill you. You are the weakest link in all of this.'

It was sudden. Dr. Barnet's reflexes were sharp and quick. He managed to grab hold of Dr. Slander's arm, and with the other arm, went to stab him with the hypodermic. But he missed his arm because Dr. Slanders' jerked his arm and screamed so loud it took Dr. Barnet by surprise. A gentle man and refined usually, Dr. Barnet could not abide loud noises. The sudden intervention of shock gave Dr. Slanders his opportunity to get away from him.

A sudden rush and a scuffle as Dr. Slanders, in fear of his life, ran out, closely followed by Dr. Barnet. The situation was falling apart and was not going according to plan. But this was working for Clara, as she was trying to undo her bindings. The knot had not been intended to keep her forever in its promise to its creator.

Alone in the dissection, Clara bent down to untie the knot at her feet. Tears of frustration welled up in her eyes, for her hands were buckling under her panic. Is this how it was going to end? Frantic.

Running upstairs, and now overhead, two large men

were chasing each other. The noise above didn't need too much imagination to understand what was happening. One man tried to escape for his life while the other needed to kill his partner to save his reputation and the money.

Perhaps it was because Clara had heard one man screaming for his life, which made her determined to push that bit harder to save her own life. Rocking from side to side enabled her to stretch her muscles further. She leaned forward, and with a jerk, caught hold of the thread of one end. Another lurch and her teeth had a more secure grip.

She had it, and then she pulled back. One link unfolded and loosened the rest of the knot. While up above, their world went silent. Lurching forward, she tore her teeth into the link of this next knot, so clumsily done but still able to bind her tight. The rope was tearing into her flesh and burning, but the price of her life was worth more than a little grazing. Now she found she could pull her feet towards her while her fingers, which had grown red from restriction, were reaching out and stumbling to undo herself.

How fast she could untie herself when she previously she believed she would be stuck forever. And there it was, and then it happened. She was free. Her legs and wrists were scored fractiously, but the numbness caused her the worse problem.

Another yell came from above, two rooms away, and then a thud before all went silent. Peace for a few seconds. But not for long. One of them was coming slowly down the stairs. Which one of them was the winner of this battle?

Leaving her bounds, her eyes searched about the room for her escape. There was only one choice but to go by the only entrance. As Clara entered the main office from the connecting door, Dr. Barnet walked in.

He looked at Clara as if he didn't know her for a few seconds.

'I have lost a dear and genuine friend. We had known each other for over thirty years,' and then he grinned. 'And now it is time for me to deal with you.'

'You have gone mad,' Clara terrified screamed at him.

'On the contrary, this has all been planned out and calculated; I even expected Franklin's objection to willingly make himself a sacrifice. It all went so surprisingly easy that I feel I have been robbed. There is not much time now, and I need to kill you before the others return. And then I have to tidy up everything. You know, killing people involves a great deal of hard physical work.'

He had placed himself in the entrance. The only way for Clara to get out was to go through him, which was precisely what he wanted.

'When you plan someone's death, you have to be very meticulous. You cannot afford to go wrong in any way,' said Dr. Barnet as if he was giving a medical lecture. 'The first time we did, it was a learning curve, and we learned many things from it. I can honestly tell you that there is nothing like killing someone. We only possess our lives, and to take that is to take everything.'

Dr. Barnet took out a piece of silk from his pocket and began twisting it around his hands as he slowly moved towards Clara with his back to the entrance.

'Can you imagine how it feels to take someone's life?'

He smiled and looked exhilarated.

'I thought I would be repulsed, but I wasn't. It was truly a beautiful and emotional moment that you share with this person as you watch them cross over. I wonder if the newly dead find what they are looking for.'

'I thought you said you don't believe in taking people's

lives and it is better someone else does it,' said Clara, watching the silk wrapping between his fingers while walking towards her.

'You've been paying attention to me. How flattering. But no, I lied. Some people cling on to life greedily, and that is when I become impatient. When I plunged that needle into Miss Lamont, she opened her eyes wide and stared at me. The child was so surprised, and she asked me what I was doing. I told her I was killing her.'

Again, Dr. Barnet's eyes strayed to another ring in time.

'She asked me why. I told her the truth, which was she was worth more dead. Just like her father, I, too, was after her money. Then she said the most surprising thing. She said, thank you for telling her the truth. And then she died peacefully.' He shrugged.

Gradually, Dr. Barnet was moving closer towards Clara. The chair, which proved no protection, was thrown to the floor to give Clara that few extra seconds of life.

'Aren't you going to be as compliant as Charisse? Be a good girl.'

'No, I want to live,' said Clara savagely.

There were pile of papers on the desk. Running her arms across them, Clara flung them into the air, giving them flight to fan the world with paper birds' wings straight into Dr. Barnet's face. Annoyed, he chased them aside, which allowed Clara to run out of this entrapping room.

'I'm disappointed with you, Miss Tinder,' called out Dr. Barnet, coming up behind Clara as she ran to the front entrance.

Her real chance to flee. Grabbing hold of the front door, hands running all over it, she found the doorknob as if she were blind and then tried it, but it was locked.

A tap on the shoulder from behind.

'I've got you now.'

'No,' screamed Clara, whose faster spirit turned on her heel and ran.

But where to run to when there was no place to run? Inevitability was the word running through her head, and this was not the first time that Dr. Barnet had planned for her to die. When would the others come back to the commune? If they returned early, her life would be saved.

Her eyes, like madness, were darting everywhere for somewhere to hide from Dr. Barnet. Out through the back door, she sprinted into the garden and into the sunlight. No one dies on a sunny day; it was like going against the laws of nature.

At this time of the day, the air was heavy with the perfume of flowers, roses, wonderful hummingbird sage had just opened up its sack and yawned minty tones into the air, but there was no mistaking the oleander. It seemed to call and beckoning to her amid the fragrant white and yellow flowers.

Heady and drowsy with fear from its perfume, Clara stopped to think about where she was and what she would do. Dr. Barnet had stumbled and was now pulling himself up off the ground. Once again, he was back in pursuit of her. She turned before fleeing deeper into the garden.

A scream. There was someone in the foliage, a shadow ruffling as it moved. Was this also someone intent on killing her?

She screamed again and then burst into tears. She didn't want to die. She had to fight for her life, and it was tiring; she was still so frail and unwell.

Panic seized her, Clara went to run, and then changed her mind. It cost her dearly for her lost time, made up for his lost time. When out came a hand and this time caught hold of Clara and kept her.

'Your death could have been easier for you, Miss Tinder, a peaceful one. One injection and you would have fallen asleep forever, but now I am going to have to kill you physically.'

The silk scarf went around her neck, and her struggles meant nothing as the silk tightened on her flesh. She kicked and thrashed her hands, but she could not scream anymore as the silken killer pressed against her windpipe.

'I should mention to you, Miss Tinder, how grateful I am for your legacy. Really, I am looking forward to owning the Picasso. How thoughtful you were.'

He pulled her backward with him as he fell to the ground. She tried to scream, finding herself lying on his chest. He was still holding her, but now the silk scarf around her neck had lost its grip.

Oh dear, oh dear. She pushed herself up from him, and he allowed her to move freely. Was this another of his games? Was he doing this to let her get away from him? The thrill of the kill was in the chase. But you take these opportunities when you can, which might be her chance to run and evade him.

And yet, she turned to see what this all meant. An expression of delight shined from Dr. Barnet's eyes as if he were casting them on the Picasso even now. He looked so ecstatically happy; he didn't appear worried that she was getting away. Perhaps the reason was the hole in his forehead, like one of those frustrating and ugly zits that had just erupted.

25

___

'We were anxious about you,' said Anise, returning to the beautiful room overlooking Cote D'Azur. The sky had dropped into the sea, surrounded by the golden collar of the bay.

The panorama was not only just breath-taking but left one so speechless that one was prepared to dedicate one's soul to it. Raphael was lounging on the sofa, and he, too, found it very difficult to tear himself away from the view. But he turned when his wife spoke to him and nodded, and then smiled hastily at Clara as he cleared his thoughts.

'Raphael,' snapped Anise. 'Pay attention. You will see this view for the rest of your days.'

Like a schoolboy, he folded up his legs and swung around to face their visitor.

'Of course, we knew your capabilities,' Anise said. 'We did not doubt that you would succeed. Tea?' she offered, like the perfect hostess. 'Suddenly, now that we are in France once again, we find that we have become very popular with the English even in these troubled times.'

Anise picked up the silver teapot and poured the dark golden liquid into the most delicate of cups.

'When one has money—thanks to you, money has no prejudice, no race, or religion, no opinions on anything. But I understand that you too have come to this understanding.' She smiled secretly, as if she had got what everyone else wanted and would not share it, ever.

'I thought I owed it to you to tell you what I knew about Charisse,' said Clara.

Nothing had changed in her estimation of what she thought about this spoiled couple. That she was the operative to have given them what they wanted in the first place; Charisse's money goaded her into the unfairness. She would have been much happier if the money went to the commune instead of these two. But people like Raphael and Anise inevitably always triumph. Playing the injured victim these days was a winner.

'Well,' smiled Anise. 'It was very kind of you to travel all this way. Perhaps you could make this journey a holiday while you are here. Take in the sights of this beautiful country and, of course, its history.'

So, this was not an invitation for her to stay with them how crafty Anise was.

'Raphael was desperately upset to hear about his daughter, inconsolable, I feared for his reason. But we are pulling together as a family, helped by the wonderful gift that his daughter, dear Charisse, has bequeathed to us. Poor Charisse, such an unhappy child.'

'I remember Charisse as a baby,' it was a thought which suddenly occurred to Raphael.

'Yes, she was never a pretty child.' Anise orchestrated the direction of the conversation. 'Poor thing, but you can't have it all, I suppose.'

Do you really want to know anything about your daughter? Clara thought angrily to herself. About how interesting she was and how kind and caring she was to others. In fact, if she had lived, she would have been a conquering spirit for good. The surprising fact was that Charisse had cherished a dream that she could become a doctor once she was well. Her fortune could have done so much good for the underprivileged, but that's an ongoing battle. People often choose to live their lives on the paths which have been directed for them by others. But not Charisse.

Was she going to tell them what she had come here to say, or would her nature not wanting to hurt or offend advise her to keep quiet about it? After all, this was also her views? But if you allow others to dictate everything that has happened, then this becomes history, and history is not written from silence.

'In fact, Charisse would sooner her money had gone to anyone else other than you.'

Clara had spoken in that sudden impact of rage. Anise looked up and smiled.

'But we got it in the end.'

That was how she remembered this couple. Both were smiling and feeling their success. It didn't matter how they got the money; the beautiful couple was born to be rich. While Clara walked away, feeling that she was the ugly monster. The ogre that had come across these beautiful fairies and wanted to spoil their happiness.

Life just didn't work out fair sometimes. Was this what it was all about? Dr. Barnet wanted to join the super-rich set, and he wanted to do it now. He would have been rich if he allowed time and work to take him there. But how rich is rich? Perhaps it's never enough.

Poor Dr. Barnet, although goodness knows why she felt

sorry for him because if he had his way, he would have taken her life too. But he was shot instead of her. This was something she couldn't get into her head. Such a great change of fortune it was for her.

The cleaner which Dr. Barnet had contracted had got the wrong person. When Clara realized he was well and truly dead, her first instincts came in bouts. To scream, to laugh, and then what she finally did was to run away in case the killer thought better of it and reloaded his gun.

Oh, that was a scary time as well, running around in a time of confusion. History had changed in an instance that meant she would live instead of dying, which takes a great deal of reorganizing and planning.

A future—Clara had a destiny to carry on with, and a secure future now, which meant she had money—and plenty of it. And that was another thing when it came to her fee. Anise simply smiled and raised the subject herself.

'Congratulations to you, Miss Tinder, now that you are a very wealthy woman. It would be an insult to offer you the wages now.' She smiled, keeping her gold doubloons locked tight inside her cheeks. 'You wouldn't even notice it.'

But I would, Clara told herself. I would notice that you would have appreciated me and everything I tried to do to get to the truth. But you will always be a barrier to a pleasant reality.

And then Clara realized something remarkable about herself that some would try to detract and conceal and even lie about the truth, but not her. Not anymore. Warts and all, the only genuine history about our lives is in the telling of the truth.

REVIEW

I would appreciate it if you reviewed my book as this would make my day.

Thank You...

9 781915 778109